THE SPANDAU COMPLICATION

THE SPANDAU
COMPLICATION

BOB ORKAND

CASEMATE
Philadelphia & Oxford

Published in the United States of America and Great Britain in 2021 by
CASEMATE PUBLISHERS
1950 Lawrence Road, Havertown, PA 19083, USA
and
The Old Music Hall, 106–108 Cowley Road, Oxford OX4 1JE, UK

Paperback Edition: ISBN 978-1-63624-026-8
Digital Edition: ISBN 978-1-63624-027-5

A CIP record for this book is available from the British Library

Printed and bound in the United States by Integrated Books International

Typeset in India by Lapiz Digital Services, Chennai.

For a complete list of Casemate titles, please contact:

CASEMATE PUBLISHERS (US)
Telephone (610) 853-9131
Fax (610) 853-9146
Email: casemate@casematepublishers.com
www.casematepublishers.com

CASEMATE PUBLISHERS (UK)
Telephone (01865) 241249
Email: casemate-uk@casematepublishers.co.uk
www.casematepublishers.co.uk

Foreword

This is a work of fiction, so by definition the events depicted herein didn't really happen.

But to be fair, some of them really did occur. Others I made up. And some I just skewed a bit to conform to my narrative and help advance the plot.

The trouble is that as the years have passed—and what took place in Berlin back in 1966 is certainly a long time ago—my memory has increasingly begun to confuse what actually happened with what might have happened. At one point in my life, I was reputed to have an especially keen memory, which I think is alluded to at several points in this story. But my wife—who is several years younger than me—tells me that my recollection of events isn't what it used to be as I get older and grayer.

I suppose that she's right. Anyway, I just wanted to forewarn you that I've populated this story with some people and events—Willy Brandt, General Andrew O'Meara, Ambassador George McGhee, Ambassador Pyotr Abrassimov, Reverend Billy Graham, Colonel Lazarev of Spandau Prison, the release from Spandau of Speer and von Schirach, the pistol-pointing incident at the train station, Wall patrols into East Berlin—that really were part of the West Berlin landscape in the 1960s. Yes, there was an East Berlin tugboat skipper who moved the pilings in the Griebnitzsee and there was a MiG that crashed into the river and the Allies took it apart underwater, but not exactly as I've described.

But I hope you get the point. Any references to real people—living or dead—are products of my imagination. Most of these people, of course, have long since passed on to their eternal rewards, even Andy O'Meara, who lived to the ripe old age of 98. I didn't intend to criticize or discredit anyone in this book, which is—as I said at the outset—entirely a work of fiction.

And if I've confused or garbled any facts, figures or events pertinent to my narrative, please know that the errors are mine, and not my publisher's. I've done my best to set the record straight, as best I can recall.

But Berlin in the Cold War era was a world apart from reality and I was then a young man. Now the once-divided city has become a powerful factor in global economics and diplomacy and I am no longer young, growing increasingly forgetful as I age. Please forgive me if fact and fiction collide in this story.

So to begin …

Harrison ("Harry") Holbrook Jr.
Lt. Col., Infantry, U.S. Army (Ret.)
Rockford, Illinois

From 1945–1989, Berlin—110 miles behind the Iron Curtain—was divided into four occupation zones. The zones of the three western allies comprised West Berlin, while East Berlin consisted of the Soviet Sector. The Berlin Wall, built in 1961, divided West and East Berlin and encircled all of West Berlin. When the Wall was breached in November 1989, it effectively ended the 44-year Cold War between the Soviet Union and the western allies.

1

Lichterfelde-West Bahnhof
West Berlin
1930 hours, 5 May 1966

Captain Vasily Komarov of the Soviet Army in Berlin—part of the Group of Soviet Forces in Germany—had had a bad day, marked by constant moaning, groaning, and bitching from his seven-months-pregnant wife. He was determined to take out his anger on someone or something as he commenced his nightly duties at the Lichterfelde-West train station in West Berlin.

The U.S. Army duty train being readied for its nightly crossing between West Berlin and West Germany—transiting 110 miles of hostile East Germany—was under the supervision of Second Lieutenant Gordon J. Hauser, a 1965 ROTC graduate of Norwich University in Vermont.

Tonight's run would be Hauser's fourth as train commander since completing the Transportation Officer Basic Course at Fort Eustis, Virginia, and subsequently being assigned to the Berlin Brigade. Together with its British and French allies garrisoning their respective sectors of the Divided City 110 miles behind the

Iron Curtain, America's 6,000-man Berlin Brigade was the world's sole remaining vestige of a post-World War II occupation force.

As commander of the train during its three-hour run from West Berlin to Helmstedt in West Germany, and then on to Frankfurt am Main, Lieutenant Hauser headed a team of one Transportation Corps staff sergeant, two Military Police corporals, and a radio-telephone operator to keep the train in constant contact with headquarters back in West Berlin. The two MPs had been added to the duty train's complement back in 1948, when Soviet soldiers—presumably in search of black marketeers—had attempted to illegally board what was essentially an American train.

In the intervening years, train incidents between the two occupying powers had been few and far between, but Hauser had been cautioned to be on his guard. The Russian army's recently installed captain as its representative at Lichterfelde-West had been giving the American train commanders a hard time. Tonight would be Hauser's initial encounter with Captain Komarov.

Lieutenant Hauser, a 23-year-old native of Lexington, Massachusetts, looked on as the East German locomotive was coupled at the front of the train. By Allied agreement, ever since the end of World War II, the duty train—consisting usually of three sleeping cars, a mail car, a freight car, and an escort car serving as headquarters for the American military personnel—was pulled across East Germany by an East German locomotive and manned by a crew from that nation, until it arrived at Helmstedt, the first stop in the Federal Republic of Germany, or West Germany. At that point, the East German locomotive and crew were detached to make ready for the next train heading back to Berlin, whereupon a U.S. Army locomotive took its place.

The previous Soviet train inspector at Lichterfelde-West had been a relatively easy-going captain who spoke passable English with the second lieutenants escorting the duty trains,

2

often pausing to mooch an American cigarette or two from his counterparts.

But Captain Komarov, according to Lieutenant Hauser's fellow train commanders, was proving to be difficult to work with, stubbornly insisting that things be done his way. Hauser had been cautioned to be alert for possible trouble.

Armed with his Makarov 9mm semi-automatic pistol, Komarov walked up and down the track at the train station, seemingly looking for trouble spots. As he passed Lieutenant Hauser on each round, he'd either ignore the lieutenant or pause to examine the train in such a manner that Hauser was forced to move around him.

Hauser had just finished inspecting the coupling of the locomotive to the first car, finding it satisfactory. But Komarov came up beside him and in broken English ordered that the coupling be redone. Hauser, satisfied that the coupling was correct and concerned that the train would be thrown off schedule, said "*Nyet*" to the Russian and raised his hand to signal the engineer to move the train forward.

Komarov drew his pistol from its holster and pointed it a few inches away from the lieutenant's nose. "Correct the coupling," he ordered, "or the train will remain here!"

Hauser had no choice but to obey. One of the MP corporals drew alongside and asked if he should intervene, but Hauser put a hand on his arm and told him to stand down, that things were under control.

From the escort car, the radio-telephone operator called the Rail Traffic Office a few miles away, reporting that a Soviet Army captain had just threatened the U.S. Army's duty train commander with a pistol to the face. While the report was being evaluated and forwarded to higher headquarters, the train began to move forward on its delayed transit to West Germany.

"By whose authority did you non-concur?" the U.S. Commander Berlin (USCOB) thundered at his information officer, Major Harrison ("Harry") Holbrook Jr.

Holbrook, the USCOB staff officer in charge of dealing with the news media on all matters involving the command and its principal subordinate unit—the Berlin Brigade—had stuck his neck out and put thumbs down on the Berlin State Department's intent to issue a press release about the previous night's pistol-threatening incident at the Lichterfelde-West *Bahnhof*.

Holbrook, 34, had been commissioned 12 years earlier from Penn State's ROTC program. He stood an even 6 feet tall, weighed 170 pounds, and needed glasses to read the large volume of paperwork that appeared on his desk each morning.

Holbrook was considered by his superiors and peers to be a competent officer, certainly not a water-walker, but one who was steady, reliable, and cool under pressure. In other words, destined for promotion to lieutenant colonel when his time came, but not really in line for responsibilities above and beyond light colonelcy.

Thus, it was somewhat unlike Holbrook the morning after Captain Komarov's tirade at the *Bahnhof* to non-concur—that is to blatantly disagree with and put the kibosh on—the State Department's carefully worded proposed press release to news media in Berlin and everywhere else that there had been a major incident in West Berlin involving an armed threat from a Soviet Army officer against a U.S. Army lieutenant who was doing his duty as a train commander.

As a consequence, Holbrook now stood on the carpet—literally— in front of Major General John S. Caraway, the U.S. Commander

4

Berlin, and was being called upon to explain his actions in defiance of the State Department's supposedly superior world view.

Holbrook was no genius, nor would he ever be mistaken for John Wayne. But neither was he anyone's dummy. He was fully aware that two months earlier in March 1966, President Lyndon Baines Johnson had visited U.S. Army Europe (USAREUR) headquarters in Heidelberg and had instructed General Andrew P. O'Meara, the four-star commander of all U.S. Army forces on the continent, in the frankest of terms: "General, whatever you do, don't rock the boat with the fucking Russians in Berlin. I've got a war a-building on the other side of the world and I haven't got enough god-dammed troops to fight a second war with the fucking Russians. Is that understood?"

Based on the President's not-so-gentle guidance against rocking the boat with the Russkies while the American military buildup in South Vietnam was proceeding apace, Holbrook had been somewhat mystified at the haste with which his State Department counterparts at the U.S. Mission Berlin (USBER) had cobbled together an announcement which clearly—in Major Harrison Holbrook's considered judgment—went against the grain of Lyndon Johnson's directive to General O'Meara.

LBJ's introduction of American ground combat elements into the struggle for Vietnam, beginning with the arrival of U.S. Marines at Da Nang in March 1965, had precipitated a "draw down" of combat arms officers out of USAREUR, as majors and captains were needed desperately either to go directly to Vietnam as combatants or else to be reassigned to Continental United States (CONUS) to become part of the expanding training base at stateside military installations such as Fort Benning, Fort Bragg, Fort Sill, and elsewhere. In previous drawdowns, Berlin had been left unaffected but this time around no USAREUR element escaped the axe.

As a consequence, as Holbrook had scanned the roster of field grade officers still assigned to USCOB and the Berlin Brigade, it had dawned on him that he was the sole remaining U.S. Army infantry major left in Berlin. Every other wearer of gold oak leaves and crossed rifles had been drawn down, sent summarily either to report to the 90th Replacement Battalion depot at Long Binh, Vietnam (nicknamed "Camp LBJ" for Long Binh Junction and for the chief executive who was sending troops there), or to help replenish the training base in CONUS.

The reason that Holbrook was still in Berlin, still occupying his plush field-grade housing at 12 Goldfinkweg in the upscale Dahlem neighborhood where his backyard overlooked Berlin's famed Grunewald forest and park, was that General Caraway (nicknamed "Bourbon John" by his subordinates because of his predilection for the famed alcoholic beverage of his native Kentucky) had put Holbrook's name on a listing of absolutely essential officers who shouldn't be drawn down under any circumstances. It wasn't that Holbrook himself was indispensable; rather, a competent, school-trained press officer was essential to the Berlin headquarters, and Harry Holbrook had managed to finish as honor graduate of his class at the Defense Information School.

As Holbrook stood on General Caraway's oriental carpet in a modified position of attention waiting to be dressed down—maybe fired—he wondered if the USCOB was regretting his earlier decision to spare him from the drawdown and perhaps was already making arrangements to promptly ship his sorry ass to Camp LBJ.

Harry Holbrook, whose Army career had consisted up to this point of not making any waves—well, not any big ones anyway—realized that he had indeed stirred up a hornet's nest. Despite the seriousness of his immediate prospects, he almost chuckled to himself about his mixed metaphors while waiting for General Caraway to look up from his stack of papers and recognize him.

"Well, Holbrook, what in the world gave you the right to intervene in Minister Calhoun's decision to notify the press about last night's incident at the train station?"

Minister Ernest C. Calhoun was the top State Department official in Berlin. His office, known as the U.S. Mission or USBER, shared space at Clayallee 127 with the Office of the U.S. Commander Berlin. The large U-shaped building had been built for the German air force in the late 1930s and had served under Reichsmarschall Hermann Göring during World War II as a consolidated air defense headquarters for all of the Third Reich.

Clayallee had been known as "Kronprinzenallee" for most of its history and had been renamed in 1949 to honor General Lucius D. Clay, hero of the 1948–49 Berlin Airlift, which had saved West Berlin's two million occupants, along with their hay-starved horses, from starvation.

The American ambassador to the Federal Republic of Germany (West Germany), "Big George" McGhee, had his embassy in the sleepy little Rhine River village of Bonn, birthplace of Ludwig van Beethoven. Subordinate to the ambassador was USBER, headed by a minister, currently Ernest C. Calhoun.

Calhoun's deputy was Peter V. Day and his press officer was John Brogan. Relations between military personnel and State Department officials at Clayallee 127 were, as might be expected, often at odds, with both components trying to outpoint the other or sometimes affixing blame when things became fouled up, as was all-too-often the case.

USBER had its own wing in the headquarters building. It was unusual to see a uniformed member of the USCOB staff on USBER turf; the reverse was also true—hence, the frequent lack of coordination and shared information between the two staffs.

General Caraway awaited with growing impatience Major Holbrook's response to who had authorized his non-concurrence.

"Sir, to begin with, I seriously doubt that Minister Calhoun was personally involved in the drafting of the press release or that he was involved in the decision to release it. My understanding is that Pete Day and John Brogan considered it imperative that we get out front with a statement about the Russian captain's actions."

"You haven't answered my question, Holbrook," the USCOB shot back. "Who or what gave *you* the authority to undermine what the State Department considered to be a prudent course of action, highly advisable under the circumstances?"

Once again Holbrook dodged Caraway's question. "Sir, in light of President Johnson's recent guidance to USAREUR that any confrontation with the Russians should be avoided during this Vietnam buildup, I felt that what State was proposing contravened"—here Holbrook prided himself on coming up with such an adroit verb—"the President's guidance. In addition," he continued, "the press hasn't been paying much attention these days to routine activities at the train stations. I doubt that Hugh Erb has any stringers at the *Bahnhof*." The Associated Press's Berlin bureau chief, Erb was considered by many to be the most important newsman in West Berlin.

General Caraway's capillaried red nose—made so by his inherent fondness for the golden produce of his native state—seemed to grow progressively redder as Holbrook evaded USCOB's direct question but instead looked intently at the eyes of the seated general, whose bushy eyebrows quivered with unhappiness and impatience. But Holbrook had been reserving his *pièce de résistance*—his career-saving stroke of genius—for this very moment, and now he deftly laid it on the general.

"Sir, I coordinated my decision with Colonel Hill in Heidelberg. He fully supported my position and told me that he seconded my decision to non-concur."

Caraway sat back in his chair, stunned at this new development, which—if true—changed the equation enormously. In the general's hierarchy of potentially disastrous occurrences, an all-out attack by Russian forces against West Berlin ranked third, censure by the State

Department back home at Foggy Bottom in Washington was second, while in first place—at the very forefront of Caraway's catalogue of nightmares—stood the fierce Irish irascibility of General Andrew P. O'Meara, the four-star USAREUR commander in Heidelberg, along with the good will of key USAREUR staffers such as Colonel L. Gordon Hill, O'Meara's press officer, who was reportedly headed to a promotion to brigadier general and a key Pentagon billet in the very near future.

"Colonel Hill, you say? Your response was coordinated with Hill?"

"Yes sir. He felt, as I did, that the State Department was overreacting to a relatively minor activity by a single Russian officer and that it doesn't represent a change of heart by either the Russians or East Germans. In view of the President's cautions against 'rocking the boat' with the Soviets, Colonel Hill agreed that we should take our chances that the incident won't attract attention."

Caraway mulled this over. "So what happens if Erb or some German newsman finds out about the incident?"

"Sir, at that point we run with State's press release, using it as a response to query. We have nothing to hide. We just don't want to maximize one unfortunate incident."

Caraway considered this. He knew that he would have to spread oil on troubled waters with Calhoun and Day, who would be irked that Holbrook hadn't been axed and sent packing to the 90th repple depple (slang for "replacement depot") in Vietnam. But on the other hand, if Holbrook was right and if the press wasn't likely to hear about the incident, then the President might think favorably of Caraway's firm grip on events taking place in Berlin.

"That'll be all, Holbrook. Keep me informed—immediately—if the press noses around about this."

"Will do, sir," Major Harrison Holbrook said, saluting sharply as he left the USCOB's office, and hiding a bit of a shit-eating grin.

Information Division (ID)
Officer of the U.S. Commander Berlin
Clayallee and Saargemünder Strasse
Dahlem, Zehlendorf
West Berlin
1330 hours, 6 May 1966

Frau Gertraud Haupt, secretary to the USCOB information officer, came into Harry Holbrook's office with the day's official correspondence and mail.

"This one looks like it may be of interest, Major Holbrook," she said, extending a handsome embossed envelope with some sort of red insignia on it.

"Well, let's see what it says, Gertie." Frau Haupt—53 years old and with bleached blonde hair to offset the onset of graying—hated the nickname the Americans had assigned her, but after 11 years on the job to a succession of information officers and their staffers, she'd grown pretty much inured to it.

After all, 90 percent of the costs of keeping 6,000 American soldiers and their families in Berlin was being underwritten by the West Berlin Senat. Without the American presence, it was widely believed, West Berlin—a virtual island in a Red Sea— would have been swallowed up by the Soviet Union shortly after World War II.

Holbrook used his letter opener to make a neat slit in the impressive envelope and drew out a formal-looking cardstock invitation. At the top of the invitation, in bright red and yellow colors, stood the hammer and sickle emblem of the Soviet Union.

He read, "The presence of Major Harrison Holbrook, Office of the United States Commander Berlin, is hereby requested at a luncheon, 1230 hours Wednesday, 15 May 1966, Dining Room of the Commandant, Spandau Prison, British Sector, Berlin."

Holbrook whistled softly to himself, then passed the invitation to Frau Haupt. "What do you think, Gertie?"

Frau Haupt studied the invitation. She had never seen one before in all her years at the USCOB headquarters. "I think it is quite an honor to be invited, Major Holbrook. Apparently it is the Russians' turn to guard the prison next month and their commandant has invited you to their luncheon."

Holbrook knew, of course, that the four occupying powers rotated guardianship of Spandau Prison—with its three remaining aging Nazi prisoners—on a monthly basis. Along with garrisoning a platoon-sized guard force at the prison in the British sector, it had become traditional for the prison commandant (who also rotated with his troops) to host a lavish luncheon at some point during his monthly tenure.

"Gertie, please check with Colonel Semsch's secretary and see if he's free for a couple of minutes."

Lieutenant Colonel Phil Semsch, the USCOB intelligence officer, or G-2, was seemingly aware of everything taking place on both sides of the five-year-old Berlin Wall. Semsch, who spoke just about every conceivable Western European language, and his wife, had become close personal friends of Harry Holbrook and had more or less "looked after" him during his divorce-enforced bachelorhood. Holbrook's ex-wife and their two children lived in Ligonier, Pennsylvania.

"Colonel Semsch will be free in 15 minutes," Gertie called from the outer office.

"Good. Tell them I'll be there."

A quarter-hour later, Holbrook, carrying the Soviet invitation in its envelope, walked the long hallway down to the intelligence officer's suite of offices.

"Come in, Harry. What's up?" Semsch said. It was unusual for the information officer to visit the highly classified intelligence office area, although Holbrook had the necessary Top Secret security clearances.

Without replying verbally, Holbrook handed over the envelope containing the Russian invitation.

Semsch opened it and raised an eyebrow. "Interesting, Harry. It's not that unusual for the Sovs to invite higher-ranking officers from the USCOB and brigade staffs, but I'm not aware that they've invited any majors before. Of course, you're probably the last infantry major left in Berlin, so Colonel Lazarev probably wants to know how weakened our remaining forces are."

Continuing his musings, Semsch said, "I've been to a number of these luncheons hosted by the Russians, Brits and French. Each one tries to outdo the other in the elaborateness of the food and drink. The Russians haven't invited me in a year or so and I wonder … Grace," he called out to his secretary, "have we seen an invitation in today's mail?"

"I haven't gotten the mail yet, sir. I'm on the way."

Grace Wertman, American wife of Master Sergeant Millard Wertman of the Berlin Brigade, was back a few minutes later with the mail. "Is this what you're looking for, sir?" she said, handing over an envelope very similar to the one received by Holbrook.

"Thanks, Grace," said Semsch, opening the envelope. "Looks like I'm coming too, Harry. Grace, here's the invite with Colonel Lazarev's RSVP number. Please accept for Major Holbrook and myself and then mark it on my calendar for May 15."

Semsch turned back to Holbrook, his fingers steepled in thought. As a career intelligence officer, he was plugged in to the manifold spycraft networks functioning around the clock on both sides of the Berlin Wall.

"Harry, there may be something unusual going on here. I can't quite put my finger on it yet. I'm tied up for the rest of today so I can't get away, but you might check and see if Gene Bird can see you. He might have some insights into this."

Lieutenant Colonel Eugene K. Bird, the U.S. commandant of Spandau Prison three months out of every year, maintained an office down the corridor from General Caraway, whom he assisted when not on prison duties. (In coming years, Bird would get in serious hot water for collaborating with imprisoned Nazi war criminal Deputy Führer Rudolf Hess in the writing of a book entitled *Prisoner #7* about Hess and Spandau. Bird would be placed under house arrest in Berlin, relieved of his Spandau duties, and sent into early retirement.)

Bird was available when Holbrook knocked on his office door. He had relatively little to do when not at Spandau, but he was of course an invited guest at the monthly luncheons hosted by his fellow commandants, as was the case with all four prison commanders.

Bird glanced at Holbrook's invitation, then held up an identical one he had received. "It's probably no big deal, Holbrook. Colonel Lazarev mentioned to me a while back that he was tired of seeing the same old faces at these monthly luncheons, so it's possible that he's looking for some newer, younger blood. I wouldn't make too big a deal of it. You'll accept, of course?"

Harry Holbrook assured him that he'd be there, that he'd already made arrangements to travel to the British sector and Spandau in Phil Semsch's car, and that he was looking forward to the visit.

2

En route to Spandau Prison
Wilhelmstrasse, Borough of Spandau
British Sector, West Berlin
1130 hours, 15 May 1966

Colonel Semsch's sedan—a 1962 four-door Ford Galaxie painted olive drab and flying two metal miniature American flags above its left and right fenders—headed north from Zehlendorf to the 19th-century prison on Wilhelmstrasse in the borough of Spandau.

Semsch, the ranking officer in the car, sat in the right rear seat, while Holbrook sat to his left. The car was driven by Specialist Four Norman Hellerstein.

"Harry," said Semsch, "this is Norm Hellerstein. He's a trained intelligence specialist, has a poli-sci degree from NYU, and enlisted in the Army for a three-year hitch so he could see some of Europe before he returns to school with Uncle Sam's financial help to get master's and law degrees. It wouldn't surprise me if someday he's either a judge in New York or a professor at NYU."

Hellerstein waved hello at Holbrook, looking into the rearview mirror. "Happy to meet you, Major."

"You too, Hellerstein. How long have you been doing this?"

"Driving for Colonel Semsch in Berlin? Around a year, I think. I also help out in the office when the colonel doesn't need me to chauffeur him around."

"Hellerstein has an excellent handle on what's taking place in East Berlin," Semsch explained. "He's developed some contacts over there, particularly through a synagogue across the Wall on Oranienburger Strasse that has been very useful on occasion. The Jewish population of Berlin has been chewed up by the Germans and Russians and they regard Americans and the Brits very favorably. They've come up with some good information, and they have a pipeline to Norm that I'm not cleared for," Semsch joked.

"Let's talk about what you're likely to experience at the luncheon, Harry," Semsch continued, changing the subject. "In addition to Colonel Lazarev and perhaps five or six Soviet Army officers—just about all of them spooks, of course—the British and French will each have a couple of representatives. From our side—you, me, Bird, and maybe one or two from State. Pete Day maybe. Perhaps John Brogan.

"You'll probably be the lowest-ranking American there," Semsch continued, "so presumably far down the table from Lazarev. Much of the conversation around you will be in Russian, maybe French, so you won't understand it. But listen carefully and we'll compare notes when we get back to the car.

"By the way," Semsch added as an afterthought, "the Sovs trot out some of their best vodka for these occasions. After all, each of the four powers tries to outdo one another in their hospitality each month. So the waiters—all of them professional Russian soldiers from the platoon guarding the three Nazis—will be pouring shot glasses filled with vodka all through the meal. Don't let them get you drunk."

Semsch knew, of course, that his friend Holbrook had self-imposed strict limits when it came to alcohol. "Any questions, Harry?"

"Tell me about the three prisoners. I don't know as much about them as I should."

"Right, good point. Well, of course you've heard of Rudolf Hess, who was Hitler's Deputy Führer. He was probably the third-ranking Nazi, after Hitler and Göring. Oddly enough, Hess was born in Egypt to a successful German businessman and his wife and didn't come to Germany until he was 14. Hess fought in World War I, had a distinguished record that included two war wounds, and ended up as a pilot, which is key to his story. He was an early convert to Nazism, was arrested and jailed with Hitler after a failed uprising, and actually was Hitler's stenographer for *Mein Kampf* while they were cellmates at Landsberg Prison.

"Remarkably, sometime in early 1941 before Hitler stabbed Stalin in the back by invading Russia, Hess got into a Luftwaffe uniform, commandeered a Messerschmitt, and flew to Scotland to broker a peace deal of sorts with some duke he'd met in Berlin during the '36 Olympics. In essence, he was trying to convince the British that Hitler had no plans to invade the British Isles and would be content with controlling the continent. Churchill wasn't persuaded, the Brits felt that Hess was probably crazy, and they put his ass in prison for the rest of the war as a ranking Nazi.

"Back in Berlin, Hitler and his cohorts arrived at a similar conclusion that Hess was insane. They disowned him, denied any knowledge of his flight and bargaining attempts, and in effect were totally embarrassed by his actions.

"At the Nuremberg Trials, Hess went nuts, stared off into space, claimed amnesia, but swore loyalty to Hitler, who by then had committed suicide in the Führerbunker here in Berlin. Hess got a life sentence. He's 70 or 71 now and undoubtedly will die in Spandau."

Holbrook thoughtfully took all of this in. "So he really wasn't in the military chain of command during the war?"

"That's right. He went into a British prison before Pearl Harbor and stayed there until he was flown to Nuremberg in 1945 to stand trial as a war criminal. But because he'd been Hitler's Deputy Führer—along with Göring—and because of his flight to Scotland, from which he parachuted, by the way, Hess is the best known of the three prisoners still here.

"Originally, seven Nazis were sentenced to Spandau at the Nuremberg Trials. Four of them have either died or been released, leaving the three who are still here."

Holbrook had a thought. "Why all this fuss and bother about keeping three old men behind bars, involving soldiers from four nations as prison guards? Couldn't money and effort be saved by releasing them?"

"Good point, Harry. I think the key words here are symbolism and memory. The Russians don't want their people and the world to ever forget what the Nazis did to their country. So these 'three old men,' as you correctly call them, are the last living symbols that we know of the leadership that represented the enemy in World War II.

"There are pressures from some quarters," Semsch continued, "to release these last three and let them die in their homes. I think perhaps our State Department people might go along with that and save some money. But the key point is that the Russians will never agree to it. Even when it might be down to one last prisoner—and that'll probably be Hess—the Russians will want to keep him behind bars.

"There's one other consideration too. For three months of every year, the Russians can maintain an armed presence—maybe 30 men or so—here in West Berlin. That's their prison-guard platoon. So they can nose around, see what's happening, and report back to Moscow on developments on our side of the Wall. It's not a big deal, but it's one more leg up for them."

Holbrook took it all in. "What about the other two inmates?"

"Neither one is or was as visible as Hess," Semsch said. "Albert Speer was Hitler's minister of armaments. But more importantly, Speer was put in charge of building the concentration camps: Speer either had them built or expanded, using slave labor that he worked to death. It's probably because of the mistreatment of those people that he got a 20-year sentence at Nuremberg. His 20 years are almost up and he'll probably be released later this year unless there are complications, such as the Russians protesting and lobbying to keep Speer and von Schirach in Spandau until they die, like Hess's death sentence.

"Baldur von Schirach, believe it or not, had an American-born mother. His grandparents lived in Pennsylvania. One of his indirect ancestors actually signed the Declaration of Independence. He was a vicious anti-Semite and was convicted of deporting Jews from Vienna to the Nazi death camps. Like Speer, he got a 20-year sentence and will probably be released sometime this fall.

"So, in a couple of months, Harry, this huge prison will become home to only one man, Rudolf Hess. It's costing the Berlin Senat something like $800,000 a year to keep the prison in operation since they're paying all of its costs, just like they're paying 90 percent of the costs of keeping the three Western Allies here. But given the alternative—the Russians overrunning West Berlin at the first opportunity—I guess the Senat figures it's worth it. Nevertheless, if it wasn't for the Russians' stubborn insistence that Spandau be kept open until the last Nazi dies, everyone else would be only too happy to see the damn place closed down and leveled so it doesn't become a neo-Nazi symbol. Who knows? Someday this acreage might even become some sort of shopping center after Hess dies."

"We're coming up on the prison, sir," Hellerstein called from the front seat, alerting his two passengers that Russian sentries at the prison gates would soon be in sight.

The 90-year-old prison, which at one time had held as many as 600 inmates—reduced now to just three aging Nazis—looked to Harry Holbrook like some kind of medieval castle or fortress with its two crenellated towers flanking the front gate.

Two Soviet sentries in dress uniforms—obviously forewarned about their commandant's distinguished group of visitors arriving for lunch today—did a quick scan of the sedan's interior before coming to a port arms salute and then pushing a lever to open the gate's two massive doors for the drive through into the prison courtyard.

Semsch and Holbrook, both wearing their standard AG44 Army Green uniforms with gold-braided service caps, exited the sedan and went into the prison's outer rooms, walking through doors held open by Russian soldiers in postures of rigid attention.

They checked their caps at a reception desk, where the receptionist gave them both numbered slips to retrieve their caps when they left. She placed their caps on a shelf behind her, where, Holbrook noted, headgear from all four occupying nations was already represented.

Soviet prison commandant Colonel Dmitri Lazarev proved to be a gracious host. He offered his guests frosted shot glasses of vodka, which Semsch accepted but Holbrook declined in favor of soda water. Holbrook didn't know how well he could hold himself against dyed-in-the-wool Russian vodka.

Semsch was acquainted with a few of the 18 or so guests. He knew, of course, the two USBER people, Day and Brogan, and had seen the two British lieutenant colonels at other functions, but was unfamiliar with the half-dozen Soviet officers who were keeping busy with their shot glasses.

Holbrook was surprised to see the commander of French forces in Berlin, Général de Brigade François Binoche, in the gathering. Binoche, whom he had met before, was known to be a famously private, introverted man who avoided public appearances as much as possible.

Yet another surprise for young Holbrook was the seating plan. Instead of being seated far down Colonel Lazarev's table together with the most junior officers present, lo and behold Holbrook was seated to Lazarev's left, with Binoche directly across the table from him in the place of honor to Lazarev's right. Harry thought that the Russian lieutenant had screwed up in ushering him to a seat so close to the host, but there was his tented name sign—"Major Holbrook, U.S. Army"—right in front of him.

With his guests seated, Lazarev rose with his vodka glass in hand and welcomed them in Russian, French (with a nod to Binoche), and passable, if heavily accented, English. He then proposed a toast to future four-power cooperation and—seeing that Holbrook lacked a shot glass full of vodka—pressed one into Holbrook's hand and gestured with his forearm for him to drink up.

The vodka tore at the roof of Holbrook's throat. No sooner were they seated than Russian orderlies were refilling everyone's glass. Holbrook tried to put his hand over his shot glass to prevent its being refilled but Lazarev gently brushed it aside, motioning the orderly to refill it.

"It is the best Moscovich vodka, Major Holbrook. I had it brought to Berlin from Moscow especially for this luncheon, which is also true of much of the food we shall eat. So please relax and enjoy yourself. You can always take a nap when you get back home," he said with a wink.

Holbrook had no choice but to comply.

The meal was elaborate, confirming what Phil Semsch had told him about each of the four powers vying to outdo one another at the Spandau luncheons. There was herring, borscht, a main course of *kotleti* (cutlets), and a dessert of *medovik* (honey cake), served with hot tea in glasses.

With the meal coming to an end, Lazarev tapped his water glass with a spoon and, nodding to the French brigadier, told everyone that his honored guest, Général de Brigade Binoche, a distinguished hero of the Great Patriotic War who had lost an arm fighting against the Nazis, had an important announcement.

Binoche rose and took off his spectacles so he could look down the table to its end. He spoke first in French, pausing occasionally to translate key thoughts into English. A Soviet lieutenant had quietly appeared next to Colonel Lazarev to translate into the colonel's ear.

"What I am about to share with you should be kept from the news media to the maximum extent possible. Sometime shortly—perhaps within a week or two—President de Gaulle is planning to announce that France is withdrawing all its military forces from NATO because of policy differences. He will request the withdrawal of all American and foreign forces, air bases and depots from France and will ask the NATO headquarters to relocate from Paris, all to be accomplished by April 1 next year."

Binoche paused to let his startling news sink in, then continued. "My chief purpose in sharing this advanced information with you is to assure you that President de Gaulle has called me personally to inform me that the decision for France to leave NATO's military structure will have absolutely no—repeat *non*—impact on my nation's presence here in Berlin.

"Our position is that my brigade, like all your forces in Berlin, is here as an occupying power, not as a member of NATO. The repositioning of NATO forces and its headquarters away from France, together with my country's withdrawal from the military aspects of the NATO alliance, has absolutely no impact whatever on our role here in Berlin.

"President de Gaulle," Binoche continued, "regards the presence of French soldiers in Berlin as an historic obligation. We are privileged to be here, along with the soldiers of your countries, to ensure that the evils of Nazism can never rise again and also to make certain that these last three remaining criminals of the 'Great Patriotic War'—as your nation terms it, Colonel Lazarev—can never cause trouble again."

As Binoche seated himself, the others around the table rose and applauded him. They were impressed with his frankness and now had to hurry back to their respective headquarters to pass the word to their superiors. Day and Brogan were whispering to themselves, while Phil Semsch looked stunned, as Holbrook eyed the rest of the table, assessing their reactions.

"Quite an announcement, Major Holbrook, wouldn't you say?" said Colonel Lazarev, leaning in to Holbrook.

"Yes sir. I see that Colonel Semsch is getting ready to depart. I'm riding with him so I'd better excuse myself."

"Yes, yes, of course. But please be sure to take your correct hat, Major Holbrook. The last time I hosted the luncheon here, one of the officers—I forget which—took home the wrong hat and there was quite a 'rat race,' as you would call it, to figure out whom it belonged to."

"I'll be careful, sir. Thank you again for inviting me."

"My pleasure, Major. Perhaps we shall do it again."

Holbrook went with Semsch to the reception desk, where many of the guests were submitting their hat-check tickets. As the attendant handed Holbrook his service cap, she said, "Please make certain that I have given you the correct cap, Major."

Holbrook wondered why such a fuss was being made about his cap. He checked inside and there, tucked safely inside a plastic holder stitched into the cap's underside, was his calling card, reading, "Harrison Weldon Holbrook Jr., Major, United States Army, Infantry."

"It's my hat, all right," he reassured the attendant. "*Danke schön,*" he said, and followed Phil Semsch out the door to Hellerstein's waiting sedan.

"Well, that was quite a stunning announcement," said Semsch as the car pulled away from the prison. "I hope that François doesn't get his tit in a wringer for giving us a head's up about what Charles the Great is about to spring on NATO."

"What's behind the move?"

"De Gaulle has been pissed for some time about the so-called 'special relationship' that's evolved between the Brits and us. He feels that France has been relegated to second-team status and this is his way of getting back at us. The man's got an enormous ego and this sounds like just one of the stupid things he's capable of doing. He'll probably want to remain a member of NATO for diplomatic reasons, but if Binoche is right, France's military role in NATO is over and done with. Except for here in Berlin, of course, which has nothing to do with NATO."

Holbrook nodded his understanding. "Phil, a couple of funny things took place as the lunch was breaking up."

"There were lots of funny things today, Harry. For example, how come Lazarev seated you in a position of honor right near the head of the table, when there were far more ranking people down the table? No offense, you understand, but I'm sure Pete Day and Brogan were jealous as hell."

Holbrook thought about that for a couple of moments. "Yes, that was weird. But listen to this. Just as the lunch was breaking up, Lazarev leaned in to me and whispered that I needed to be sure I took home the correct hat. Then, at the desk the German girl said almost the same thing—to make sure I had the right hat. I wondered what the heck was going on, that my hat had become so important."

Semsch thought about it. "Let me see your cap, Harry." Holbrook took it off his head and passed it to the intelligence officer.

"Nothing unusual about the outside or the brim," Semsch reported, as he turned the cap over. "There's a calling card in the little envelope. The Army hasn't used calling cards for years, Harry. They're like a vestigial remnant of the days when we placed cards in a tray when calling on the post commander at the New Year's Day reception at his quarters."

"I know that, Phil. I used to go to those dumb receptions when I was a young lieutenant, but now I use the calling cards when I'm dealing with the media and—in this instance—to claim my correct service hat from a reception desk." Holbrook reached out to take the cap back from Semsch, and as he did so he removed the calling card from its plastic holder.

As the card came out of its holder, a small white piece of notebook paper, carefully folded to business card size, fell out of the hat and onto the floor of the sedan. Both officers looked at it in stunned amazement.

Harry Holbrook reached down and picked up the piece of paper. He read to himself:

KaDeWe
Men's shoes
1930, 22 May

and then passed the note to Semsch without comment.

Semsch didn't know what to make of it either. "Harry, you're sure that Colonel Lazarev specifically reminded you to be sure to take the correct hat?"

"Yep, and so did the hat-check girl. It appears they were trying to tell me something."

"I think you're right. I need to talk with some people about this and see if they come to the same conclusion—that Lazarev and some others apparently want you to meet with someone in the men's shoe department at KaDeWe next Wednesday. We've no idea why, but this looks important enough to follow through on. You agree?"

"I do. You need to keep the note, I guess?"

"Right. You've memorized the date and time?"

"Roger that. You'll keep me posted on what's decided about my going to KaDeWe?"

"Of course, Harry. I suppose now we know why Lazarev wanted you sitting right next to him, so he could clue you in about looking into your hat."

Holbrook knew all about one of the largest department stores anywhere in Europe. He had recently bought some civilian shirts and underwear at the massive six-story establishment. Its full name was *Kaufhaus des Westens*, or Department Store of the West. Opened in 1907 by Jewish merchants, it had been demolished by American and British bombers during World War II and then rebuilt, reopening in 1950 to crowds of eager Berliners anxious to buy consumer goods in the postwar period.

Semsch was pondering Harry's visit to the store. "You'll drive your POV"—privately owned vehicle—"of course. And you'll wear civvies. The intent is that you'll appear to be just a regular American shopper. You know where the shoe department is?"

"Yes, it's on the first floor, part of the overall men's clothing department. I know exactly where it's located. Will you have anyone following me?"

Semsch thought about this for a moment. "Harry, I need to coordinate this with some people." Harry supposed this was a reference to the State Department intelligence types, the CIA spooks and probably even General Caraway. "Whether or not we shadow you to KaDeWe is none of your concern. If we do, I promise you, you won't even notice. Any problems with that?"

"No, I guess not. What happens now?"

"I'll try to see the General when we get back to the head shed. I'll see what his guidance is and we'll take it from there."

"Got it," said Holbrook.

General Caraway's Office
USCOB headquarters
Clayallee and Saargemünder Strasse
Dahlem, Zehlendorf
West Berlin
1715 hours, 15 May 1966

Major General Paul Caraway, the U.S. Commander Berlin, looked around at the small group seated at his round conference table.

Present were the American minister, Ernest Calhoun; his deputy, Peter Day; Roger Halvorsen, on paper a State Department attaché, but in actuality the CIA's station chief in Berlin; and Lieutenant Colonel Philip Semsch, who was standing.

Caraway, having heard Semsch's briefing and evaluation of the situation, began the discussion.

"If the Russians have something to tell us, why in the world did they pick an idiot like Holbrook to convey it?"

Semsch, who knew that the USCOB was still smarting from the way Harry Holbrook had outfoxed him a month ago over the *Bahnhof* incident, responded, "Sir, I believe that Colonel Lazarev, or more likely whoever in the East is behind this venture, deliberately chose someone who isn't part of the intelligence structure. As your information officer, Major Holbrook is privy to many secrets which he needs to keep from the press in many instances. In other words, I think that Harry's reputation was known to the Russians and they feel they can trust him and rely on him."

At this, Caraway, Calhoun, and Day all swallowed hard and looked down at their notepads. Holbrook's recent one-upmanship of them all still rankled in their craws. But the Russian plotters had chosen Holbrook as their point of contact—for whatever unknown reason—and there matters stood.

Semsch continued, addressing the USCOB. "Sir, I recommend that we authorize Major Holbrook to make this meeting next Wednesday and then take follow-up action as necessary."

Calhoun, Day, and Halvorsen all exchanged glances and nodded to one another.

General Caraway was still unsettled with the choice of Holbrook. "Mary Beth," he called out to his administrative assistant, "get Major Holbrook in here right away."

"Yes sir," she replied. Six minutes later an out-of-breath Harry Holbrook was ushered into the room.

"You wanted to see me, sir?"

"Sit down, Holbrook," the general said, motioning Major Holbrook to the table where the others sat, now including Colonel Semsch. "Tell us exactly what it was that Colonel Lazarev said to you at the luncheon. And how did you come to be invited?"

"Sir, I have no idea why I was invited. I was surprised to receive the invitation and even more surprised to be seated next to Colonel Lazarev. He was very open and friendly, telling me all about his daughter, who's an A-plus student in aeronautical engineering at Moscow State University. He asked about my own marital status, seemed to know I was divorced with two children, asked if I'd been to Vietnam yet and how I felt about the war there, et cetera."

"But how did he approach you about your hat?"

"As the luncheon was ending and people were starting to stand up and leave, he leaned over and whispered to me that I needed to be sure to retrieve my own service cap, that at a previous luncheon someone made off with the wrong cap. I didn't think anything

27

of it," Holbrook continued, "but then at the check-in desk, as the receptionist handed me my cap—after I'd surrendered my claim ticket—she told me to make sure that I had the correct headgear. Later, in the car, Colonel Semsch and I discovered the note"—he nodded at the message now lying in the center of the conference table—"hidden behind the calling card."

Pete Day was itching to get involved in the inquiry. "You're absolutely certain you've had no prior contact with the Russians?"

"None, sir. None whatsoever."

General Caraway knitted his formidable eyebrows. "Under the circumstances, Holbrook, it seems we have no alternative other than to let you follow through on this. My preference," he said, nodding at the CIA station chief and Semsch, "would be to let a seasoned intelligence professional handle the situation. But under the circumstances the Russians have presented us with, it appears we have no recourse other than to entrust you with the task."

The USCOB looked around the table to ensure that all present understood his reluctance to allow this uninitiated loose cannon named Holbrook to handle such a delicate assignment. All—with the exception of Semsch—nodded sagely in agreement that there was simply no alternative other than to trust this uninitiated major with such an important mission.

"All right, Holbrook, that'll be all," the general said. Holbrook knew he had been dismissed under a cloud of "I wish we had someone better qualified than this neophyte."

Back in his office, Holbrook glanced at the wall clock. 1800 hours. Too late for what he had in mind, but Frau Haupt was still at her desk. "Gertie, get word now to Hugh Erb and Dieter Goos of *Morgenpost* that I need to see them both for a meeting tomorrow morning. Suggest 0900 hours if they can make it. If not, ask what's convenient for both of them. And tell them to bring their tape recorders."

Information Division (ID)
USCOB headquarters
Clayalle and Saargemünder Strasse
Dahlem, Zehlendorf
West Berlin
0945 hours, 16 May 1966

Hubert J. Erb, the Associated Press bureau chief in Berlin, and Dieter Goos, the military reporter for *Die Berliner Morgenpost*, one of the city's most respected newspapers, sat down in front of Harry Holbrook's desk, portable Uher reel-to-reel tape recorders at the ready. Goos, Holbrook noted, had a much more up-to-date model than the AP newsman.

"Thanks for coming, Hugh and Dieter. I have something important to share with you on deep background, not for attribution, and embargoed until it's publicly announced by the French. I've worked closely with both of you and I feel I can trust you better than some of the others who cover the military scene."

Hugh Erb, probably around 40, Holbrook estimated, had graduated from some university in Buffalo, New York. He'd taken an ROTC commission as an artillery officer and been sent to Korea, where he'd served in the 187th Airborne Regimental Combat Team under a rising brigadier general named William Westmoreland. After his discharge from the Army, Erb had gone to work for the AP in New York City and in February 1965 had been on a bus traveling through Harlem and Washington Heights—the only white person on board—when he thought he heard what sounded like gunshots.

Although his fellow passengers dismissed the noise as a backfiring automobile, Erb's nose for news kicked in. He pulled the bus's emergency cord and dismounted at Broadway and West 165th Street. He saw policemen and a crowd rushing toward the second floor

29

of the Audubon Ballroom and discovered that African-American nationalist leader Malcolm X had been shot and killed by some disaffected members of the Nation of Islam while getting ready to address an estimated 400 attendees at an African-American conference on unity.

Erb's story on the assassination of Malcolm X scooped the competition by almost 30 minutes, resulting in his rapid ascent through the AP hierarchy and a year later landing him the plum position of AP bureau chief in West Berlin. Erb, whose father had emigrated to the United States from Cologne in West Germany, and who had subsequently returned to Germany after the war, had married a blonde German girl whom he met while visiting his father in Cologne. Erb and his wife Krista had a five-year-old son named Klaus, whom Holbrook had met.

Dieter Goos was younger than Erb, around 30, Holbrook believed. He was a conscientious follower of the military scene in West Berlin, attended key functions, briefings, etc., and didn't hesitate to come to Holbrook with intelligent and logical questions about what was taking place in the American sector.

"Hugh, Dieter," Harry Holbrook began as both turned on their Uhers, "I learned yesterday that sometime in the next few days, probably less than a week from now, President de Gaulle is planning on announcing that France is withdrawing its forces from NATO and is kicking the NATO headquarters out of the Fontainebleau section of Paris. The NATO headquarters will have to leave France, along with all non-French armed forces personnel, ammunition, and supply depots and weaponry. All non-French military personnel and equipment will also be required to leave French soil."

Holbrook paused while the two journalists absorbed this astonishing development. "The good news," Holbrook continued, "is that it has no effect on our French brigade here in Berlin. General Binoche and his men will stay on with no impact on them."

Goos raised a hand to speak. "That would be because the status of the French soldiers in Berlin is still that of an occupying power, without relationship to NATO. Would that be correct, Major Holbrook?"

"Correct, Dieter. De Gaulle is miffed at the close ties between Britain and the United States, feels that he has his own nuclear arsenal to defend France, and to hell with the rest of Western Europe."

Erb spoke for the first time. "Everything you've said is embargoed until de Gaulle makes his announcement. Is that right, Harry?"

"Totally, Hugh. I'm telling you this in strictest confidence so you can do your background research, history of the French in NATO and Berlin, et cetera. Under no circumstances can you contact Binoche or anyone who's not in this room right now. I hope that's understood, because if this leaks, my ass will be on the next flight to Saigon and you'll have to take your chances with the next USCOB spokesman."

The reporters turned off their tape recorders, nodded in acquiescence at Holbrook's deep-background admonition, thanked him for sharing the information with them, and left the office.

Holbrook knew that once again he was sticking his neck out. But he felt that he owed a heads-up to two diligent, hard-working newsmen and, if it backfired, well, his reputation in Berlin was already lower than whale shit. Plus, if he needed a favor sometime in the future from Erb or Goos, he knew he could call on them and remind them that they owed him.

3

KaDeWe Department Store
Tauentzienstrasse 21–24
Intersection of Schöneberg/Charlottenburg Districts
Central West Berlin
1900 hours, 22 May 1966

Major Harrison Holbrook parked his POV, a dark blue 1961 Chevrolet Impala that he'd retained under terms of his divorce from Holly, in the parking lot.

He was 30 minutes early for his appointment at 1930 hours, as recommended by Phil Semsch, so that he could nose around the store to see if anything was amiss.

Earlier that afternoon, Holbrook had been killing time—waiting for his clandestine rendezvous at KaDeWe—by reading the story in the *Stars & Stripes* military newspaper about France's decision to disengage from its military role in NATO.

Twenty-four hours earlier, French President Charles de Gaulle had told a press conference in Paris that France was withdrawing all its military forces from NATO and that U.S. and other European armed forces had to be out of France by April 1, 1967.

When U.S. Secretary of State Dean Rusk briefed President Lyndon B. Johnson on the sudden, unexpected turn of events, LBJ flew off the handle and gave Rusk a direct order: "Ask him about the cemeteries, Dean!"

What had happened was that after Rusk had informed LBJ that all U.S. troops and equipment were to be removed from French soil by April 1, Johnson became enraged and insisted that Rusk query de Gaulle on whether the eviction notice included the American dead who had fought and died on French soil on behalf of French freedom and now lay buried in cemeteries in France. Whereupon Rusk asked de Gaulle to his face at the end of a meeting if the order to leave France included the more than 60,000 American soldiers buried in France who were killed fighting on behalf of France and the Western Allies in two world wars. De Gaulle, embarrassed by the question (which was what LBJ had intended), rose, left the meeting, and never responded.

Holbrook hadn't yet learned all these details as he strode through the huge, elaborate department store in his blue blazer, with an open-necked light blue dress shirt and khakis. He had deliberately selected a pair of well-worn, down-at-the-heel (literally) brown lace-up shoes so he would clearly be in need of a replacement pair.

The men's department, he knew, was on the first floor. To get there, he had to pass a memorial in the store's exact center which read, "Places of terror that we are never allowed to forget," followed by a listing of the major Nazi death camps such as Buchenwald and Auschwitz.

If he was being followed by anyone from Phil Semsch's operation, or by anyone else whether friend or foe, Holbrook was unable to pick up the surveillance. True, he wasn't a trained counterspy expert, but with his eyeglasses in place he had pretty keen eyesight.

The merchandise was gorgeous. Pricey to be sure, but beautiful. He saw sports jackets and slacks he could drool over. Someday, he mused, when he got back to dating again, he would love to be wearing clothing like this, if he could afford it on a major's pay and with child-support responsibilities.

At precisely 1930 hours, Holbrook arrived at the KaDeWe men's shoe department. There were no other shoppers in that section of the store as far as he could see and he began to browse through the displays.

As he examined shoes, looking at sole bottoms to be see how many marks each pair cost, (doing mental arithmetic to convert four German marks into one U.S. dollar), he was unaware that a clerk had come up quietly behind him.

"*Guten Abend, mein Herr,*" the clerk said behind him. Then, as if realizing he was dealing with an American soldier because of the close haircut, he corrected himself, saying, "Good evening, sir. How may I be of service to you?"

"I need a pair of brown shoes," Holbrook said. "As you can see, the ones I'm wearing have pretty much outlived their usefulness."

"Of course, sir. We offer a complete selection of quality footwear. Would the gentleman be interested in a slip-on? A loafer? Perhaps we should start with a lace-up, since that is what you are now wearing."

"Yes, good idea."

"Please have a seat anywhere, sir, so I can measure you for the best possible fit. Wednesday evenings are usually one of our slower traffic times, so we can take all the time necessary to ensure a perfect fit to your satisfaction."

The shoe clerk was probably in his mid-40s, Holbrook guessed, with glasses and a receding hairline. He was dressed in a black suit with a vest and a starched white shirt underneath. In short, a typical Berlin male department store clerk.

Holbrook chose a seat and the clerk brought over a small stool on which he sat, with a sloped side facing his customer so a foot could be placed on it.

"Please be kind enough to remove both shoes, sir," he said, examining the insides of one for its size. "10 ½, double E. A fairly wide foot, would you say, sir?"

"I suppose so," Holbrook, replied, wondering when the clerk was going to get down to business or whether this was all a bit of theatrical nonsense.

"This is a standard, lace-up shoe, sir. Would the gentleman prefer one similar to it or some other style, perhaps?'

"No, lace-up will be fine."

"Please excuse me for a few minutes. I will go the stockroom on the other side of the department to bring out some sample brown lace-up shoes that I think will be satisfactory."

With the clerk out of sight for several minutes, Holbrook used the opportunity to glance casually around the men's department. Other than an idle clerk positioned at a cash register, he was pretty sure there was no one else in the department.

The clerk returned a few minutes later, carrying a stack of six or seven shoeboxes. "These are all your size, sir, and I am hoping that there is one among them that will be satisfactory for you."

As he slipped the first pair of shoes on Holbrook's feet, using a plastic shoehorn to insert each shoe and then lace them up, the clerk began speaking in a discreet whisper. "I have just confirmed your identity, Major Holbrook, so we may talk in confidence. My name is Gunther and I am your direct and only contact in this matter."

Just as Holbrook was about to ask what the project was, the clerk raised a hand to hush him. "All in good time, Major. Exactly two weeks from today, June 5, at approximately 1215 hours, a Soviet MiG-21 airplane will be flown from Schönefeld Airport in East Berlin and will be crash-landed in the Griebnitzsee. That is a lake in the Wannsee District of West Berlin. Do you know it?"

Holbrook nodded. He was familiar with the lake—about 2 miles long and maybe the width of three football fields. The dividing line between West Berlin and East Germany ran exactly down the middle of the lake, and a couple of months ago an East German barge skipper had been caught at dawn pulling up the demarcation pilings—tall wooden telephone-pole-like markers—and moving them eastward, thereby expanding the size of East Germany at the expense of West Berlin. USBER officials had protested with the Ulbricht regime in East Germany, whereupon it was attributed to a careless mistake by the barge captain, who had misunderstood his instructions.

Holbrook's breath had caught at mention of the MiG-21. He was vaguely familiar with the fact that it was a fairly recent addition to the Soviet Air Forces and that its NATO code name was "Fishbed." It was rumored that it posed a highly maneuverable threat to American warplanes such as the F-4 Phantom.

Gunther continued. "The pilot of the airplane is a Soviet Air Forces captain who wishes to defect to the West, together with his wife, who is currently being allowed to study music in Vienna. He is offering the MiG as his down payment for moving him and his wife to the United States and providing them with a new life.

"Do you have any questions, Major Holbrook? You were selected for this assignment because you have a reputation in your headquarters of having a remarkable memory with a fine grasp of important details. Nothing can be written down and you must store it entirely in your head until everything has been accomplished. Is that agreeable to you?"

As Gunther was speaking, he was continuing to try different shoes on Holbrook's feet, pausing to ask Holbrook if they fit, how he liked them, etc.

Holbrook wondered how Gunther and his associates knew about his reputation in the USCOB headquarters for having an exceptional memory. Holbrook himself had had no idea that he had a special memory, but it had finally become clear to him why he had been the contact for Colonel Lazarev, Gunther, and whoever else was working with them.

"Major, that is all we are to accomplish this evening. I would ask you at this point to inform your commanding general and his officials—in the greatest of secrecy—that this defection is going to take place during lunch hour on June 5. Captain Vasilevsky—his name—will parachute into the Grunewald near the West Berlin side of the lake after making certain that his airplane has been steered into the water. Steps will be taken to make it appear that he aimed his malfunctioning airplane into the lake to protect the lives of innocent Berliners.

"You and I will meet here again one week from tonight at a new time, 1830 hours. You will return the shoes you are about to purchase because you have decided that you want a slip-on pair instead. Do you have any immediate questions?"

There were a thousand things that Holbrook wanted to ask, but he opted to wait for next week.

It was just as well, because Gunther raised the volume of his voice at that point, saying, "Very well, sir, I think this pair is an excellent choice and if you will just step this way, I will process your payment and wrap them for you."

Holbrook carried his bagged purchase to his car in the KaDeWe parking lot. As he slid into the driver's seat, a slouching figure sat up in the rear seat—Phil Semsch, in civvies.

"What happened, Harry?" No preambles, no apologies for breaking into Holbrook's Chevy Impala.

So, Harry Holbrook—he of the legendary memory that apparently was renowned throughout all of Berlin, even on both sides of the Wall—gave Semsch a word-for-word replay of the conversation as he drove back toward Dahlem and home.

General Caraway's office
USCOB headquarters
Clayallee and Saargemünder Strasse
Dahlem, Zehlendorf
West Berlin
0830 hours, 23 May 1966

General Caraway had summoned on a basis of urgency the previous attendees at his conference table, with the addition of Colonel Charles Hazeltine, the USCOB chief of staff. This time, Major Holbrook was included and was seated at the table. He had just given his second account of the previous night's rendezvous at KaDeWe and watched the incredulous reactions of the group.

Halvorsen, the CIA station chief, was first to speak. "This is an incredible development, General. The MiG-21 has been in service for only a few years and we've never been able to lay our hands on one up to this point."

"But what the hell good is it to us at the bottom of a lake?"

Halvorsen had an immediate answer. "Sir, we can cordon off our side of the Griebnitzsee in all directions so the Soviets can't muscle their way in. They won't have a platoon at Spandau next month, but they will have soldiers guarding the War Memorial who can be rushed to the lake. It will take some time to move reinforcements from East Berlin. So we fence off our side of the lake and send underwater divers to take photos of the plane and all its equipment. If we can hold the Russians off for a couple of days, there might even be time to bring some of the avionics to the surface, take them apart, analyze their coding, and photograph everything before we return the plane to them."

"Who says we have to return the plane?" said Caraway.

Minister Calhoun was quick to respond. "General, that airplane must be returned to the Soviets as promptly as possible. Perhaps we can stall them for a few days with some technical excuses, as Mr. Halvorsen proposes, but that airplane is a piece of Soviet property and must be returned. Failure to do would constitute an international incident."

Hazeltine spoke for the first time. "Who lifts the plane out of the lake?"

Colonel Semsch had an answer. "We let the Russians do it by themselves, under close supervision of one or two of our rifle companies. After we've gotten every single bit of usable information out of the plane, we then become gracious hosts and invite our Russian brothers in arms to bring their heavy equipment and retrieve the MiG-21."

"What about the pilot?" asked USBER's Pete Day. "Holbrook, what do you know about the pilot?"

"Very little, sir. His name is Captain Vasilevsky and he plans to parachute out of his plane at the last minute after making certain that it won't crash into any West Berlin neighborhoods. He and his wife—she's in Vienna studying music—want to defect to the U.S. and are offering the MiG as their airfare, so to speak."

General Caraway chose not to be amused by Major Holbrook's clever wordplay. "Is that all you know about him, Holbrook?"

"Sir, I'm assuming that I'll learn more when I meet with Gunther at KaDeWe next Wednesday. At this point, that's just about all I was told," Holbrook said. He chose not to inform the group, other than Semsch whom he had already told, that he'd been chosen for his role as go-between because of his allegedly fabulous memory. But he felt confident that he had passed along to them just about every word—verbatim—that had been exchanged between Gunther and himself.

"What's our next step, gentlemen?" said General Caraway. "And we've got to keep this under tight wraps so we don't blow the whole opportunity."

"Right, sir," said the CIA's Halvorsen. "I assume that Colonel Hazeltine will line up a rifle company or so from one of the brigade's battalions," at which suggestion Hazeltine nodded and made a note on his writing tablet.

"Then," Halvorsen continued, "we need to each discreetly inform our higher headquarters of what's about to take place on June 5. The problem is that each of them—and I know Langley well—will want to send observers who will only gum up the works. Minister Calhoun, if you could get word to the White House about what's happening and have President Johnson's new chief of staff, Marvin Watson, order them all to stand aside, that would address that problem,"

Calhoun nodded in agreement, turned to his deputy Pete Day, and got assent. He made a note to phone Watson after he'd called Bonn on a secure line to brief Ambassador George McGhee.

"What about SCUBA divers?" Caraway asked. "Navy SEALs, I suppose? We could ask EUCOM for the loan of some SEALs."

"Sir, the Brits have some very fine underwater divers," said Colonel Semsch, "and it might be useful to get them involved in this, along with our own Navy SEALs, in the spirit of cooperation."

"That makes eminent sense, Phil," said Minister Calhoun. "Excellent idea."

Holbrook had remained silent during this operational portion of the meeting. Having passed along the details of his KaDeWe meeting, he had little or nothing to contribute. His sense of things was that Caraway was being given good advice, and Holbrook was already beginning to make plans for his meeting that afternoon with his Volksfest contractors when Caraway brought him back to reality.

"Holbrook, are you really and truly confident that you can handle the pressures accompanying this assignment? You haven't been trained in any of the intelligence-gathering techniques that we've been discussing and I wonder if the challenges of this very important situation are above your pay grade?"

"Sir, as a first lieutenant I served for two years as aide-de-camp to Major General William Breckinridge when he was chief of the Army Security Agency. ASA, as you know, is the Army component of the National Security Agency. I traveled with General Breckinridge all around the world, visiting ASA installations and activities, some of them classified, such as under the roof of our embassy in Cairo, Egypt. The general and I went to Shemya Island in the western Aleutians; Sinop on the Black Sea coast; Asmara, Eritrea; Cheltenham, the British signals intelligence headquarters; and a bunch of other locations. I still carry my Top Secret/Crypto security clearance.

"In short, General, I know how to keep a secret and I'm used to working under pressure. For some reason"—here again Holbrook chose not to mention his vaunted memory skills—"some people in East Berlin or East Germany singled me out for this job. There's no problem, sir. I can handle it."

Caraway still looked skeptical. "Very well, then," he said reluctantly. "Gentlemen, let's begin the necessary coordination steps and reconvene here Saturday morning at 10." Turning to Calhoun, he asked, "Will that be agreeable, Ernest?"

Calhoun assented and the meeting broke up.

Information Division (ID)
USCOB headquarters
Clayallee and Saargemünder Strasse
Dahlem, Zehlendorf
West Berlin
1400 hours, 23 May 1966

A major component of Major Harrison Holbrook's responsibilities, apart from his current role as a *sub-rosa* intelligence operative, was the planning, coordination and execution of the annual German-American Volksfest, or people's festival.

Each summer in late July and August when the weather was optimal, the U.S. command in West Berlin hosted an annual outdoors Volksfest, attracting an estimated half a million Berliners. This had been going on since 1961, the year the Berlin Wall was erected. The Volksfest took place at a site where Clayallee and Argentinische Allee intersected in Dahlem, a few minutes from the USCOB headquarters and near the Thomas A. Roberts elementary school for the children of American military and civilian personnel stationed in Berlin.

Volksfest planning under Holbrook's supervision had commenced almost as soon as the 1965 event had concluded in mid-August. Holbrook was responsible for a huge network of contractors, beer vendors, restaurateurs, musicians, performing actors, souvenir vendors, and endlessly on, it sometimes seemed.

Holbrook's deputy information officer, a civilian named J. Paul Scholl, was the hands-on leg man for Volksfest planning, on an almost year-round basis. Scholl, a 48-year-old long-time Berlin resident who'd married a German woman and had two children with her, sported a widow's peak hairline and a dapper mustache that he played with constantly when cogitating or perhaps plotting his next romantic conquest among the pretty German secretaries employed at USCOB and USBER.

With the opening of the fifth Volksfest only two months away, it was time, Holbrook felt, to bring the key players together and review progress to date despite his important involvement in the MiG-21 affair.

Holbrook looked around the table in his conference room, making sure that all the usual key operatives were present: Paul Scholl; Frau Ingeborg Jochem, Scholl's right-hand assistant; as well as Werner Bauer and Ernst Zimmermann, the two principal German contractors who were responsible for construction of Volksfest buildings and beer tents, signing up musical talent, etc.

For the first time, Holbrook had invited the brigade's special services officer, a civilian named Dan Silvestri, to the Volksfest meeting, and Silvestri wondered why.

"I'm getting a very favorable reaction from the West Berlin German community," Holbrook began, "that we've decided to repeat last year's Wild West theme. As we discovered at last year's Volksfest, the Berliners are fascinated, literally thrilled, with anything dealing with cowboys and Indians. Werner and Ernst, I'm under the impression that last year we sold more cowboy hats, toy pistols, Indian headdresses, and so on in the souvenir booths, than in the three previous Volksfests combined."

The two contractors nodded in agreement. "And the Dodge City Saloon sold more beer than any other four *Bierhalles* combined," noted Bauer.

All Volksfest proceeds, after deductions for expenses arising from construction costs, food and beverages, and manpower, were donated to the West Berlin Senat and earmarked for university scholarships for needy students. The 1965 net proceeds had amounted to more than half a million Deutschemarks, or about 125,000 U.S. dollars, so the Volksfest was a major operation, both in terms of German–American relations and the scholarship assistance it provided.

After all reports had been presented and Frau Jochem had recorded her scrupulously accurate minutes of the meeting, Holbrook turned to the special services man, Dan Silvestri, who had responsibility for virtually every form of recreation in the American sector: intramural sports, golf tournaments, baseball, touch football and soccer leagues.

"Dan, I'll bet you're wondering why I invited you." Silvestri nodded. "Two things I had in mind," Holbrook explained. "First, in view of the Berliners' love for all things cowboys and Indians, I was wondering about staging a John Wayne film festival at the Outpost Theater." The Outpost was the movie theater on Clayallee that showed fairly recent Hollywood movies to American soldiers and their families. The theater seated about 750, but no one was seated while the National Anthem was being played before each performance. The 1964 Walt Disney musical fantasy *Mary Poppins* was currently being shown at the Outpost.

Holbrook continued, "I know that we normally require American ID cards to get into the Outpost, but I'll bet that if we opened the theater up to Berliners during the Volksfest, charging maybe one mark (twenty-five cents) for adults and children, we could make a bundle and entertain a lot of people. So, Dan, I'd like you to check with your film distributors and see if any John Wayne films come in a German-language version. Even if they don't, I have an idea how we can use German-speaking translators to narrate while the film is running."

"No problem, Major," said Silvestri. "What's the other thing?"

"Boats, Dan, boats. I'd like to make your special services rowboats available to the Berliners to row around on the lake behind the Volksfest grounds. Most of them are too poor to have ever been in a boat. We'd need life jackets, of course, and close supervision by some of the brigade's soldiers, but I believe it could be done. We'd charge maybe six marks for a family to take a boat out for 30 minutes. Something like that."

Then Holbrook arrived at a key moment of his meeting. "How many rowboats do you have, Dan?"

"As of this morning, I've got 13 operational boats and two more in maintenance getting fresh coats of olive drab paint. Barring any accidents, I'm thinking we should have 15 boats available by Volksfest time."

"That's great, Dan. Let's plan on it," Holbrook said. "Anything else we need to discuss? If not, let's all get back to work," and he adjourned the meeting.

After everyone had filed out of the conference room, Scholl stayed behind to ask Holbrook, "What was that all about, Harry? We've never used boats before, and it opens us up to all sorts of liabilities if there's a boating accident."

"I know, Paul. It may be impractical but I was just wondering if it could be done. We'll see."

44

Office of the U.S. Commander Berlin
Clayallee and Saargemünder Strasse
Dahlem, Zehlendorf
West Berlin
1010 hours, 25 May 1966

General Caraway convened his MiG-21 meeting a few minutes after 1000 hours, after everyone had been offered coffee and doughnuts. With the inclusion of Brigadier General Walter J. Hay, who commanded the Berlin Brigade, once again there was no room for Harry Holbrook at Caraway's round table, and he was consigned to a back-bencher seat near the door of the conference room.

"Thank you all for coming," the USCOB began. "I appreciate your giving up a Saturday morning, particularly on this beautiful day for golfing. And Walter," he said, nodding to the one-star general who was his second in command in Berlin, "thank you for joining this important task force. I believe that Colonel Hazeltine has brought you up to speed on everything we know at this time."

Hay nodded in agreement. "That's affirmative, sir. Charles has filled me in on the situation as we know it."

Walter Hay was a 6-foot-2-inch good-looking officer who commanded respect just by his physical appearance. Compared with the shorter, dour, two-star general that Hay reported to, he looked like a Hollywood casting director's dream. Hay had been an honor graduate of the University of Wyoming's ROTC "Cowboy Battalion" and was clearly headed for a second star and possibly even a third, factors which occasioned more than a trifling amount of jealousy on the part of his immediate supervisor, Caraway.

"To begin with," Caraway said, "I've asked Roger to update us on what he's learned about the Russian defector."

45

Halvorsen, the CIA station chief in Berlin, fingered his handwritten notes and nodded. "Thank you, General. Langley has been able to verify that there is in fact a Captain Alexi Vasilevsky assigned to Schönefeld Airport, about 10 miles southeast of East Berlin. Schönefeld, as we know," Halvorsen continued, "serves as headquarters to the Soviet Air Forces in Germany, so it's not terribly surprising that a couple of MiG-21s are based there. The plane is basically a jet fighter and interceptor, so it's well-suited to patrol the territory around Berlin, particularly to the west and the three air corridors between West Germany and West Berlin.

"Captain Vasilevsky is around 30 years old, married, no children, and is considered one of the Russians' best pilots. He's apparently being groomed to take command of a MiG-21 squadron sometime in the next two or three years."

"What about his wife?" asked Minister Calhoun.

"Yes sir, she is indeed in Vienna, as Harry told us last time. She is a concert violinist with the Moscow Philharmonic Orchestra and is highly regarded, we believe. In fact, the orchestra's director, Kiril Kondrashin, arranged for her to spend a year in Vienna, working under and learning from its principal conductor, Wolfgang Sawallisch, who was born in Munich and took the orchestra on a tour of the U.S. two years ago."

"Any word, Roger, on the captain's political leanings?" asked Pete Day of the State Department.

"Not a word, Pete. As far as we can tell, he's a loyal supporter of Brezhnev and the Communist Party; otherwise, he wouldn't be entrusted with a MiG-21. So we really don't know what his motivation for defecting is. It would be helpful, Major Holbrook," he said, looking over his shoulder at Holbrook sitting by the door, "if you could glean any information about this from your contact at KaDeWe."

"I'll certainly try, sir."

General Caraway was concerned about the logistics of the operation. "Holbrook, you told us that the pilot plans to parachute out into the Griebnitzsee. Just in case he lands by accident outside the American sector, I'm wondering if we ought to alert the British and French about the possible arrival of a Soviet parachutist in their sector midday on June 5."

"With all due respect, sir," said Phil Semsch, "I'd advise against it. The French in particular leak like a sieve when it comes to controlling classified information and word would get back to Ulbricht in a hurry"—Walter Ulbricht was the leader of the German Democratic Republic, or East Germany—"and the captain would be arrested."

There was concurrence around the table not to inform the Western Allies in advance of the pending defection and Caraway dropped the idea.

"Let's talk about controlling the site," he said. "How do we protect our side of the Griebnitzsee, and what about the East German side? "

Colonel Hazeltine, the USCOB chief of staff, replied, "Sir, there's a patrol path along the lake's southern and western shores. I've arranged with General Hay for a reinforced rifle company from the second of the sixth (2nd Battalion, 6th Infantry Regiment of the Berlin Brigade) to take up positions on the southern shore by 0900 on the 5th. The brigade will also pitch four squad tents in that vicinity: one for a mess tent, one for a command post, and two for the off-duty soldiers to rest on portable cots. Concertina wire will be strung by the 42nd Engineer Company all along our side of the lake to protect the site against any intrusion by the Russians, Vopos, or curious Berliners." The Vopos were the *Volkspolizei*, or East German people's police.

Heads turned toward Hay, who nodded in agreement and added, "The company will be under the command of Captain Stephen Zaijek, probably the best company commander I have in the brigade. His men will carry their M14 rifles and M60 machine guns, with full combat loads of live ammunition. I've coordinated that with General O'Meara's people in USAREUR and they approve. Some of the M60s will be pedestal-mounted on our jeeps."

Calhoun and Day of USBER blanched at the thought of the 19-year-old riflemen of the brigade carrying live ball ammunition to the site but they realized the very real likelihood of Soviet interference from the western, or East German, side of the Griebnitzsee, where the Russian pilot was planning to ditch his aircraft.

"What about protecting the western side of the lake?" Caraway asked. "We assume that the Russians will rush their guards from the War Memorial to the lake as soon as they realize that the MiG is at the bottom."

Semsch replied, "Yes, that's undoubtedly what will happen, General. We can't legally deny their Memorial guards access to the East German side of the lake, since rights of access are protected under the four-power agreement. Isn't that so, Minister?" at which point Calhoun and Day nodded in assent.

"So what we have to do," Semsch continued, "is allow the Soviets access to the East German side of the lake, but prevent them from interfering with our underwater salvage efforts until we're finally able to turn the airplane over to them."

"But how do we do that, Semsch?" Caraway asked. "How do we keep them from intervening as we examine the plane underwater, or prevent them firing at our efforts?"

"Sir," Semsch answered, "the lake is only 869 feet at its maximum width, although it's just under 2 miles in length. It would be possible, I suppose, for them to try to bring longer-range weapons with them, but we would prevent that at Checkpoint Charlie."

As the participants pondered the implications of keeping the Russians at bay on their side of the lake in East German territory, a voice came from a seat near the door.

"Boats," said the voice. Heads turned in its direction.

"We station rowboats in the middle of the lake, right where the dividing line is," said Harry Holbrook, "and we tie them to the pilings that mark the political boundary between West Berlin and East Germany. Each boat should contain three or four armed riflemen."

"Good idea, Holbrook," said General Caraway with just a note of sarcasm. "But we don't have any boats."

"Actually, sir, we do. We have 13 operational rowboats, with two more in the shop being painted. That's 15. We add the three Ducks that the Engineer Company has, and we've got 18 craft that can be spaced out along the 2-mile length of the lake."

General Hay spoke. "I can confirm that the brigade's Engineer Company has three Ducks. The Duck can move on land or water and would seem to be well suited for this mission."

"And where are the other 15 boats, Holbrook?" asked General Caraway. Apparently, the youthful major had shot his mouth off once again without thinking.

"They're in our Special Services Department, sir, available for recreational use by our soldiers and their families. We'd pull all 15 boats from service, of course, a week or so before the MiG is due."

"And why are you so confident about the number of boats and their availability, Holbrook?"

"I spoke with Dan Silvestri yesterday afternoon, sir. He's the brigade's special services officer, as you know."

"Yes, yes, of course." Caraway looked around the table. "What do you think, gentlemen?"

They all nodded in approval at Holbrook's suggestion and General Hay made a note to nail it down with Silvestri.

"I think that will do it for today, gentlemen. When is your next meeting at KaDeWe, Holbrook?"

"May 29, sir, at 1830 hours."

"We'll re-convene on May 30," said the USCOB, "to see what Holbrook has learned. Meanwhile, continue close coordination with your respective headquarters, reminding everyone that if this is leaked, a golden opportunity will have been lost. Are there any questions? If not, the meeting is adjourned. Thank you all for coming."

4

KaDeWe Department Store
Tauentzienstrasse 21–24
Intersection of Schöneberg/Charlottenberg Districts
Central West Berlin
1815 hours, 29 May 1966

Carrying a paper sack containing the box of unworn shoes he was returning, Harry Holbrook entered the massive KaDeWe department store and spent a few minutes surveying the customer traffic. As before, he was wearing casual civilian clothes, a pair of starched blue jeans, with a Penn State T-shirt. But he had substituted running shoes for the down-at-the-heel shoes he had worn to the previous KaDeWe meeting.

Satisfied that nothing seemed amiss, he entered the men's shoe department and began looking for his contact. There was no need to browse among the shoes on display since his task was clearly to return an unwanted pair. His contact, Gunther, appeared to be finishing up the fitting of shoes on another customer, so Holbrook waited patiently near a cash register.

Another clerk approached him. "How may I be of assistance, sir?"

"I'm waiting for him," Holbrook said, nodding in Gunther's direction, "and he's busy right now, it seems. He sold me a pair of shoes last week and I wanted to try something else."

"That is no problem, sir. I would be more than happy to assist the gentleman."

"No, I'll wait for him. He was very helpful last week. What was his name again?"

"That would be Gunther, sir. He is one of our longest-serving assistants in the men's shoe department. May I inform him that you are waiting?"

"Thanks, no need to. I'll just wait and look around."

"Very well, sir. May I at least relieve you of the pair you are returning?"

"Yes, thank you."

Holbrook began to scan the shoe displays, occasionally turning shoes over to examine the price tag attached to the sole bottoms. He had pretty much decided to trade in the lace-up pair for a more casual pair of slip-ons, maybe with a tassel. Doing so, he wondered how Berliners, only 20 years or so after Allied bombings and Russian devastation, had come up with the resiliency to be able to afford these kinds of prices for a pair of men's shoes.

He was almost afraid to look at the cost of the high-fashion women's shoes at the other end of the store and perhaps even glad that he no longer had a wife to spend money on such articles of clothing. Maybe not. Marriage had its usefulness, he had to concede, and in some ways he missed it, particularly the absence of his two children, who were in process of forgetting about him a little more as each day passed.

Quietly, as before, Gunther was beside him. "I was sorry to learn from my colleague that the shoes were not entirely satisfactory, sir."

"No, no, the shoes were fine. It's just that I changed my mind and decided to get something a little more casual. Slip-ons or loafers maybe."

"Absolutely, sir. Was the size correct, 10½ double E, I believe?"

"Yes, the fit was perfect."

"Please allow me to visit the stockroom and locate a selection of shoes in that size and style. Brown again? Perhaps burgundy? Cordovan maybe?"

"Yes, any of those might work, I suppose." Holbrook didn't want to dilly-dally over the color of the shoes; he was there for a specific purpose, but he recognized that Gunther was correct and that the semblance of a normal shoe sale needed to be maintained.

While Gunther was away in the stockroom, Holbrook realized that it was 1900 hours and the other clerk had apparently left for the night. Once again, he'd be alone with Gunther in the shoe department, as the clerk had probably planned.

Gunther came back, carrying two stacks of men's shoeboxes and setting them down next to the stool on which he sat. "I am hopeful, sir, that among these shoes there will be a pair that will be highly satisfactory to you," and he began to try on various styles for Holbrook's appraisal.

"Have you been able to make necessary arrangements for June 5, Major?"

"Yes, everything will be in readiness. Where does Captain Vasilevsky plan to land after he parachutes from his plane? Can you give me a physical description of him—height, weight, for instance?"

"Certainly. After he steers his plane so that it is heading for the eastern side of the Griebnitzsee, he will parachute into the Grunewald, which is the largest green area in the entire city of Berlin. You are familiar with the Grunewald, sir?"

"Yes. In fact, my house on Goldfinkweg backs up to the Grunewald and my backyard fence gives access to the Grunewald. On that basis, we can bring Captain Vasilevsky to my quarters, change him out of his flying suit, and prepare to get him out of Berlin as rapidly as possible. What does he look like?"

"Alexi is not as tall as you, perhaps one and three-quarter meters."

"Five foot eight," Holbrook calculated aloud.

"Precisely. He weighs about 75 kilograms."

"About 165 pounds," Holbrook estimated.

"Yes. He has brown hair and brown eyes."

"How about facial hair? Mustache? Beard?"

"Yes, he does wear a mustache," Gunther said.

"We'll shave that off at my house," Holbrook thought aloud.

"Have arrangements been made to get his wife out of Vienna? That is a most important part of his willingness to move to the West and cooperate with your officials."

"To be sure. We have confirmed that she is studying with the Viennese orchestra and American agents know where she lives. She will be flown with a female CIA agent to Frankfurt to join her husband there while he is being debriefed."

"Debriefed? I am not sure what that means." Gunther said.

"Questioned. Interrogated. The CIA and military officials will have all sorts of questions for him before he is relocated to the United States. They will want to talk to him while everything is still fresh in his memory about his airplane, the numbers and types of planes at Schönefeld, the organization of the Soviet Air Forces, their missions, etc. It will take a few days and his wife will be able to shop or visit in Frankfurt, escorted by the female CIA officer.

"I will be meeting tomorrow with the USCOB, General Caraway, and members of his staff, and we will make final arrangements to ensure the safety of Captain Vasilevsky and his wife, as well as to safeguard the wreckage of his airplane."

Holbrook raised the volume of his voice. "This pair is exactly what I had in mind. Please wrap it up for me. Is there any additional cost?"

"None whatsoever, sir. It has been my pleasure serving you."

General Caraway welcomed the group, which Harry Holbrook had begun to think of as the MiG-21 Task Force. Caraway called on Holbrook for a report on the previous night's KaDeWe encounter, which Holbrook did. Everyone seemed satisfied with the planning arrangements.

"What do you all think at this point?" the USCOB asked.

The CIA's Halvorsen was first to respond. "It all sounds legitimate, sir. Jenny Moss, one of our agents in Vienna, has made contact with Captain Vasilevsky's wife, will pick her up at the concert hall the morning of June 5, and has reservations for the two of them on a Lufthansa flight that gets into Frankfurt at 12 noon. They'll be met at Rhein Main Airport and driven directly to our CIA offices in the IG Farben Building. Since USAREUR is also located in the headquarters building, she and Captain Vasilevsky can be reunited there."

"Holbrook," said General Caraway, "when and how will the captain be arriving in Frankfurt?" Holbrook then briefed the group, which he had already coordinated with Phil Semsch, on his imaginative plan to smuggle Captain Vasilevsky out of Berlin and across the 110-mile gauntlet into West Germany.

"Not bad," said Halvorsen.

"Audacious, in fact," said Minister Calhoun.

"I liked it too, sir," said Semsch. "It avoids the usual bottlenecks."

Caraway, usually reluctant to approve Holbrook's ideas, was forced to concede the merits of the plan. "Very well, then," he said. "That's what we'll do."

"General Hay," said Holbrook, "one more request. Captain Vasilevsky plans to parachute into the Grunewald, which is a huge area, more than 7,000 acres, I believe. It would help if you could dispatch perhaps two platoons from the brigade to be positioned in the forest and the park, along with a couple of jeeps, early the morning of June 5. I'm hopeful that Vasilevsky can avoid the heavily forested areas and aim for the park areas. When they locate the pilot, the jeep can be used to deliver him to the back gate of the fencing around my quarters. Here's a map of where my house is located at 12 Goldfinkweg, showing where it backs up to the Grunewald." At which point, Holbrook handed a map to the brigade commander.

"We can do that, Harry. But how do we explain the 50 or 60 soldiers rummaging through the park?"

"Sir, I'll have my community affairs person, Ingeborg Jochem, phone the city's Parks and Forest Department the morning of the 5th and tell them that a soldier has escaped from your stockade and is potentially dangerous. Therefore, all civilians are advised to stay away from the Grunewald that morning. The forest rangers and game wardens will be able to help enforce that and cordon off the park while we search."

The group came to agreement on additional coordinating details and logistical considerations. The short meeting adjourned at 1015 hours.

12 Goldfinkweg
Dahlem, Zehlendorf
West Berlin
0800, 5 June 1966

An error had been made in assigning quarters to Major Harrison Holbrook in anticipation of his arrival as an officer on the USCOB staff.

Holbrook had completed a questionnaire while still assigned as an assistant professor of military science at Ohio University, indicating that he was the father of a boy, seven, and a girl, five. The fact that the children didn't live with him but were in the custody of his ex-wife in Ligonier, Pennsylvania, was never addressed in the housing questionnaire.

As a consequence, Holbrook had been assigned field-grade housing as a married officer with a wife and two children, and was given as his quarters in Berlin a very sizable, substantial home on a beautifully landscaped street named Goldfinkweg. The house was located in an upper-class section of West Berlin known as Dahlem, a seven-minute drive to the USCOB headquarters on Clayallee.

The grey stucco two-story house with a full basement stood in a neighborhood of similar homes occupied by the families of American lieutenant colonels and majors, most of them Army, although a few were Air Force pilots working out of *Flughafen* Tempelhof or on the four-power Berlin Air Safety Center. A Navy commander serving as aide-de-camp to Minister Ernest Calhoun also lived in the neighborhood, although Holbrook rarely saw him.

The house at 12 Goldfinkweg had three large bedrooms upstairs, two and a half bathrooms, a large study, maid's room, and a full kitchen. It had been built prewar and had survived the Western Allies' destructive saturation bombing of the industrial and commercial neighborhoods in Berlin. The full basement included a steam room, with permanent wire cables used for hanging clothes coming from the washing machine for those who preferred air drying to a gas dryer.

Two middle-aged sisters had more or less come with the house as maids when Holbrook took up occupancy in late 1965. Their names were Elsie and Emmie and they came to the house twice a week to clean up after Holbrook, take care of his laundry, and leave precooked meals in the refrigerator. They had escaped from East Berlin through an underground tunnel shortly before the Wall went up in August 1961, carrying with them their only worldly possessions, which included a wicker basket full of fine KPM china.

Berlin porcelain, or *Königliche Porzellan-Manufaktur Berlin*, dated back to the 1750s and was considered on a par with some of the finest works of Dresden and Meissen, both of them now in East Germany. Shortly after Elsie and Emmie had been hired by Holbrook as housekeepers, they had brought to the house one day the basket of KPM porcelain, consisting of a like-new dinner service for eight and offered it to him for 100 U.S. dollars, explaining that they were short of funds.

Although Holbrook was now a bachelor, with no romantic ties or plans to remarry, he bought the dinner service from the women, which was now proudly displayed in the glass-fronted china cabinet that came with the other quartermaster furniture at 12 Goldfinkweg.

The house lacked a garage but a paved driveway could hold two or three cars. Holbrook's only car was a '61 Chevy Impala and, like all other privately owned vehicles driven by American personnel in Berlin, was required to be parked at night facing the street and with at least a half tank of gas at all times in case wives and children needed to be evacuated on the Autobahn to travel the 110 miles to West Germany if the Russians were to attack.

The backyard of Holbrook's house bordered on the paved walking pathways of the Grunewald, where every Sunday afternoon families of Berliners, often wearing their one and only dress clothing, with children in their finest outfits, would stroll through the Grunewald in a ritual that went back timelessly, Holbrook had learned.

A few blocks from Goldfinkweg, Hugh Erb, the AP bureau chief, lived in a house owned by his news service. From time to time, Holbrook would see Erb, his blonde German wife, and their young son strolling through the neighborhood on weekends and would wave to them if he was outdoors. Erb was a formidable newsman and Holbrook had no problem maintaining a distant, discreet friendship with him, even if their work in Berlin was often at cross purposes.

From the second-floor bedrooms at the rear of the house, Holbrook could look out over his 8-foot fence and see pedestrian traffic in the Grunewald. So, on the morning of June 5, watch from his house was being kept over activities in the huge park.

Phil Semsch was watching upstairs with a pair of high-powered binoculars. His wife Alicia was downstairs in the kitchen, preparing a lunch she thought the Soviet pilot would enjoy. Norm Hellerstein, clad in his green AG44 uniform, had laid out a similar uniform, complete with shoes, socks, and underclothes, in one of the guest bedrooms. Hellerstein's personal car, a black 1960 Volkswagen, was downstairs in the driveway, as was the Semsch family car. No military vehicles were present, in keeping with efforts not to draw undue attention to the house.

Semsch was also in radio contact with the Army captain commanding the soldiers who would scour the Grunewald for the first signs of the parachutist. Their assignment was to find Vasilevsky, then drive him in a jeep to the back fence of Holbrook's quarters, while other soldiers took possession of the pilot's parachute and awaited instructions on how to process it for forwarding to a facility where it could be examined.

Semsch and Holbrook had concocted an unorthodox plan to transport Captain Vasilevsky from West Berlin to West Germany, and had gotten approval from the MiG-21 task force to implement it. It seemed clear that once the Russians and their East German underlings had tumbled to the fact that the crash of the MiG was in fact no accident and was instead a defection, they would use plainclothes personnel to monitor passengers departing from the West Berlin airports—Tempelhof and Tegel—and would beef up their inspections of trains departing from the Lichterfelde-West *Bahnhof*.

The Semsch-Holbrook plan called for Vasilevsky, dressed as an American soldier, to be driven by Norm Hellerstein in his VW on the Autobahn connecting West Berlin and Helmstedt, the easternmost terminus of the Federal Republic of Germany, or West Germany. The two would be posing as off-duty soldiers from the Berlin Brigade on a five-day pass to Frankfurt.

This was not all that unusual. Because West Berlin was in effect an island surrounded on all sides by a formidable enemy, American military personnel and their families occasionally needed to get away from the city's confines, enjoying a few days of R&R in a less-hostile environment, away from the claustrophobia of living in an encircled city.

And so Specialist 4 Norman Hellerstein and Private First Class Eric Brogden—Vasilevsky's *nom de guerre* for his escape from the Soviet Air Forces—would be traveling as buddies headed to Frankfurt with official five-day passes signed by a brigade company commander. Hellerstein would drive his VW bug, would converse with the pilot in his fluent Russian, and would do any necessary talking if they were stopped by East German guards at any point along the Autobahn.

Holbrook had added yet another wrinkle into the deception operation. A mustachioed civilian built much along the lines of Captain Vasilevsky would attempt to board the Army's duty train that evening at the Lichterfelde-West train station. He would carry papers and identification indicating that he was a Department of the Army civilian going to a meeting in Frankfurt if questioned by Russian inspectors at the *Bahnhof*.

Downstairs at 12 Goldfinkweg, Alicia Semsch was preparing what she hoped would be a late lunch—at 2, maybe 3, p.m.?—for the defecting captain, along with her husband, Harry Holbrook, and Norm Hellerstein. She knew how to prepare borscht, the cold beet soup beloved by many Russians, and had brought with her that morning fresh beets, buttermilk, yogurt, cucumbers, radishes, some green onions, hard-boiled eggs, and sour cream.

She had also bought at the commissary some dark pumpernickel bread and several varieties of jams and jellies to be eaten with the beet soup. She knew from having entertained Hellerstein at family dinners at the Semsch quarters that he had no qualms about eating ham, so she was also making some ham and cheese sandwiches, along with celery sticks and potato chips, to be placed in a cooler in Hellerstein's car—along with a six-pack of Cokes—to sustain the two "R&R-bound soldiers" during their 339-mile, five-and-a-half-hour trip to Frankfurt.

Holbrook's home phone rang and he picked it up. "Holbrook? Hazeltine here," said the USCOB chief of staff. "I'm at the lake and things seem to be in good shape here. What's happening at your end?"

"I think we're all set, sir," Holbrook replied, and then gave a rundown on what was taking place in his house.

"Sounds good, Harry. We've got the special services rowboats moored to the pilings with armed soldiers in them, as you suggested. That was a pretty good idea. The general may think you're an asshole, but I've got to admit you do some good work."

"Thanks, sir. Have the divers arrived?"

"Yep, they're getting rigged in one of the tents right next to the one I'm in. We've got four divers that the Navy sent up from Italy and another four that the Brits brought in from somewhere in the British Army of the Rhine. There's a platoon or so from the 3rd of the 6th getting ready to move out and patrol the park when it gets a little later in the morning."

"Have you been able to keep the rubberneckers away from the lake, sir? I mean, nosy people from all the headquarters involved who want to get in on the action?"

"Yes indeed. As you recommended, we placed concertina wire all along our side of the lake, with only one entrance to the site, which the MPs are manning. No one, regardless of their rank or position, is admitted unless I authorize it. Anything else we need to do, Harry?"

"No sir, looks like we're pretty well set."

"Roger and out," said Hazeltine, signing off as if they were speaking on radios.

As his MiG-21 plowed into the eastern side of the 2-mile-long lake, Captain Alexi Vasilevsky had already opened his bubble canopy, deployed his ejection seat, and was guiding his parachute—an unfamiliar process for him—into an unforested portion of the Grunewald.

He was met by three American soldiers armed with their M14 rifles, who assisted him out of his parachute harness and began rolling the chute up, as instructed. One of the Americans offered a cigarette to help break the ice, which Vasilevsky—a nonsmoker—politely refused by gesturing with his hands.

A few moments later, a jeep with an American lieutenant in the passenger seat drove up. The lieutenant climbed in the back, offered the front seat to the pilot, and told the driver to proceed to the back fence of the house on Goldfinkweg.

Semsch, monitoring the process from an upstairs window, noticed that the American SEALs and British Royal Engineer divers were already deploying into the lake, their underwater cameras at the ready. As the jeep neared Holbrook's house, he could see that a man wearing a Soviet Air Forces Nomex-type flight suit was seated in the front passenger seat.

"He's coming," Semsch called downstairs. "They'll be here in four or five minutes."

Semsch, Holbrook, and Hellerstein hurried out of the house, opening a sliding glass door that faced the backyard, and moved quickly to the fence, which Holbrook unlocked and opened as the jeep drew up.

The U.S. lieutenant who had retrieved the Russian pilot didn't know whom to salute, since Semsch and Holbrook were both in civilian clothes and the only person in uniform was a Spec 4.

"Lieutenant Delgado reporting, sir," he said to the group at large. "Here's the man who parachuted out of the plane."

"Well done, Lieutenant," said Semsch. "Please tell your men that the mission has been accomplished and they did everything just perfectly."

"Roger that, sir."

Hellerstein, with his Russian language skills, took over. He introduced Semsch and Holbrook and, as they walked through the backyard toward the house, told Vasilevsky where they were headed and what was going to take place.

The pilot nodded in agreement. "What about my wife in Vienna?" he asked.

"We have her safe and sound," Hellerstein said. "The CIA picked her up from the rehearsal room at the Konzerthaus about 0945 hours this morning and she is now on a Lufthansa flight to Rhein Main in Frankfurt. She will be waiting for you at the IG Farben building when you arrive."

Vasilevsky sighed with relief.

Semsch then issued instructions to the defector, which Hellerstein translated. "We'd like you to go upstairs, Alexei, and wash up. I'm sure you'd like a hot shower. There are razors in the bathroom to shave and get rid of your mustache. In the bedroom you'll find a change of underwear and a U.S. Army uniform, just like the one Hellerstein is wearing. It even has a nametag on it with your new name for the crossing into West Germany.

"When you come downstairs, we're hoping that you will look like a member of the Berlin Brigade, wearing the Berlin shoulder patch and all. My wife has fixed a late lunch for us all. There's even time for a nap, since you're probably exhausted by now. There's no rush because you won't be leaving the house until 1900 hours, when Hellerstein and you will begin your drive on the Autobahn to Helmstedt and on to Frankfurt. You'll be riding in his Volkswagen."

"Why do we drive? Would not an airplane be faster?"

Semsch's reply was translated. "Once the Russians and Vopos are aware of your disappearance, it's very likely that they will send agents in civilian clothes to the two principal airports in West Berlin and also to the *Bahnhofs*, since these are the most likely exit points out of West Berlin. We figure that by letting several hours elapse while we wait here, the intensity of the search will die down and they'll begin a thorough search of possible hiding places here in the city. You and Hellerstein, we hope, will look like a couple of GIs driving to the West on an R&R. There's also a diversion planned at the most likely train station, to take some pressure off the Autobahn. Now, let's go about turning you into an American soldier."

Alicia Semsch interrupted her husband to produce a Wahl haircutting clipper she had bought at the PX a few days earlier. "Captain," she said via her husband's translation, "before you get undressed, I'm going to give you an official GI haircut," and she also showed him a bed sheet she planned to drape over him.

Upstairs, Vasilevsky found a nearly new, freshly pressed Army Green uniform, socks, underwear, and black dress shoes. His new name, he noticed on the pinned-on black plastic name tag, was Brogden. As a passenger in the Volkswagen being driven by Hellerstein on the Autobahn through East Germany, he was hopeful that he wouldn't be called upon to speak by any inquiring border guards. If challenged, he would just hand over his R&R pass.

Hazeltine phoned. The Army Security Agency technicians monitoring Russian and East German radio and telephone communications reported a huge increase in electronic traffic, along with implementation of a general alert in East Berlin. Guards from the Soviet War Memorial in the Tiergarten (Deer Garden, or Animal Garden) in central Berlin were being relieved of duty and were being rushed to the crash site as soon as transportation for them could be dispatched from East Berlin. The vehicles would then need to be processed through American MPs at Checkpoint Charlie, who had been instructed to carefully examine every inch of these vehicles, using discreet delaying tactics.

At the Griebnitzsee, Hazeltine reported, the U.S. and British dive teams were already busy at work examining the crashed MiG-21. A diver in the plane's cockpit was photographing every component. Several systems—such as the fire-control mechanism, computer code transceiver, radar and anti-jamming systems—had already been detached and hoisted to the surface for more thorough examination. The divers had been told that the Soviets and East Germans were going to be detained from the site for a total of 12 hours, time they would require to assemble personnel, access the East–West crossing point at Checkpoint Charlie, transit the heavy West Berlin evening traffic, and then be routed around the Allied-controlled eastern side of the lake.

It had also been anticipated that Soviet bloc heavy equipment capable of lifting the airplane's debris from the lake bottom would be arriving from East Germany, but that might require another 24 hours before showing up.

Meanwhile, any Soviet officials who attempted to access the Griebnitzsee would be detained by American MPs and USBER personnel, who would politely explain that necessary diplomatic clearances allowing access to the site were being processed by the American Embassy in Bonn, and would be issued immediately upon receipt, not before. It was therefore requested that any Soviet visitors should wait patiently in their parked vehicles, a quarter mile from the lake. It was inevitable that a diplomatic protest would be filed by the Russians and East Germans, but by then, it was expected, the Western Allies would know everything worth knowing about the latest Soviet air weapon.

Captain Vasilevsky, shorn and shaven, came downstairs wearing his uniform as Private First Class Eric Brogden of the Berlin

Brigade. In his well-worn Dockers men's wallet were his military ID card, Social Security card, USAREUR driver's license, two condoms, a photo of his German girlfriend, 110 U.S. dollars, and 76 Deutschemarks, all arranged by Phil Semsch's deputy G-2 (intelligence officer).

He was told how authentic he looked and was ushered into Holbrook's dining room, where he ate hungrily all of the meal prepared by Alicia Semsch.

"Very good!" he commented, as translated by Hellerstein. "How did you learn to make borscht like that?" he asked Mrs. Semsch.

"My mother taught me," she said modestly.

Semsch asked Hellerstein to convey the following: "We have about three hours before beginning the drive on the Autobahn. Since you'll be traveling about 550 kilometers late at night, may I suggest you go upstairs and take a nap? We'll wake you when it's time to leave."

Holbrook phoned the Griebnitzsee command post and was connected with Colonel Hazeltine's deputy chief of staff. He reported on happenings at his quarters and asked how things were proceeding at the lake. "Everything seems to be under control," he was told. "There are four Russian officials, two in army uniforms, who are being made to sit in their vehicle until we get clearance from Bonn to admit them to the site. They are most unhappy with us and plan to file a diplomatic protest in the strongest possible terms."

"No surprise there," said Holbrook. "Is the search going well?"

"Like clockwork. These divers really know their stuff."

"Sounds good, sir. The car carrying Pfc. Brogden will leave from here about 1900 hours, tied in with the train boarding at the *Bahnhof.*"

"Good job, Harry."

Lichterfelde-West Bahnhof
West Berlin
1920 hours, 5 June 1966

Soviet Army Captain Vasily Komarov sensed something suspicious in the mustachioed man waiting in line to board the nightly U.S. Army duty train to Helmstedt and Frankfurt. The man was wearing a tweed peak newsboy cap pulled low over his face and had on a military-style tan trench coat with the collar up. He seemed to be looking around as if someone was pursuing him.

Komarov, as was the case at all other access points in and out of West Berlin, had been furnished photos of the apparently defecting Soviet Air Forces pilot and was on alert. The man he was eyeing appeared to be about the same height as Vasilevsky. Although it was difficult to estimate his weight under the coat, it appeared to be consistent with Vasilevsky's body frame.

Reacting quickly, Komarov pulled a radio from his web belt and ordered an immediate alert throughout the *Bahnhof*. Everything came to an immediate halt, not only at the duty train but throughout the entire train station as whistle blasts punctured the air while *Volkspolizei* guards descended on the platform where the duty train was boarding.

First Lieutenant Gordon J. Hauser, having been promoted after finishing his mandatory 18 months as a second lieutenant, ran up to Komarov and confronted him.

"What the hell are you doing, Captain?"

"None of your business, Hauser. A wanted criminal is being pursued and I have reason to believe that he is possibly attempting to board this train and escape to the zonal border. My orders are to apprehend him and you would be well advised not to interfere. This is a matter of internal Soviet security and you have no jurisdiction in it."

"That may well be, Captain Komarov," the lieutenant shot back, "but this is my train and any delays are my responsibility, not yours."

"Fuck you, Hauser. You are a pimple on the face of progress." Komarov turned his back on Hauser and began deploying his arriving policemen to line up the duty train passengers for interrogation before boarding.

The four female passengers were allowed to board without questioning. But each of the 17 male passengers was ordered to produce military identification cards or the civilian equivalent and was given a cursory body search, presumably for concealed weapons.

Midway through the line of male passengers, Komarov came upon the suspicious person who bore somewhat of a resemblance to Captain Vasilevsky. Satisfied that the remaining male passengers were not a threat, he turned to Lieutenant Hauser and said for everyone to hear, "This man is being detained for further questioning. All other passengers may proceed to board."

Assisted by two burly Vopo officers, the suspect was carted off to Komarov's office in the *Bahnhof*'s interior.

The suspect was pushed into a straight-back chair. "Papers and identification, please," the Soviet captain ordered, almost as if he was portraying a Gestapo *Oberleutnant* in a black and white World War II film. The man reached inside his topcoat, causing the guards to shift their AK-47s to an alert position, and drew forth folded papers and a U.S. passport.

Komarov held the papers up to the brightest available light in his small train-station office and scrutinized them carefully. "So," he said at last, "you are a civilian employee of the U.S. Commander Berlin, according to this documentation."

"That is correct, Captain."

"And how long have you been in this position?"

"Going on nine or ten years, I believe."

"What was your purpose in traveling on the train to the West?"

"I am going to Frankfurt to coordinate with a U.S. Army officer who works in the American headquarters in the IG Farben building."

As the civilian spoke, Komarov realized that the resemblance to the missing pilot was superficial at best. In addition, his English was perfect and the dossier on Vasilevsky had indicated that he spoke no English.

"You are free to go. Thank you for your cooperation." He spoke in German to the senior of the Vopo guards. "Tell that idiot Hauser that he is free to move his train."

J. Paul Scholl, deputy to Major Harrison Holbrook, USCOB information officer, gathered up his personal papers and left Komarov's office with a sly grin that Komarov couldn't see. Harry's deception had worked.

Scholl had no intention of taking the train to West Germany. Instead, he got into his POV and drove home, but only after a quick stop at a local night spot to see if some promising female flesh might be available.

5

Office of the Chief of Staff
U.S. Commander Berlin
Clayallee and Saargemünder Strasse
Dahlem, Zehlendorf
West Berlin
0845 hours, 6 June 1966

"Have a seat, Harry," USCOB chief of staff Colonel Charles Hazeltine said to Harry Holbrook. "You did real good yesterday."

"How did it turn out, sir?"

"Vasilevsky and his wife were reunited in the USAREUR building. The CIA had sent a couple of agents from Langley—one male, one female—to interrogate them both, the captain about his MiG and the Russian air force in general, and the wife about cultural affairs. The sessions were both very useful, I understand. The Vasilevskys are being flown to the U.S. later today in the same special-mission plane that brought the agents to Germany."

"What about the MiG's wreckage, sir?"

"Harry, we got access to every damn nut and bolt on that plane. The components that were removed for examination ashore were all studied and photographed before they were returned to the wreckage. There's no indication that the Russians tumbled to what

69

we were doing underwater; they probably have their suspicions but nothing provable.

"By the way, Harry, that ruse using Paul Scholl to impersonate the defector was a gem. It focused attention on the train station and diverted it away from the Autobahn. Very clever."

"Thanks, sir. Scholl told me this morning that he really enjoyed the play-acting, and it gives him some more ammunition as he pursues all the available females in West Berlin."

Hazeltine's face betrayed the hint of a smile. "Yes, I'd heard that he does have that reputation. But he's a good man, isn't he?"

"Yes, he is, sir. I gave Hugh Erb of AP and Dieter Goos of *Morgenpost* a very limited heads-up from my phone at the house after the SEALs had finished their work, just to let them know what was going on. It's a pretty big story for them. Scholl is at work right now on a press release for the other media types."

"Good, Harry. I'll have to clear it with the general and he'll probably run it by Calhoun. You know how it goes."

"Yes sir. I've been down that road before, as you know."

Back in his office, Holbrook asked Gertie to get Dan Silvestri, the special services officer, on the phone. "Dan, I want to thank you so much for the loan of those rowboats. I guess you've heard by now how we used them yesterday at the lake."

"I did indeed, Harry. I'm glad we could help out. By the way, I've got some news for *you*, for a change."

"What's up?"

"Only this: Herb Alpert and the Tijuana Brass are coming here and will put on a performance for the American community three weeks from now, on Saturday, June 25."

"Wow, that *is* news! He's very big back home right now, I understand."

"Bigger than big, Harry. His recording of 'A Taste of Honey' made Record of the Year last year and he's doing just as well—maybe even better—this year."

"To what do we owe the honor, Dan? What brings him to Berlin?"

"Well, he was scheduled to perform at a couple of the Army and Air Force bases in the Zone, part of a USO tour, and I believe that Andy O'Meara was so pleased with the job the brigade did with the missing MiG that he encouraged Alpert to spend a day with us in Berlin. It'll be a Saturday afternoon concert and I'm thinking the best venue for it would be the high school gymnasium. We can use the bleachers on both sides of the gym and then put a couple of hundred folding chairs on the gym floor. I'll probably have to promise the basketball coach that I'll refinish his floor later this summer before the school year starts, but he's a pretty agreeable guy."

"Good plan, Dan. I'll get a press release out about it in the next day or two. Paul Scholl will be in touch with you for details."

"I've got a section reserved for the USCOB and brigade brass. You want a couple of tickets?"

"One will be fine. I'm batching it these days."

"You got it, Harry."

Office of the U.S. Commander Berlin
Clayallee and Saargemünder Strasse
Dahlem, Zehlendorf
West Berlin
1430 hours, 6 June 1996

General Caraway was smiling. There was even a little spring in the USCOB's step as he greeted the members of his MiG task force the morning after the successful operation to do an underwater analysis of the MiG-21 and get its pilot and his wife to safety in the United States.

"General O'Meara phoned me from Heidelberg late last night," the general explained. "He had received complimentary messages from several people in Washington, including someone from the

White House, and he wanted to share the good news with us. I want to pass on to each of you my compliments on a highly sensitive mission that was accomplished with the utmost professionalism and outstanding competence."

Harry Holbrook, fully aware that the Irish wrath of USAREUR's four-star commander Andrew P. O'Meara ranked at the very peak of Major General John Caraway's pyramid of nightmares, was happy for the entire command and satisfied with his own participation in the adventure.

Caraway then proceeded to update the group on the mission's outcome, with supporting details provided by Colonel Semsch. "I don't have to tell you, gentlemen, how valuable the information already being studied and analyzed by the CIA, Army and Air Force intelligence and other government agencies is going to prove. And the fact that this group was able to carry out the delicate assignment without a hitch is an elegant tribute to your professionalism."

"Sir," said Colonel Semsch, "I'd like to extend particular congratulations to Major Holbrook, who was our liaison with the man at KaDeWe and who also devised the imaginative plan to get Captain Vasilevsky to West Germany using my driver as his cover. I think we are all indebted to Holbrook."

A few in the room began to applaud until General Caraway held up his hand. "Yes, to be sure, Holbrook, well done. Thank you, everyone. This task force is hereby dissolved."

Walking down the corridor with Phil Semsch, Holbrook mentioned the considerable contributions of Specialist Four Norman Hellerstein in helping effect the pilot's escape.

"You mean *Sergeant* Norman Hellerstein, Harry. I promoted him this morning and will write him up for a Commendation Medal later today, using as few details as possible in the citation."

"Is Hellerstein in the office? I'd like to thank him."

"I'm pretty sure he's available, Harry. Why don't you wait in my conference room and I'll send him in."

A few minutes later, Sergeant Norman Hellerstein came into the conference room and closed the door, still wearing on his uniform sleeves the sewn-on cloth insignia that displayed the gold U.S. seal eagle against an olive drab background, denoting the rank of specialist four.

"I hear you're out of uniform, Norm," Holbrook said, shaking the hand of the new sergeant.

"Thanks, sir. I just got promoted this morning and there was no time to get to the tailor shop to get these sewn on," Hellerstein said, displaying in his hand a pair of three gold cloth chevrons denoting a buck sergeant.

"Thanks for everything you did yesterday. Let's sit down and you can tell me some of the details about the Autobahn trip."

"Not much to tell, sir. A couple of Vopos stopped us a couple of miles out of Berlin and asked to see our papers. I handed over my five-day pass and the one for 'Pfc. Brogden.' I didn't let on that I spoke German and I pretended to misunderstand the guards a couple of times, kind of playing dumb. There was no need for Captain Vasilevsky to speak, since I'd told him to keep his window rolled up the entire trip.

"We made it to Helmstedt in a little under two hours, stopped for gas and a pit stop at a gas station there. An MP sedan was waiting for us when we got back on the Autobahn and escorted us the rest of the way to Frankfurt and USAREUR headquarters. The MPs must have had radio contact with people in the Farben building, because a full colonel, probably from Army intelligence, greeted us at the entranceway, along with two civilians who I assume were CIA types. They told Captain Vasilevsky that his wife was waiting upstairs and took him to the elevators.

"I shook his hand just before they took him away. He thanked me in Russian and I replied that I was privileged to have helped him begin a new life in the West. The MPs offered to lead me to the enlisted barracks where I'd be staying overnight, so I followed them there. I had breakfast there and then began the drive back here to Berlin. I don't think it could have gone much better, sir."

"Well done, Norm. I've got one other thing in mind for you, which I've discussed with Colonel Semsch and which has his OK. Please check it out with him when you have a moment."

"What's up, sir?"

"Are you familiar with the Jewish synagogue in East Berlin that sits on Oranienburger Strasse?"

"I know where it is. I've driven past it dozens of times when I do a Wall patrol but I've never been in it. I know that the main building was demolished during the war and what's left of the Jewish community over there meets in an annex next door. I'm not a very observant Jew and I don't believe I've been in a *shul* since my *bar mitzvah* about ten years ago. Why do you ask, sir?"

"The shoe clerk at KaDeWe—Gunther was his name, or maybe it was just the name he was using with me—at our final meeting asked me if I knew about the synagogue. I told him that I was vaguely aware of it—like you, from my Wall patrols—but that's all."

"Wall patrols," as they were termed, were trips into East Berlin by officers of USCOB and the Berlin Brigade in official U.S. Army sedans flying small American flags from both front fenders. The patrols, conducted at all hours of the day and night, were used to assert the right of access that the Western Allies had to enter East Berlin at any hour. The Soviets had a similar right of access with respect to West Berlin.

A uniformed soldier who, like Hellerstein, was part of Semsch's intelligence operation, would drive the sedan into East Berlin through Checkpoint Charlie and would then proceed along varying designated routes, with an officer in the back seat. Although the primary purpose of the patrols was to constantly demonstrate right of access, a secondary purpose was to see if any new activities, such as troop or equipment movements, were taking place in the East.

Holbrook was on the Wall patrol roster and pulled the disruptive duty about once every three or four months—usually, it seemed to him, at the most inconvenient time of the early morning. He seemed to land the 0330 or 0445 patrols more often than his peers, he felt, even though it probably wasn't the case.

"So what do you want me to do, sir?"

"Clear all this with Colonel Semsch, of course. But the next time you have an opportunity to drive your VW into East Berlin—maybe on a Saturday afternoon for some shopping or sightseeing—stop by the synagogue and tell them that you're a friend of Gunther's from KaDeWe. If my hunch is correct, it may be a relationship that might prove productive someplace down the road. Maybe not, but at least it's worth a shot."

"No problem, sir. I'll let you know when I make contact."

Back in his office, Holbrook said, "Gertie, please see if you can get Mrs. Semsch on the phone. She's probably at home, I suspect."

A few minutes later, Frau Haupt called out, "Mrs. Semsch on Line 1, sir."

"Alicia? Harry Holbrook. I just wanted to thank you for what you did the other day with my guest. You really helped us out with the haircut and the borscht and everything. Norm Hellerstein just got promoted by Phil and will probably be getting a Commendation Medal but neither works for civilians like yourself. So I just wanted to say 'thank you' for playing a big role on a very important assignment."

"Thanks, Harry. Phil has filled me in in a general way about what was going on and I'm glad that I could help. Say, I'm planning a nice roast beef dinner Sunday afternoon after church. How'd you like to come over?"

"That's very kind of you, Alicia. I'd be happy to come."

"Great. How does 2 p.m. sound?"

"Perfect. I'll bring a bottle of red wine. Merlot okay?"

"Excellent. Any chance you'll be bringing a guest with you?'

Holbrook knew that Alicia was just digging, as women sometimes do, into whether he was dating anyone. "Nope, just me. I'm looking forward to it. Thanks, Alicia."

6

Information Division (ID)
Headquarters, U.S. Commander Berlin
Clayallee and Saargemünder Strasse
Dahlem, Zehlendorf
West Berlin
0900 hours, 13 June 1966

"Mr. Erb is on Line 1, Major Holbrook," Frau Haupt called from the outer office.

"Put him on, Gertie." The Associated Press bureau chief was a formidable presence among the newsmen in Berlin and Holbrook had always gotten along well with him.

"What's up, Hugh?"

"First, Major, I wanted to thank you for the heads-up about the MiG crashing into the Griebnitzsee. I filed my story exactly 33 minutes before Fleming got wind of what was going on."

Joe Fleming of UPI—United Press International, the wire-service rival of Erb's Associated Press—was constantly playing catch-up with Erb. Fleming wasn't as aggressive or as accurate as Erb in probing for news, and as a result the AP newsman usually won out in their races to be first with the news. The fact that Harry Holbrook was in Erb's corner didn't help Fleming either.

"Can you tell me where the pilot and his wife are now, Major?"

"Off the record and not for attribution, Hugh?"

"Absolutely."

"Last I heard they were both at Langley being debriefed by the CIA."

"Is there any truth to the rumor that we sent Navy SEALs into the lake to take pictures of the MiG?"

"I can't comment on that, Hugh, you know that. What else was on your mind?"

"It's a personal matter. Any chance I could stop by your office this afternoon and visit with you?'

"Sure thing. Hold on a sec. Gertie," Holbrook called out, "what's a good time for Hugh Erb to stop by this afternoon?"

"You are free after 1500 hours, sir."

"Hugh, how about 3:30?"

"I'll be there. Thanks, Major."

Erb arrived promptly at 1530 hours and was shown in to Holbrook's office by Frau Haupt. Holbrook offered a seat and asked her to bring coffee for two. "What can I do for you, Hugh?"

"My father passed away last night." Erb was somber as he shared the news.

"I'm sorry to hear that. I would sometimes see him walking your young son when I was on the driveway washing my car. He would usually wave his cane at me while holding on to Klausi's hand. That's right, isn't it? Your son is Klaus, nicknamed Klausi?"

"Yes, you're correct. Good memory. My dad was 81, lived a good long life, but was in poor health the last couple of months. He passed away in his sleep last night and Klausi is absolutely heartbroken."

"How can I help?"

"My father was born and raised in Cologne, a few miles north of Bonn in what's now West Germany. He came to America as a young man and settled in Buffalo, New York, where I was born.

When my mother passed away a few years ago, we flew her coffin back to Cologne for burial there. All the remaining members of our family still live in Cologne, or are buried there, and Papa wanted to be buried in the family plot in the Cologne cemetery." Erb paused, waiting for a reaction from Holbrook.

Holbrook nodded, waiting for his visitor to continue, wondering what this had to do with him.

"Major, in order for my father, in his coffin, to get to the West, it will have to be moved by train or truck and the goddamned Vopos will open it and search it for contraband. I don't want those bastards touching my father's body!"

"I understand, Hugh. What's the alternative?"

Erb looked him in the eye. "Your duty train."

"I don't understand, Hugh. You want me to move your father's coffin on the duty train?"

"I've been told that you recently authorized a shipment on the train of Gary Stindt's professional papers. Is that correct?"

Stindt headed the NBC bureau in Berlin. "Yes, that's true. Gary had a couple of boxes of professional papers he was shipping back to New York, and I approved them to travel as freight on the baggage car that holds soldiers' possessions."

Erb gave the USCOB information officer his most serious scrutiny. "Major, I have a large box of professional papers that I need to get to Frankfurt."

Holbrook sat back in his chair and steepled his fingers. "Let me get this straight, Hugh. You want me to authorize the shipment of your father's body on the duty train, disguised as professional papers?"

"That's correct. I'll take care of packaging Papa's remains in an oversized carton with books and papers around it."

Holbrook pondered his options. The easiest thing would be to turn down Erb's request, on grounds that it violated the four-power agreement. If he went to "Bourbon John" Caraway with the request, as he really was obligated to do, the USCOB would scream in anguish with nightmares about what would ensue if General O'Meara ever got wind of it.

And the last option open to Holbrook was the one he chose. "Okay, Hugh. We'll do it. Let me know a day in advance about when you're ready to ship your *professional papers*."

Erb rose from his chair. "Thanks, Major. Would it be possible for the funeral services for my father to be held at the brigade chapel by Father Mulcahy? That shouldn't be a problem, should it?"

"Not a problem. You're an Army veteran from the Korean War. Matter of fact, you served under General Westmoreland as an artillery forward observer, correct? I'll probably be going to work for Westmoreland somewhere in Vietnam later this year."

Erb raised an eyebrow that Holbrook was aware of his Army background. "That's right. One final request: I'd like you to be one of the pallbearers at the funeral. I'm going to ask Captain Larsen to be another pallbearer, and the other four will be some of my media colleagues. I'll schedule the service with Chaplain Mulcahy and let you know."

Jerry Larsen, Holbrook knew, had joined the brigade's aviation section a few months ago. He had arrived directly from Vietnam, where he had flown the large CH-47 Chinook helicopters carrying South Vietnamese special forces soldiers into battle against the Viet Cong in the days before Lyndon Johnson committed the first American combat units. Erb had apparently befriended the pilot in hopes of gaining early insights into what was taking place in Vietnam.

"Sure thing, Hugh. I'd be proud to be a pallbearer."

After Erb left, Holbrook went to Frau Haupt's desk. "Gertie, Erb's dad has died. Let's send flowers from all of us in the Information Division. Order them from the PX and charge them to my ID account. That's the same one we used for the socks and underwear we bought there last week. Have the flowers delivered to Erb's house.

79

I don't have the street address but it's right in the neighborhood where I live."

"I can call his office, Major, and get the address."

"*Danke,* Frau Haupt," said Holbrook.

Berlin Brigade chapel
Clayallee
Dahlem, Zehlendorf
West Berlin
1000 hours, 14 June 1966

Fewer than 20 people were present at the Berlin Brigade chapel for the funeral of Papa Erb. Hugh Erb with his wife Krista and son Klaus were seated in the front pew, with the six pallbearers right behind them. Holbrook and Captain Larsen wore their dress blue uniforms with earned combat decorations, of which Larsen had a bundle from his Vietnam service. Holbrook had none, since he hadn't been to Vietnam yet.

Chaplain (Major) Charles Mulcahy officiated and spoke thought-fully about how the elder Erb had forged a rich life for himself in America that had produced so eminent a son and grandson, and would now be returned to his roots in Cologne.

Hugh Erb delivered a farewell message, wiping away a tear or two as he spoke, while Krista consoled young Klausi. With the service ended, the six pallbearers solemnly carried the casket of Papa Erb to the German hearse that had been arranged with the funeral home.

Erb phoned two days later to inform Holbrook that his box of "professional papers" was ready for shipment that night on the duty train. Holbrook, wearing his duty uniform, met Erb's station wagon at the Lichterfelde-West *Bahnhof* at 1900 hours and helped locate a cart to move the heavy box to the train's baggage car.

"What is in that box?" asked the ever-present, ever-vigilant Captain Komarov.

"That is none of your business, Captain," said Holbrook. "Here are papers authorizing its shipment to Frankfurt, signed by an officer of the United States Commander Berlin."

Komarov scrutinized the shipment papers signed by Major Harrison Holbrook, looked derisively at Holbrook and Erb, and then moved on down the train to see what trouble he could stir up.

"You're traveling with the train I assume, Hugh," said Holbrook.

"Yes, I need to be sure that no one disturbs my 'professional papers.'"

"The Vopos have no authority over the train while it's crossing East Germany. Let's go meet the train commander and I'll introduce you as a colleague."

"Thanks for everything, Harry. You're a good friend."

Holbrook reached into his inside jacket pocket. "Here's a couple of reserved-seat tickets for Krista and you for the Herb Alpert concert on the 25th. Let's go find our duty train commander."

Introductions made with Lieutenant Hauser, Holbrook got into his car and drove home, wondering if there were any edible leftovers available in his refrigerator.

Berlin American High School gymnasium
Am Hegewinkel
Dahlem, Zehlendorf
West Berlin
1500 hours, 25 June 1966

The high school gymnasium was filling up quickly with American families and soldiers from the Berlin Brigade. People were still coming through the gym doors, anxious to see and hear Herb Alpert and the Tijuana Brass.

The group's best-selling albums included *Whipped Cream* (6 million copies sold in the U.S.) and *Going Places*. By year's end, Alpert's group had sold 13 million recordings, outselling the Beatles and—just two months before the concert in Berlin—had four different albums on Billboard's Top 10 charts.

In other words, the American families and soldiers in West Berlin were fortunate indeed to have landed Herb Alpert and the Tijuana Brass for a Saturday afternoon concert. Holbrook, wearing casual civvies, shook hands with Dan Silvestri as he entered the gym and headed for the reserved-seat section.

As he found a seat, he passed Hugh and Krista Erb. Erb gave him a signal—forefinger and thumb joined in a circle—that all had gone well on the funeral trip to Cologne—and mouthed a "thank you." Holbrook waved in acknowledgement.

Taking his folding metal chair, he saw that he was seated next to a colleague, Major Lillian Baker of the G-1 (personnel) section of the USCOB headquarters. He knew her slightly, a good-looking, well-built brunette probably in her early thirties, without a wedding ring. But he had never been in contact with her outside of meetings in the headquarters building.

"Hi, Lil," he said as he sat down.

"Welcome, Harry. Haven't seen you in a while."

"Oh, I've been busy, I suppose."

"I hear you were involved in that MiG incident at the Griebnitzsee."

"Yeah, there was a lot of press interest in it, as you can imagine."

"And maybe something more, as well. I had to process an ARCOM"—Army Commendation Medal—"for Phil Semsch's newly promoted sergeant, so methinks there was more going on with it than meets the eye."

"Well, it all turned out for the best, Lil. Dan Silvestri tells me that the reason Herb Alpert is here today is because General O'Meara wanted to reward USCOB and the brigade for the job we did with the MiG and the pilot."

"Okay, Harry, if that's all you can share with me that's fine. But tell me this: how come you've never asked me out?"

Holbrook's jaw dropped. He was used to being put on the spot by Berlin's newsmen but he'd never been confronted so directly by an attractive female. Even sitting down, he had to admit that Lil Baker looked good in her flowered top and blue jeans.

While he was framing a reply, Baker had more to say. "I know you're not queer, Harry. I've been through your personnel records jacket and I know that you're divorced with a couple of kids in Pennsylvania. You're 34, going on 35, so what's your problem in asking out a reasonably good-looking single woman on a dinner date?"

Harry Holbrook was having a tough time coping with the directness of this "reasonably good-looking single woman." The bottom line was that he'd considered once or twice about asking Lil Baker out for a date but never really thought she'd be interested in him. That admission, he thought, might very well be his best response to her.

"Lil, I never really considered that you'd have much in common with me."

"Are you a red-blooded American boy or not, Harry?"

"Of course I am."

"Good, that's settled. So you'll buy me dinner this evening at the O Club?"

"Be my pleasure, ma'am," he replied, thankful that the hustle and bustle of the incoming crowd had drowned out the likelihood of anyone else listening in on what he regarded as a very private conversation.

Herb Alpert and his group were greeted with a roar from the overflow crowd as they moved with their instruments to the roped-off center of the gymnasium, where their sound equipment, piano, and music stands had been set up on a raised platform.

The seven-member mariachi-style band, led by Alpert playing trumpet, was enjoying major hits back home in the States, such as "The Lonely Bull," "A Taste of Honey," and an album titled *Whipped Cream and Other Delights*, which had been a huge success in 1965.

When "Tijuana Taxi" with its honking car horns was played, the audience roared its approval, demanding two encores when the regular set ended.

The concert over, Holbrook walked Lil Baker to her car. "Do we have a date, Holbrook?" she asked.

"We do, Lil. Let's go home and change and I'll pick you up at seven. You live in the female bachelor officer quarters, right?"

"Correct, Harry. I'll be waiting at the door of the BOQ at seven."

Harnack House Officers' Club
Ihnestrasse 16
Dahlem, Zehlendorf
West Berlin
1930 hours, 25 June 1966

Holbrook went home to shave and shower. He phoned the Officers' Club, located in the Harnack House, and made a reservation for 7:15 p.m. The historic building in Dahlem, which had opened in 1929 as a scientific conference center and research campus, had once been used by scientists such as Albert Einstein, Max Planck, Fritz Haber, and Otto Hahn for research purposes. An estimated 35 Nobel Prize winners had done work at the site prior to World War II.

The American occupation army used the Harnack House and the beautifully landscaped acreage behind the building for indoor and outdoor social gatherings. The food was pretty good, perhaps not of the quality of West Berlin's finer restaurants, but certainly better than the GI mess halls.

Lil Baker looked lovely when Holbrook drove up in his five-year-old Impala. An independent female, she had no intention of waiting for Holbrook to exit the car and open the passenger door for her. "Stay where you are, Holbrook. I'm good at opening car doors," she said.

Clad in a black sheath dress that showed off her slender figure, along with stockings and high heels, Baker drew admiring glances from a number of male officers—and perhaps a few envious appraisals from female guests—as she and Holbrook entered the club and were led to their table.

Holbrook was wearing a navy blue suit with a blue button-down shirt and Countess Mara striped tie, but no one seemed to be paying him any attention.

"Lil, I had no idea you were this good-looking," a somewhat tongue-tied Harry Holbrook—spokesman, of all things, for the U.S. Commander Berlin—said as they sat down.

"Harry," she confided, "you have no fricking idea what you've been missing all these months you've been neglecting me."

"Neglecting you? I've watched you at a number of staff meetings and I've admired the way you look and the way you present yourself."

"So how come you've never asked me for a date?"

"It never occurred to me that you might be interested in me. I'm sure you could take your pick of any of the eligible bachelors in the command, and even some of the married ones if you wanted to."

"You're wrong, Harry. I was waiting for you to get off your fat ass and invite me out."

"Well, here we are at long last, Lil. Let's pick a bottle of wine to celebrate."

They drank some wine, consumed two very palatable surf 'n' turf steak and lobster dinners, and washed it all down with a glass of Remy Martin VSOP cognac that left them with a warm glow.

"Let's get out of here, Harry," Baker said.

Holbrook was surprised at the directness of the suggestion. "Where are we going?"

"Drive me back to the BOQ so I can get my car and I'll follow you to your quarters."

12 Goldfinkweg
Dahlem, Zehlendorf
West Berlin
2115 hours, 26 June 1966

They parked their cars in the driveway at 12 Goldfinkweg, each facing out toward the street as required by USCOB regulations.

Lil Baker appraised the spartan, humble furnishings of the Holbrook manor. "This place looks like a quartermaster warehouse, Harry. Just one piece after another of standard military-bought furniture. Not a personal touch anywhere."

Holbrook felt a need to explain. "I'm really not into buying knick-knacks and throw pillows and all those little things that women crave. The TV is mine and the turntable for my LPs, but everything else is Uncle Sam's, I guess."

"Let's have a look at your LPs, then."

Harry brought the albums out from a closet. Peggy Lee, Errol Garner, Tony Bennett, Sinatra, Earl "Fatha" Hines, Sergio Mendes, Carmen Cavallaro, Sarah Vaughn, The Four Lads, The Beatles, Astrud Gilberto and Antonio Carlos Jobim, and a dozen or so more.

"Not bad," Baker assessed. "Did you know that Sergio Mendes was pretty much a protege of Herb Alpert?"

"No, I didn't," Harry said. "Do you want something to drink?"

"Nope, I'm good. Let's check out the upstairs."

As they reached the second-floor landing, Lil removed her high-heel shoes and set them down near the stairs. "So these are the bedrooms?"

"Yes, I sleep in the middle one." Lil noticed that the bed had been carefully made up, the adjacent bathroom was spotless, and no clothes had been left out, all signs of a potentially domesticable male.

"Which bathroom should I use to change?" she said.

"Change?"

"Yes, change. I plan to change out of these clothes and into something far less confining. Do you have any objections?"

Once again, Holbrook was taken aback by her forwardness. "No, certainly not. Whatever you want. Here, use this one. Emmie and Elsie were here this morning, so they're all clean."

As he pondered the probable course of coming events, Holbrook realized that he might not have any condoms. It had been so long—perhaps a year and a half—since he'd slept with a woman that he didn't keep tabs on essential components of mating, such as condoms. But he had a sudden recollection that there might be one or two in the medicine cabinet of his master bathroom and sure enough, he found a couple, which he placed next to the lamp on his bedside table.

Lil emerged from another bathroom wearing only a black see-through thigh-length negligee she had apparently brought with her in her purse. Noticing the two still-wrapped condoms, she pretended to exclaim theatrically, "Oh my, sir, what fate lieth in store for me? Art thou preparing to pierce the pearl of my virginhood?"

Holbrook, slow thinker that he sometimes was, was clearly no one's utter fool. He was already shedding his necktie and shirt while Baker began tugging at his belt buckle.

"Lil, I gotta tell ya. I haven't slept with a woman in a long time and I'm probably not very good at this. I just hope I don't disappoint you."

"Well, just let me get in the saddle, cowboy and let's go for a ride." With both of them fully undressed, she pushed him back on the bed, opened a condom packet to embed on his quite-ready member, and proceeded to mount him.

As she began rocking back and forth, humming "This Guy's in Love With You" from the Herb Alpert repertoire, she put her face close to Holbrook's ear and whispered, "See, Harry, that wasn't so painful, was it?"

Holbrook just lay back in his post-coital stupor and lazed.

Seeing what was happening, Lil barked out, "Holbrook, don't you dare fall asleep on me. We've got another go-round coming in 15 minutes or so!"

Holbrook managed to stay awake.

12 Goldfinkweg
Dahlem, Zehlendorf
West Berlin
1010 hours, 26 June 1966

Lil found some bacon and eggs in Holbrook's understocked refrigerator, brewed some excellent coffee, made buttered toast, and they were enjoying a late Sunday morning breakfast—clad in a couple of Holbrook's frayed bathrobes—in the dining nook of his quarters.

With a cup of coffee just below her lips, Lil asked, "Why did you get divorced, Harry? I've had worse experiences in bed than last night with you."

"Thanks for the compliment, Lil," Harry said wryly. "As they say in the *gangster* movies, it really wasn't personal. Holly just disliked the Army and all the disruptions it caused. She got used to running things her way while I was in Korea or away on field exercises, so when I was home it became uncomfortable for both of us. She's a good woman, a good mother for the kids. She and I were just incompatible, and it took us too many years to realize it."

Lil nodded, as she nibbled at her toast. As a personnel officer, she had heard similar stories more often than not. "Harry, I've got some things to take care of in the office this afternoon. Let's do one more roll in the hay and then I'll head home to clean up and change clothes."

Whereupon they went upstairs, perfected a couple of warmup foreplay maneuvers and satisfied themselves once again that they were fully compatible sexually. Fully dressed, they went downstairs for sweet partings.

"Harry, that was a wonderful night and day. I had a really great time. Can we do it again in a couple of weeks?"

"I'd like to, Lil. Very much so. I'll have very fond memories of last night."

There was one more quick kiss on the lips at the door, then out she went.

7

Clayallee, in front of USCOB headquarters
Dahlem, Zehlendorf
West Berlin
1100 hours, 4 July 1966

The Fourth of July—Independence Day back home—was always a big deal in the American sector of West Berlin.

It was an annual occasion to literally "show the flag" to the 2 million West Berliners, who were ever-mindful that the only thing preventing their being flattened by an Iron Curtain descending on them from four sides and crushing them were the 6,000 American soldiers of the Berlin Brigade who—with their counterparts in the British and French sectors of the divided city—were the only thing keeping the Soviet wolves at bay. Middle-aged Berliners who had lived through the war and survived it had ugly memories of the raping and pillaging done by rampaging Russian soldiers just two decades ago. Therefore, the deterrent presence of the American troops ensured that any attack against West Berlin constituted an attack upon the United States itself. This fact was a constant reassurance to most Berliners.

Three years earlier, John F. Kennedy had stood on a platform at Rathaus Schöneberg (the city hall of the borough of Tempelhof-Schöneberg) and had told hundreds of thousands of cheering West Berliners "*Ich bin ein Berliner!*" The people loved it.

Each July 4, members of the Berlin Brigade marched in parade formation, banners flying in the summer breezes, to celebrate the independence of their own nation and to help remind Berliners that they stood ready to protect and preserve the independence of West Berlin. With their love of ceremonies, rituals, and parades, the Germans would line the sides of Clayallee, waving small American flags and cheering their protectors.

General Hay, as commander of the Berlin Brigade, had overall control of and responsibility for the parade. Harry Holbrook's responsibilities were to issue parade advisories, make press passes available, ensure a reserved bleacher area for reporters, photographers, and TV cameramen, and be otherwise generally available to answer questions about the who, what, where, when, why, and how of the ceremony.

Hay began the march at the head of his troops, then peeled away as they passed the covered reviewing stand to join General Caraway, Minister Calhoun, West Berlin Mayor Willy Brandt, and other dignitaries on the stand. As a last-minute surprise—perhaps to thank the brigade for its work with the Soviet MiG—President Lyndon B. Johnson had dispatched his vice president, Hubert H. Humphrey, to attend the parade.

The last-minute addition of Humphrey to the list of guests had caused Holbrook to scramble to get out a press release about it. Helped by Paul Scholl, Holbrook's release was able to point out that, much as then-Vice President Lyndon B. Johnson had been sent by President John F. Kennedy to West Berlin a few days after the Wall went up in August 1961, so LBJ was dispatching his own vice president, Humphrey, to reaffirm America's commitment to the survival of West Berlin.

Behind the marching soldiers—carrying their M14 rifles at right shoulder arms led by their banners and guidons—paraded the M48 tanks of Company F, 40th Armor, along with the Brigade's M113 armored personnel carriers and its battery of artillery. The 298th Army Band, a component of the brigade, played spirited martial music during the parade, including familiar John Philip Sousa compositions such as "The Stars and Stripes Forever," "The Thunderer," and "The Washington Post March."

The tracked vehicles would leave unpleasant ruts in the pavement of Clayallee, to be sure, but what the heck, the Senat reasoned, a little tar would repair the road's surface, while the ruts would serve as a reminder to all Berliners—on both sides of the Wall, and to the Russian masters on the eastern side—that the brigade had armor as well as artillery to ward off a Soviet attack on the city. Well, if not to ward it off, at least to delay it until reinforcements could be rushed from elsewhere in West Germany and Europe and perhaps introduce USAREUR's tactical nuclear weapons into the equation.

It was traditional that, following the parade, the USCOB and his brigade commander would jointly host a reception for invited guests at the Harnack House. Weather permitting, the event took place on the beautifully landscaped grounds immediately behind the historic building. On this glorious Independence Day, there was no question that the reception would be held out of doors, with open-sided caterer-type tents protecting the food and drink and serving as refuges if the weather turned bad.

Vice President Humphrey joined Generals Caraway and Hay and Minister Calhoun in the receiving line, with Caraway's aide-de-camp at its head to introduce each arriving guest. As Holbrook passed through the line, exchanging handshakes with each dignitary, he was reminded that the introductions duty had once fallen upon his youthful shoulders when he was a general's aide-de-camp.

Most of the higher-ranking American Army officers were clad in their summer white uniforms, while others wore the less formal summer tan uniform. The latter group included Harry Holbrook, for whom the cost of a white uniform would have been prohibitive, given his limited spending power after paying his child-support obligations. As he'd checked his standard green service cap in at the Harneck House reception desk before proceeding outdoors, he couldn't help but notice—not without a little envy—the large amount of summer white caps on the shelf.

German waiters who were regular Harnack House staffers carried around trays with champagne flutes. Holbrook accepted a glass. Brigadier Kenneth Huddleston, who commanded the 3,100 members of the British Berlin Infantry Brigade, took one at the same time, saying quietly to Holbrook, "Excellent work on the Soviet airplane, Major."

"Thank you, General," Holbrook responded. He was surprised that the Brits were aware of his role in the caper.

Harry began to mingle among the crowd, shaking hands and saying "hello" as he went. He waved to Hugh Erb and his wife Krista, went over to shake hands with *Morgenpost*'s Dieter Goos and was introduced to Goos's very pregnant wife, greeted Joe Fleming of UPI, NBC's Gary Stindt, and Mark White, the AFN radio station manager.

"Hi, Mark, long time no see," he said. AFN, the worldwide American Forces Network, had a radio station in Berlin with White as its general manager. A television capability was still in the works, Holbrook knew. The station, with its powerful signal, reached every nook and cranny of Berlin on both sides of the Wall and could also be heard—when atmospherics permitted—hundreds of miles into East Germany. It was intended as a news and entertainment medium, not as a U.S. propaganda arm, but it nevertheless served a very useful purpose in broadcasting the essence of democracy to people trapped behind the Iron Curtain.

Holbrook knew for a fact that young people in West and East Berlin were using the American language accents of Mark White and his announcers to hone their English-speaking skills and practice the rhythms and nuances of the very fickle English language.

He'd been scouting the crowd to see if Major Lillian Baker was among the invited guests, and suddenly she was walking toward him, gorgeous in her well-fitting summer white uniform. "How nice to see you, Major Holbrook," she said formally, extending her right hand.

"My pleasure, Major Baker. How have you been since the last time we met?"

"Very well, thank you. I'm thinking it might be an opportune time for us to schedule a follow-up session in the very near future," Lil said.

"I agree completely, Major Baker. May I call you tomorrow at your office?"

"Please do. I'll look forward to it," and she wandered off to hobnob with other guests.

As dusk came on, Holbrook realized how tired he was after the long day, with all the energy required to get things ready for the parade. There was going to be a fireworks display at 2100 hours emanating from McNair Barracks, where the brigade was headquartered and where its barracks were, but Harry was simply too worn out to stay for the show.

He said a few goodbyes, retrieved his cap from the reception desk inside the Harnack House, and got in his Chevy for the drive home.

A few minutes away from the Harnack House, he suddenly thought of something. He pulled over, braked his car, and reached for the hat on the seat beside him.

He was right, he realized. There was a note tucked inside the hat, carefully placed behind his calling card.

Office of the Intelligence Officer
Headquarters, U.S. Commander Berlin
Clayallee and Saargemünder Strasse
Dahlem, Zehlendorf
West Berlin
0845 hours, 5 July 1966

"I'll be damned, Harry!" said Lieutenant Colonel Philip Semsch, the USCOB intelligence officer. "What the hell is going on, that you're all of a sudden a conduit for clandestine information?"

"Darned if I know, Phil. The shoe clerk at KaDeWe said something along the lines of 'I had a great memory for details' but that's the extent of it."

The unfolded note from his cap lay on Semsch's desk.

Bausch Porzellan
Tempelhof Luftbrücke
1745 hours, 7 July 1966

"That's a porcelain shop near Tempelhof Airport, right?" Semsch asked.

"That's correct. It's right on the square at the airport entrance, kind of facing the Luftbrücke monument. I've been in there a couple of times to become more familiar with the KPM china service that I bought from my housekeepers to help them out financially. It's a very nice store, full of recent Meissen porcelain and some older stuff from KPM and Dresden."

The Luftbrücke (air bridge) monument was a memorial to the 1948–49 Berlin Airlift that kept more than 2.5 million West Berliners from starvation when the Soviet Union shut down rail, water, and Autobahn access to the Divided City in a futile effort to coerce the three nations occupying West Berlin to abandon the city and leave it to be absorbed into the Soviet empire.

But U.S. Army General Lucius D. Clay, military governor of the American Zone of West Germany, had other ideas. Clay got on the horn to Lieutenant General Curtis E. LeMay in Wiesbaden, commander of all U.S. Air Force elements in Europe, and inquired if LeMay's fleet of twin-engine C-47 "Gooney Bird" transports could carry coal.

LeMay replied, "We must have a bad connection, General. It sounds like you're asking me if my planes can carry *coal*," to which Clay replied, "That's just what I said, Curt. Coal!" LeMay replied, "General, the Air Force can carry anything. How much coal do you want us to haul?" and began Operation *Vittles*, a round-the-clock airlift that saw cargo planes landing at Tempelhof every 90 seconds with cargoes of food, clothing, water, medicine, hay for the starving horses still in use for postwar transit and, yes, coal to keep the Berliners from freezing during wintry nights.

The Russians backed down a year later and Clay became a hero revered by every West Berliner, prompting the Berlin Senat to name a street for him immediately after the airlift had ended, with the Russians calling it quits.

Semsch pondered the next step. "Obviously, we want you to go make the meeting, Harry. I'll clear it with the general, of course, and bring him up to speed. When you finish the meeting at the porcelain store, stop by my house for a beer and let's review what you learned."

"Roger that, Phil."

Bausch Porzellan
Platz der Luftbrücke
Adjacent to Tempelhof International Airport
Boroughs of Tempelhof and Kreuzberg
West Berlin
1745 hours, 7 July 1966

"Good evening, Major Holbrook. I am Frau Bausch, owner of this shop, and I am quite sure that you have visited us previously."

Harry was wearing casual civilian clothing, but it was clear that Frau Bausch recognized him from previous visits and also because he was expected.

"Thank you, Frau Bausch. Yes, I have been to the store on one or two occasions. I bought a set of KPM dinnerware from the two sisters who look after my house and I stopped by here to learn something about fine china. Everyone here was always very courteous and attentive to me."

"Yes, we have resumed making some KPM at the rebuilt factory in the Tiergarten District. The Meissen factory in the East is producing excellent pieces of porcelain that are almost as fine as the prewar product. Please let us know if you would care for us to appraise the KPM pieces at your house sometime."

As Frau Bausch said this, she glanced at her wristwatch and saw that it had turned to the closing time of 1800 hours. She posted a "*Geschlossen*" sign on the door, lowered the door and window blinds, dimmed almost all the lights, and activated an alarm system. She was a well-groomed, stylishly coiffed middle-aged woman who carried herself with a professional bearing.

"Let us go to my office where we can enjoy a cup of tea and talk."

As she brewed the tea, Holbrook looked at the photos on her office, many of them signed by dignitaries from many Western nations. "Wow, lots of famous shoppers, Frau Bausch."

"Yes, my late husband and I were fortunate to have attracted a good many well-known customers, who came here looking for very fine porcelain that was not readily available in their own countries. We still ship many pieces each year to our clientele, many of whom, of course, live in the United States.

"My husband was killed in action fighting the Russians on the Eastern Front," she explained. Holbrook had noticed, in talking with middle-aged Berliners, that virtually all the German soldiers had supposedly been fighting Russians on the Eastern Front. So how was it possible, Holbrook had sometimes wondered, that so many well-trained, well-equipped soldiers of the *Wehrmacht* had opposed the combat divisions of Bradley and Patton during the war if everyone was facing the Russians to the east?

Frau Bausch served the tea with a platter of small biscuits. "So, you are perhaps wondering what brings you here?"

Holbrook had to swallow his cookie before replying. "Yes, I am very curious."

"The group I am with is quite familiar with the work you recently did on behalf of Captain Vasilevsky. We are aware that Natalya and Alexi are living very comfortably in a suburb of Washington called Arlington, Virginia, and that he is being well compensated by your Central Intelligence Agency. She is a violinist with the new Georgetown Symphony Orchestra, which she enjoys very much.

"In short, Major Holbrook, you and your colleagues did everything for them that we expected of you and I have been authorized to communicate to you yet another situation which we feel is important to you and the Berlin Command."

Holbrook's hand shook and tea spilled on his khaki trousers as Frau Bausch recounted what was going to happen.

8

Semsch Family Quarters
35 Drosselweg
Dahlem, Zehlendorf
West Berlin
2115 hours, 7 July 1966

Holbrook was still dabbing at the tea stains on his trousers as Phil Semsch was digesting the news of Harry's encounter at Bausch Porzellan.

Alicia Semsch had brought a damp face cloth to Holbrook to help blot the telltale stain but it was proving to be a difficult task.

Phil Semsch and Holbrook were sipping Lowenbrau beers while going over the news that Holbrook had just brought.

"So, the essence of what she told you, Harry, is that this new, emerging group of radical terrorists is planning a major strike of some kind against our presence in West Berlin—date, place, and method of attack still to be determined. Is that a fairly accurate summary of what she said?"

"Yes, that's exactly the way it came across. She apologized for the lack of specifics but promised to be in touch when they know more."

"We were aware in a general sense," said Semsch, "that left-wing factions at a number of the universities in Berlin and in the Zone have been building power, ranting against American imperialists and claiming that the West German leadership consists of a bunch of warmed-over Nazis. They've been robbing smaller banks to raise money, have torched some warehouses and commercial businesses in Stuttgart and Frankfurt, and even done some vandalism at American Army and Air Force bases in the Zone.

"They call themselves the Red Army Faction, with a branch called the Baader-Meinhof Gang, after the two radicals who founded it. Meinhof is a woman, probably 32, while Baader is younger, more college age, about 23.

"The BND (*Bundesnachrichtendienst*, or Federal Intelligence Service) has been keeping a close watch on them, sharing new developments with USAREUR, us, and the CIA. They work very closely with the CIA, in fact, and probably cooperate more closely with the CIA than the damn FBI.

"But what you're being told—that the terrorists are planning to assassinate a senior American military officer—either in West Germany or here in Berlin—to dramatize their cause and get some worldwide attention is something we've never considered up to this point." He put down his beer and leveled his gaze at Harry. "How credible do you think this is, Harry?"

Holbrook shifted in the stuffed chair he was sitting in. "I don't know. I really can't say, Phil. She seemed very knowledgeable about the MiG incident and was very current on how the Vasilevskys were doing in D.C., so it's clear that she and her associates are in close touch with the pilot and his wife."

"On a scale of one to ten, Harry, how credible do you think this information is?"

Holbrook set his beer stein down on an end table as he pondered his answer. "I'm certainly not an intelligence pro. But I remember reading reliability analyses when I was with the Army Security

Agency headquarters near Washington. At the risk of sounding stupid, I'd probably evaluate this information as a seven, maybe even a seven plus."

"That's probably a good assessment. Let's break for tonight and call it quits. I'll try to get with the general in the morning. I'll bring in USBER and Halvorsen from the CIA, and I wouldn't be surprised if the old man doesn't convene another one of his task forces. Stay loose, Harry, and be available when we need you."

"No problem. We're wrapping up preparations for the Volksfest, which begins a couple of weeks from now. Everything seems to be coming along nicely. A lot will depend on the weather, of course, but we've got lots of tentage available if the rains come down." He stood to leave, then called out in the direction of the kitchen, "Good night, Alicia," he called out in the direction of the kitchen, where Alicia was working on the children's lunches for school tomorrow at the Thomas A. Roberts Elementary School.

Office of the U.S. Commander Berlin
Clayallee and Saargemünder Strasse
Dahlem, Zehlendorf
West Berlin
1115 hours, 8 July 1966

"Roger, tell us what you know about this Red Army Faction," General Caraway said to CIA Berlin station chief Roger Halvorsen. The USCOB had re-convened his MiG-21 task force to scrutinize this latest apparent threat. Harry Holbrook had been invited and was seated at the conference table.

"General, I've spent the last couple of hours updating what we know about the group, ever since Phil briefed me on the latest developments," said Halvorsen.

"The group is just getting started and is seeking, the intel community believes, to make its first big, eye-popping statement against two prime targets: first, the United States as a worldwide symbol of unbridled imperialism and, second, the present government of the Federal Republic of Germany, which it regards as perpetuating Nazi fascism, with many of the Third Reich survivors occupying key positions in the governments of both the Federal Republic and West Berlin.

"As Phil has said, the Red Army Faction, also known as the Baader-Meinhof Group for its two principals—one male, one female—has been robbing smaller banks, committing arson on industrial warehouses and commercial buildings, and doing some low-level nuisance bombings to attract media attention and respect.

"To a large extent, these activities have been successful in engaging the news media, particularly television networks and stations in America and here in Germany. The Red Army Faction draws considerable support from leftist groups in the Federal Republic and here in Berlin on both sides of the Wall.

"Led by Andreas Baader—he's about 23—and Ulrike Meinhof, who's 32, we believe, the group has about 20 hard-core radicals backing them. Most of these people have been recruited from the universities, and it's believed that some younger university instructors are among them, heavily influencing the rhetoric and ideologies they all subscribe to."

Caraway interrupted. "What about weapons? What damage can they do?"

"Considerable damage, sir. They've managed to lay hands on many of the Soviet bloc weapons. From reports that have been assembled, they have a large quantity—perhaps 50 or 60—AK-47s, which they've used in their bank holdups. They also have a quantity of 7.62mm ammunition for the AKs. They have Semtex explosives procured from Czechoslovakia, fragmentation hand grenades,

CS tear gas to initiate riots, several types of Soviet bloc rockets and RPG-7s."

"What's an RPG-7?" USBER's Pete Day asked.

Semsch answered. "It's a rocket-propelled grenade launcher, effective against tanks and other tracked vehicles. It's lightweight, very portable, fired from the shoulder, and highly effective in the hands of a well-trained gunner. It's just a hair over a yard long, so it's easily carried and concealed. The North Vietnamese have begun using them in Vietnam against some of our Huey helicopters, particularly when the chopper is on the ground or coming in for a landing. Very nasty weapon."

"Why the name 'Red Army Faction'?" Minister Calhoun asked.

"Good question, sir," said Halvorsen. "At the outset, they wanted to be seen as part of a burgeoning communist workers' movement. In German, their name is *Rote Armee Fraktion* because they want to be perceived as a component of a much larger worldwide far-left movement. They themselves don't care for the name 'Baader-Meinhof Group.' That plays to the cult of personalities, which they scrupulously want to avoid. The press has largely developed the Baader-Meinhof tag for them; the terrorists themselves don't use that name. It runs counter to their group-think."

"Excellent report, Roger," said Caraway. Turning to the other task force members, he asked, "What is the principal threat we face from the Red Army Faction? Do they really have the ability to assassinate a key member of the military or of the government? And when I say 'government,' I'm referring jointly to the Bundestag in Bonn, the Senat here in West Berlin, the American Embassy in Bonn, and the U.S. Mission here at Clayallee."

A loud silence followed. No one wanted to contemplate the possibility that they might be terrorist targets.

"In other words," Caraway said thoughtfully and somberly, "we—along with Vice President Humphrey—were sitting ducks in the reviewing stand a couple of days ago if some terrorist had aimed an RPG-7 round at us. Well, thank goodness that public ceremony is over for a year and we don't have any large public demonstrations planned until Veterans Day in November."

"Actually we do, sir," said a low-key voice that up to this point hadn't been heard from.

Caraway instantly went on high-alert status. "What are you talking about, Holbrook?" he challenged.

"The Volksfest, sir. Two weeks away. Half a million Berliners mingling over a two-week period with military and civilian VIPs from the three occupying nations, as well as officials of the German and Berlin governments. And only MPs and a few *Berliner Polizei* for crowd control."

"Oh shit," said the USCOB.

Information Division (ID)
Headquarters, U.S. Commander Berlin
Clayallee and Saargemünder Strasse
Dahlem, Zehlendorf
West Berlin
1100 hours, 9 July 1966

"Who's got some good news?" Harry Holbrook asked as he opened the last full meeting of his Volksfest planning committee.

"I do," said Dan Silvestri, the brigade's special services officer in charge of recreation and entertainment, who had furnished the rowboats for the recent Griebnitzsee adventure.

"What've you got, Dan?" asked Holbrook.

"You wanted John Wayne western movies in German to be shown at the Outpost Theater, right, Major?"

"Right, Dan."

"Here's a list of three that I've been able to come up with so far. And I've got leads out with some other film distributors to see if others might be available." Silvestri passed around a list of the films he'd already acquired:

Der Schwarze Falke: The Searchers
Der Teufelshauptmann: She Wore a Yellow Ribbon
Die Rancher des Kleinstadt: McClintock

Everyone seemed amazed at the films Silvestri had uncovered. "My plan, Major, is to run only John Wayne westerns in German at the Outpost Theater during the two weeks of Volksfest. The first show will begin at 1100 hours when the Volksfest gates open. We'll rotate the five films, with showings at 1100, 1300, 1500, 1700, and 1900. The theater will be cleared after each performance. If I can get any additional German-language John Wayne westerns, we'll work them into the rotation.

"Admission will be one Deutschemark—that's about 25 cents," Silvestri continued, "for everyone, man, woman or child. American personnel who want to attend will of course be admitted for a mark, same as everyone else.

Paul Scholl had a question. "What about American families who want to see an American movie?"

"No problem, Paul. They're always welcome at the British NAAFI movie theater." NAAFI stood for Navy, Army, and Air Force Institution—more or less the British military's entertainment and recreation branch. The NAAFI movie house was located in the British sector, not far from Spandau Prison.

Holbrook had a thought: "Dan, the plan is to turn over all the net proceeds to the Berlin Senat to help fund education, is that right?"

"Yes, that's what we agreed to at the last meeting."

"Good. One new request: please save a small slice of the Volksfest proceeds—a total of $125,000 or so, as I recall—for our Thomas A. Roberts Elementary School. Maybe a thousand dollars, or 1,500 if we can afford it. I'm told the teachers there are very much in need of basic school supplies—writing paper, pens, pencils, rulers, and so on."

"No problem, Major," said Silvestri. "We can always take care of our own."

"What was that about, Harry?" said Scholl as the meeting ended and the group filed out.

"Colonel Hazeltine grabbed me the other day and told me he was appointing me as liaison to the TAR school. Apparently, the school principal feels somewhat excluded from contact with the brigade and wants someone to participate in her PTA meetings and serve as a go-between for the school and the military establishment. After all, she reasons, it's primarily dependents of military personnel whom she's educating.

"I figure that by bringing news about a nice check from the brigade to the first PTA meeting I attend, I can get better relations off to a good start."

"So, Hazeltine nailed you for the job, with everything else you've got going on?"

"Yep. One more chore for an overloaded major."

12 Goldfinkweg
Dahlem, Zehlendorf
West Berlin
1155 hours, 9 July 1966

Major Lillian Baker, unclad, rolled over on top of Major Harrison Holbrook Jr. and commenced what would become a very serious breast to chest communication.

"Harry, are you awake?" No response. "Holbrook, open your eyes and pay attention. There's something I need to tell you."

One Holbrookian eyeball emerged from its eyeball defilade position, followed soon after by the other.

"I know it was good for you, Lil. It was good for me too."

"Not that, you idiot. I have something important to tell you."

Holbrook roused himself on one elbow, pushing back against her supple torso. "Sounds serious."

"It is, Harry. I've been asked to go to Heidelberg."

"You mean for a TDY?"

"No, a PCS move."

Holbrook came wide awake. "What's up?"

"The WAC lieutenant colonel in the USAREUR G-1 section, who does essentially the same thing that I'm doing here, got orders transferring her to Vietnam immediately. Seems like female officers aren't exempt from the drawdown either.

"She phoned me at home last night and asked if I was interested in her job. It's a natural for me. I can step right into it and it's a light colonel billet so it'll look good on my personnel record. So I have to let them know right away if I'm available and interested."

Baker paused, waiting for Holbrook to respond. She knew what his question would be, and he knew what her answer was going to be.

"Harry, I couldn't turn the job down. It's a terrific career opportunity, a highly visible position on a very senior staff. I told Jocelyn that I'd accept."

Holbrook knew what was coming next. "How much time do you have left here?" he asked, noting that it was Saturday night, rapidly approaching Sunday morning.

"They want me at USAREUR first thing Tuesday morning, Harry. I've got to start packing and clear quarters tomorrow and Monday."

Holbrook took it like a man, or thought he did. He knew again what was coming next.

"We won't be that far apart, Harry. I can visit you here and you can always find a reason to spend a couple of days with your colleagues at USAREUR."

"Yes, of course we can do that. Good idea, Lil," he said, knowing that each of them was letting the other down as gently as possible. As the old song had it, "It was great fun while it lasted."

They made love for what would be the final time and fell asleep locked in each other's arms.

Making coffee in the morning, Holbrook found himself humming the Bob Hope-Shirley Ross duet, "Thanks for the Memory," which became Hope's signature song.

Teachers' Lounge
Thomas A. Roberts Elementary School
Hüttenberg 40
Dahlem, Zehlendorf
West Berlin
1845 hours, 28 July 1966

Miss Barbara Drew, principal of the Thomas A. Roberts school (named for an artillery colonel killed in action while leading tanks of the 2nd Armored Division in the August 1944 Battle of Normandy), called the meeting of her PTA advisory committee to order.

"Ladies and gentlemen, teachers and parents, I am so very pleased to welcome to our group Major Harrison Holbrook," she said, indicating where he was sitting. "Major Holbrook, as some of you may be aware, holds the very important position of spokesman for the United States Commander Berlin, Major General Caraway. As such, Major Holbrook is the Berlin Command's principal point of contact with the news media—not only the American press, but newsmen and women from all around the world."

Holbrook squirmed, uncomfortable in his wooden chair, as all eyes turned in his direction. There were around 20 people in the room, about equally divided, he estimated, between parents and teachers. Some of the parents were obviously couples, while others came alone. He had chosen to wear his Army Green uniform for this first meeting, indicating from the lack of significant awards and decorations that he really hadn't accomplished much in the first dozen years of his thus far undistinguished career.

Miss Drew, apparently an old maid school marm, reminded him of his first school principal when he was in kindergarten and first grade. An unmarried woman, never wed, who devoted her entire life to the education and wellbeing of hundreds—thousands, maybe, over the course of a 30- or 40-year career as an educator—of impressionable youngsters who in effect became her foster children.

Miss Drew wore her henna-colored hair in a somewhat out-of-fashion updo, high over her face. Her thick glasses hung from a green lanyard around her neck, and Holbrook was pretty sure he detected a green referee's whistle also hanging from the lanyard.

"Major Holbrook, would you care to say a few words to the group?"

Holbrook had been hoping in vain that this chore could be avoided. Apparently not. He rose, and this illustrious warrior who could stare down the icy disapprobation of the United States Commander Berlin over a train incident found himself somewhat at a loss for words.

"Miss Drew, ladies and gentlemen," he began, "I'm highly honored to be invited to be working with you in the coming school year," he lied, wondering if his fingers were crossed. "Although I don't have children in the school—my two youngsters are in Pennsylvania with their mother—I'm a strong believer in the importance of the early-school experience."

Everyone relaxed, seemingly satisfied with this homiletic garbage. Holbrook chanced imparting a little good news. "As you know, the annual German-American Volksfest kicks off in about two weeks, and arrangements have been made for the net proceeds to benefit the German schools here in West Berlin. I'm very pleased to tell you that Thomas A. Roberts will be one of the beneficiaries, so that your teachers will have a new source of funds to buy their necessary supplies."

The audience loved it. Having scored big, Holbrook took his seat amidst gentle applause.

Miss Drew was beside herself with delight. "What wonderful news, Major Holbrook! Our PTA fund is scraping bottom right now because so many of our field-grade fathers have been drawn down and sent to Vietnam or back to the United States. So any amount of money will come in very, very handy and we are very much appreciative of your efforts in this regard.

"The PTA fund," she continued, "is administered by Miss Mattersdorf, our sixth-grade math teacher. Carolyn, where are you sitting?" she asked, and scanned the room for a sign of Miss Mattersdorf.

Everyone turned to look in the teacher's direction near the rear of the teachers' lounge. Holbrook saw a very attractive young brunette, wearing glasses, a pale pink short-sleeve sweater and plaid skirt. She smiled and waved in his direction; he waved back.

Miss Drew then went through the meeting agenda she had carefully mapped out, getting ready for the coming school year that would commence in late August. The school, like most buildings in Berlin, lacked air conditioning, so the start of the fall semester was keyed to the end of summer. By late August, Berlin temperatures hit daytime highs of about 71 degrees, so classrooms were generally comfortable for teachers and students.

When the meeting had ended, most of the attendees came over to shake Holbrook's hand and welcome him to their midst. As a representative of the USCOB, he carried a fair amount of clout, they assumed.

The last to welcome him was Miss Carolyn Mattersdorf. "I look forward to working with you, Major Holbrook," she said.

"So do I," Holbrook replied, then realized that what he had said made no sense at all. "That is, I look forward to working with *you*," he corrected himself.

"How may I get in touch with you, Major?"

Holbrook reached inside his Army Green service cap, pulled out his now world-famous calling card, and scribbled on its back his office and home phone numbers. Miss Mattersdorf found a 3x5 card in her purse and provided similar information.

"I'll look forward to seeing you again, Miss Mattersdorf," he said, much like a teenage swain.

"As will I," she said. Holbrook's heart was thumping at a rapid pace.

9

12 Goldfinkweg
Dahlem, Zehlendorf
West Berlin
2055 hours, 28 July 1966

Holbrook returned home after the PTA meeting and was surprised to find the housekeepers Emmie and Ellie still there, although they had purses in hand and were getting set to leave.

"You've been working late, ladies," he said.

"We were making your lunches and dinners for the next few days, Major Holbrook. It is a good thing we were here, because you had a visitor, perhaps 30 minutes ago," Emmie said.

Visitor? He hadn't been expecting anyone. "What did he look like?"

"Not a man, a woman. She was very nicely dressed," Ellie commented. "Hair done very professionally, a beautiful, very expensive purse, good-looking clothes."

More than likely Frau Bausch, master spy Harry Holbrook concluded. "But she didn't give her name?"

"*Nein.* But she did leave an envelope," said Emmie, pointing to an envelope on the entry table.

"That's fine, ladies. Have a good evening and I'll see you Thursday."
The sisters came to the house each Monday and Thursday for housekeeping and preparing Holbrook's meals.

The envelope was made from quality linen, he could tell, as was the case with the note inside.

> *Major Holbrook, please be present at the Neue Synagoge,*
> *26–31 Oranienburger Strasse, East Berlin, at 2200 hours,*
> *4 August 1966. The side door will be open.*

Office of the Intelligence Officer
Headquarters, U.S. Commander Berlin
Clayallee and Saargemünder Strasse
Dahlem, Zehlendorf
West Berlin
0830 hours, 3 August 1966

"Smells nice, Harry," said Phil Semsch, sniffing the perfumed note Holbrook had shown him. "This looks like a follow-up to the Red Army Faction warning that Frau Bausch gave you. We're assuming, I guess, that she was the one who delivered the note to your house."

"It's the only possibility I can think of. It's got to be her, based on the maids' description. So, what do we do?"

"You'll make a Wall patrol, with Sergeant Hellerstein at the wheel. Both of you in your regular green uniforms, of course. They want you there at 2200 hours tomorrow night so you'll go through Checkpoint Charlie about 2045 or so, cruise through the East for about an hour, then end up at the synagogue.

"I'll tell Norm to park the sedan as inconspicuously as he can, and you'll both enter through the side door she mentions. He knows a couple of the Jewish people there, so that ought to facilitate the process.

"Norm will brief me first thing Thursday morning, and I'll let you know what time Caraway wants to get together to plan our response. Sound okay, Harry?"

"Okay, except for one thing."

"What's that?"

"Phil, I want credit for a Wall patrol. And I mean credit for one of those O-dark hundred patrols that whoever keeps your damned Wall patrol duty roster keeps putting me on for 0245 or 0415 hours, causing me to lose an entire night's sleep. If I do this thing with Hellerstein, I really deserve credit for a hardship patrol."

Semsch called out, "Grace, would you come in here a moment, please?" When Grace Wertman, Semsch's administrative assistant, entered his office, Semsch said to her, "Grace, the beleaguered Major Holbrook—with the very future of the Free World at stake—is terribly worried that we've got him on some kind of Wall patrol shit list, where he pulls too many of the late-at-night, early-morning stints. Would you please explain to this troubled young man how you maintain the roster?"

"Certainly, sir," and she brought in the roster where she had listed all the eligible officers who pulled Wall patrol duty, showing Major Holbrook that he pulled his fair share—and no more—of off-hour Wall patrols.

"Satisfied, Harry?" Semsch asked and Holbrook reluctantly nodded in agreement. "Grace," Semsch said, "as a one-time concession to this heroic young major who's been doing so much good work as an intelligence adjunct, let's give him late-night credit for a jaunt into the East that Norm and he are going to be making tomorrow night.

"They'll be driving through the checkpoint at 2045, but as a one-time-only concession to Major Holbrook's sensitivities, let's give him full credit as if it were one of your 'shit-list' patrols."

"There is no 'shit list,' sir," responded Grace Wertman, wife of an Army master sergeant who was used to every curse word in use by

114

the military. "There is only one roster, sir, and everyone on it is treated equally and fairly," she said to Semsch, perhaps a wee bit defensively.

"I know that, Grace. I just wanted poor picked-upon Harry Holbrook to hear it with his own ears. You know he's got a legendary memory, right?"

"So I've heard, sir," said Grace and exited Semsch's office perhaps a little huffily.

"Will there be anything else, Major Holbrook?" asked Semsch innocently.

"Fuck you, Phil," said Harry to his good friend and left.

Checkpoint Charlie, en route to East Berlin
Friedrichstrasse at its intersection with Zimmerstrasse and Mauerstrasse
Crossing point between West and East Berlin
2045 hours, 4 August 1966

Sergeant Norman Hellerstein, driving his usual U.S. Army olive drab Ford sedan with miniature American flags posted over each front fender, paused his car at the U.S. sentry booth at Checkpoint Charlie.

The MP on duty recognized Hellerstein and saluted Major Harry Holbrook seated in the right rear seat.

"Wall patrol, Norm?" he said to the driver.

"Right, Glenn. Got a couple of extra stops to make in the East, so maybe an hour or so longer than usual this time. Be okay?"

"No sweat. De La Cruz will be on duty by then, but I'll let him know when he takes over from me."

"Thanks, Glenn," said Hellerstein, putting the car in drive, zigzagging through the barricades designed to slow any trouble coming from either direction and stopping at the East German checkpoint for the usual scrutiny.

The East German border guards were very familiar with the Wall patrol process and with Hellerstein and an officer riding in the back.

They passed the sedan through with minimal inspection formalities since they expected the same courtesy when Soviet patrols on the way to West Berlin arrived at the Allied side of the Berlin Wall.

"Sir," Hellerstein said, looking over his shoulder at Holbrook, "I recommend we follow a usual Wall patrol route tonight, finishing up at the synagogue."

"Let's do it, Norm."

They drove through the streets of East Berlin, nearly devoid of traffic compared with the frenzied pace of nighttime traffic and activity—illuminated by neon lights everywhere—in the western portion of Berlin. By comparison, East Berlin was a dark, brooding, nearly deserted enclave.

Occasionally, the driver of a big truck would pass them from the opposite direction and blink his high-beam headlights at them, a gesture of "Welcome, Yank!" The practice was strictly *verboten* by the East Berlin authorities, but the truck drivers felt safe doing it in the late-night lonesome corridors of East Berlin. For them, it was a wistful reminder that they were confined to the East behind an 11-foot wall that imprisoned them to a life without many choices.

There was little activity taking place as Holbrook and Hellerstein spent the better part of an hour cruising through East Berlin at a slow pace. Around 2145, Hellerstein turned toward his passenger and inquired, "Okay to head to the synagogue now, sir?"

"Let's do it, Norm," said Holbrook.

Neue Synagoge
Oranienburger Strasse 29–31
East Berlin, German Democratic Republic (GDR)
2200 hours, 4 August 1966

The "new synagogue" was exactly one hundred years old, having replaced the "old synagogue" in 1866, when Berlin's then-burgeoning

Jewish population outgrew the older building. Count Otto von Bismarck had participated in inaugural ceremonies for the new building at a time when Jews were an accepted part of the German population. With a seating capacity of 3,000, the *Neue Synagoge* became the largest Jewish house of worship in all Germany.

During the anti-Jewish Nazi-led riots of November 1938, which became known as *Kristallnacht* (Night of Broken Glass) throughout Germany, mobs entered the building, defaced the holy Torah, broke and made piles of the wooden furniture, and set fire to them. A courageous police lieutenant, aware that the synagogue was a protected historical landmark, drew his pistol and ordered the mob to disperse, thereby saving the building from total destruction.

In 1940 Nazi authorities closed the building for prayer purposes, converting the main prayer hall to a storage warehouse for *Wehrmacht* uniforms. During World War II, British Royal Air Force bombers, in a series of bombing raids between November 1943 and March 1944, repeatedly struck the neighborhood around the synagogue, resulting in its total incineration.

The RAF bombers, showing that they didn't discriminate only against Jews, in November 1943 totally destroyed the Protestant Kaiser Wilhelm Memorial Church (*Gedächtniskirche*), which had opened its doors in 1895 on the famed boulevard-like Kurfürstendamm.

Architects argued after the war that a still-standing spire of the Memorial Church should be torn down, but public protests claimed that the spire and adjacent ruins needed to be preserved as being part of the "heart of Berlin." Accordingly, a new church was built next to the ruined spire and was consecrated a few days before Christmas 1961, just in time to overlook the four-month-old Berlin Wall. The old ruined spire remained standing.

Hellerstein parked his sedan in an inconspicuous place not far from the synagogue's side entrance, and he and Holbrook entered through the unlocked door.

"*Guten Abend*, Norman," said a voice from the semi-darkness, welcoming Hellerstein to the temple. "And you must be the famous Major Holbrook," the man said, coming forward and extending a hand to Holbrook. "Welcome to our synagogue. I am Meier Grossmann, Major, lay leader of our small congregation. Sergeant Hellerstein has visited with us previously and we are well acquainted. I am taking you now to the offices of our chief rabbi, Doctor Bernd Halbfinger," and he led them through darkened corridors to the rabbi's lighted suite of offices.

The rabbi was a middle-aged, stocky man with a yellowish beard. He was clad in black and wore a yarmulke at the rear of his balding pate. He rose and greeted the two servicemen as if they were honored guests. "*Shalom*, my friends. Welcome to our *shul*. We are waiting for someone to join us, whom we expect shortly. Meanwhile, please join with me for a cup of tea."

The rabbi spoke excellent English, Holbrook noted. "Where did you learn your very fine English, Rabbi Halbfinger?"

"Milwaukee. It is spoken there, you know," said the rabbi with a straight face.

"Milwaukee?"

"Yes, Milwaukee. It's a city in Wisconsin, if you didn't know."

"I know about Milwaukee, Rabbi. What's your connection with it?"

"Not so very much, I suppose. I was born there, attended school there, and spent two years at the University of Wisconsin campus in Milwaukee before I came to Berlin. I finished my education here, including my doctorate in religious studies from Humboldt University, met my Berliner wife at the university, and decided to live here for as long as God needs me here."

"Milwaukee," Holbrook mused. "That's where Golda Meir, the former prime minister of Israel, was from."

"Yes, to be sure. Her name was Golda Mabovitch when she left Ukraine to join her father in Milwaukee. He worked in a railroad yard, while her mother ran a small grocery store. Golda attended a teachers' college, Milwaukee State Normal School, which is now part of the University of Wisconsin-Milwaukee, my alma mater. My grandmother once told me that Golda was my great aunt, but I'm not sure that's correct. I know about Hellerstein's background, Major Holbrook, but what about yours?"

"Not much to tell, Rabbi. I grew up in a small town near Youngstown, Ohio, and graduated from Penn State with a commission from ROTC. I hadn't planned on making the Army a career, but here I am, 11 or 12 years later, still wearing the uniform."

"Have you been to Vietnam?"

"Not yet; that's where I'm going next, I believe."

"Do you have concerns about risking your life over there?"

"Not really, Rabbi. That's what I've been in training for ever since I graduated from college. Besides, I want to see for myself what's happening over there. Most of my contemporaries have already been there or are fighting there now."

"I see," said the rabbi, stroking his small beard. As he was about to ask a question, the door to his office opened and a formidable-looking young man entered.

"Ah," said the rabbi, "our new colleague arrives."

"Sorry to be late, Rabbi," said the man—probably about 30—in heavily accented English.

"Major, Norman," the rabbi said, "this is Samuel, as we call him. He comes to us from a land far to the east, as if following some kind of star to bless us with. What have you found out, Schmuel?"

"An attack is definitely in the works, Rabbi. My sources, who are very close to the terrorist group, are certain that an RPG-7 has been procured from a Czech arms dealer and that its use is being planned during the forthcoming Volksfest. That's about two weeks away, is that right, Major?"

Holbrook felt certain that Samuel was an operative of the Mossad, the State of Israel's intelligence and counterterrorism agency.

No organization in the world kept better tabs on terrorists than the Mossad.

"That's correct," he replied to the agent. "Opening ceremonies are at 11 a.m., August 13. That's a Saturday."

"And that's when all your VIPs will be present?"

"Yes. So, what you're indicating is that there's a possibility—maybe even a probability—that an RPG rocket grenade will be used at the ceremonies to take out a group of American and West Berlin officials?"

"Yes, Major. That is what I have concluded from my informed sources."

Holbrook rose. Hands were shaken all around. "If you hear anything further, Samuel, you know how to contact Norm or me?"

"I do, Major."

"Thank you, Rabbi Halbfinger, for inviting us here. Sergeant Hellerstein and I need to complete our Wall patrol. *Shalom*, Rabbi," said Holbrook.

"And to you, Harry," the rabbi replied.

En route to Checkpoint Charlie and USCOB headquarters
2256 hours, 4 August 1966

"Sound serious, Norm?" Holbrook asked as they left the synagogue and drove through East Berlin, headed back to Checkpoint Charlie, otherwise known as the Friedrichstrasse crossing point.

"Very much so, sir, I believe," said Sergeant Hellerstein.

"It's probably too late to brief Colonel Semsch tonight, I suspect," said Holbrook, glancing at his wristwatch. "It's going on 11 p.m. What do you think?"

"I agree, sir. First thing tomorrow morning will work."

"Let's do this, Norm. A soon as we get home, let's each write a recollection of what Samuel—I'm sure he's Mossad—said and the words he used to convey the terrorist threat. That way, we'll both have accurate recollections."

"I agree with you about Mossad's involvement, Major. Those people are very concerned about the damage terrorists can do."

As they arrived at the Checkpoint, Military Police Corporal Antonio De La Cruz held up his hand in greeting and saluted the rear-seat passenger, whom he couldn't see clearly.

Hellerstein cranked down his driver-side window. "Evening, Tony. All quiet?"

"Quiet as can be. Everything okay over there?" he said, nodding in the direction of the East.

"Hardly a soul moving over there."

"See you next time, Norm."

"Likewise, Tony."

Office of the Intelligence Officer
Office of the U.S. Commander Berlin
Clayallee and Saargemünder Strasse
Dahlem, Zehlendorf
West Berlin
0830 hours, 5 August 1966

"Go right in, Major Holbrook," said Grace Wertman, "he's expecting you," and pressed a button under her desk that opened the door to Semsch's secure inner office.

"Come in, Harry," said Semsch. "Norm has just finished briefing me on last night's happening." He held up a sheet of paper with handwritten notes, apparently Hellerstein's account of the Mossad agent's report.

Holbrook handed his own handwritten memo to Semsch, who could see at a glance that they were virtually identical.

121

"What's the Mossad doing in East Berlin, Phil?" asked Holbrook.

"Harry, they're everywhere that terrorism is flourishing. Think about this: just six years from now, the 1972 Summer Olympics are going to take place in Munich, right next to us in West Germany, and preparations are already well under way. What if some groups are plotting to stage some sort of major act of terrorism tied in with the Olympics, all designed to impress the world with their power?

"The Jewish people have very long memories, Harry, and can be very unforgiving when it suits them. They certainly haven't forgotten about the death camps that two of the three prisoners in Spandau were intimately involved with. Ever stop to think about how Jews will feel when Speer and von Schirach are released this fall, probably at midnight on October 1?"

"I get the picture," said Holbrook. "But what do we do about the terrorist threat at the Volksfest? Surely we can't cancel the Volksfest."

"No, I don't see that happening. The first thing I've got to do is alert the Old Man"—military sobriquet for most commanding officers, in this case General Caraway—"and he'll undoubtedly want to reconvene his task force. I've got a call in to him now. Grace," he called out, "please let me know if the general returns the call I made a little after 0800 today."

"Will do, sir."

"Harry, while we're waiting to hear from Caraway, please explain the layout of the Volksfest to me and where an attack might come from."

All of a sudden, Holbrook realized that he should have brought his Volksfest layout map with him. "Grace," he called out, "please ask Frau Haupt to bring my Volksfest map down here. Tell her it's sitting in the middle of my desk right on top."

"Will do, sir."

While they were waiting for Holbrook's map, Holbrook began to discuss the possible points of attack. "The Mossad guy seemed to lay stress on the fact that the Red Army Faction has recently bought an RPG-7 from a dealer in Czechoslovakia. That's a lethal anti-tank weapon which can blow up a whole crowd of people, in this case the VIPs at the opening ribbon-cutting ceremony. So, let's say that the terrorists have a marksman, fully trained on the RPG-7, who wants to take out Caraway, Calhoun, maybe even Mayor Brandt, all in one fell swoop. Where would he position himself for a clean shot?" Holbrook wondered.

Just then Grace Wertman brought in Holbrook's rolled-up Volksfest layout map. "Thank you, Grace, and thank you, Frau Haupt," he said, this last in a loud voice so Gertie could hear him down the hall.

He unrolled the map. "We've created a network of streets this year, marked by metal stakes in the grass and heavy-duty tape to outline the sides of each street. For example, here's O.K. Corral Strasse at its intersection with Abilene Kreuzung. A little further along you come to Dodge City Strasse."

"Clever names, Harry," said Semsch. "But where is the gunner likely to be?"

"I did some research on the RPG-7. It has a maximum effective range of about 1,100 meters, or 1,200 yards. So, if the gunner were to zero in on the opening-day ribbon-cutting ceremony taking place here"—he pointed to the map—"he would probably need to position himself somewhere within this circle." He drew an imaginary circle on the map. "The RPG-7, I've learned, is pretty susceptible to strong wind gusts, so the shooter probably wouldn't want to be firing at max range. He has just one shot at his target and then he has to run for his life, unless he considers himself a suicide bomber. So let's say he'd like to find a firing point maybe half his maximum range, say 500 or 600 yards. That brings him to the Volksfest's main drag, Wyatt Earp Strasse." He pointed to the street on the map. "We've constructed a two-story saloon, the Deadwood Biergarten, right here at the intersection of Wyatt Earp Strasse and Crazy Horse Plaza. There'll be lots of drinking downstairs and some painted women hanging out from the upstairs windows. I believe a determined assassin could overpower any women in the area, fire his weapon from an upstairs window, jump from a rear window onto a balcony, and quickly get lost as the crowd is entering the Volksfest."

"So how do we counter that?"

"Lots of MPs dressed up as cowboys and gunslingers, but toting handguns in their holsters—and with live ammunition in the chambers. The brigade has an MP company, the 287th attached to it, and perhaps 15 or 20 armed MPs wandering around the Volksfest, dressed in costumes as cowhands and gunslingers, would be a good idea, not just for the opening but for the entire two-week Volksfest run."

"That's a great idea! We need to make sure that General Hay sits in on the USCOB's task force."

"Last I heard, Phil, the 287th MP Company was commanded by a very fine captain named Charley Hines. Charley looks like an NFL wide receiver and, in fact, I believe he *was* one at Howard University, the historically Black college in Washington, D.C. I'd recommend that Hines sits in on the meetings."

"Shouldn't be a problem. These are all good thoughts, Harry." Semsch glanced at his wristwatch. "It's 0900, Harry, and I think the general should be arriving at his desk by now. I'll keep your memo from last night and Hellerstein's to show him. Since his own life may be at stake, I wouldn't be surprised if he summons the task force to meet today."

"I'll be available, Phil. That is, if he can stand having me around. You know he hates my guts."

"Well, old buddy, if you manage to save his scalp at the Volksfest, perhaps it might persuade him to form a new opinion of your worth."

"I doubt it, but we'll see. I'll be in my office all day if you need me for the meeting."

10

Office of the U.S. Commander Berlin
Clayallee and Saargemünder Strasse
Dahlem, Zehlendorf
West Berlin
1530 hours, 5 August 1966

General Caraway convened the first meeting of his new Volksfest task force, which looked very much like his MiG-21 task force of a few months ago. Military Police Captain Charles J. Hines was the only new face, wondering what the hell he was doing in this room full of military and civilian brass. Major Holbrook was present but hadn't been called upon to speak.

"How seriously should we regard this terrorist threat, Semsch?" asked the USCOB.

"In my judgment, sir, we should regard it as a very serious threat against us," the command's intelligence officer replied. He had just finished briefing the task force about the meeting that Major Holbrook had attended last night with the apparent Mossad agent and had gotten the group's full attention.

The CIA's Halvorsen was in agreement. "General, our sources in the East confirm that something is definitely going on with the Red

Army Faction people. There's an unusual amount of activity, travel around East Berlin by terrorist personnel has increased, and Phil can comment on their communications."

"That's right," said Semsch. "Our ASA detachment monitoring radio and telephone communications in East Berlin reports an increased level of traffic, much of it encoded. The Red Army Faction, we know, has had training by Soviet experts, and their commo techniques are surprisingly sophisticated. The raw data from our intercepts has been sent back to NSA at Fort Meade and we're waiting for the fully analyzed product.

"But the bottom line, General," Semsch concluded, "is that we should regard this as a very serious threat. The lives of several people in this room, including yours, sir," Semsch said, looking directly at the USCOB, "are very much at risk."

At this last comment, Caraway seemed to blanch a little. "Okay, you've convinced me. What measures should we take to avert an attack? Roger," he said, turning to the CIA station chief, "what do you think we should be doing?"

"General, as Phil has said, we will continue extensive surveillance of the Faction's radio and telephone signals. In view of the impending threat, Langley has made arrangements with NSA to assign a very high priority to the analysis of communications traffic originating from East Berlin. Our sources over there have all been alerted to the threat and so far have pretty much confirmed that something is taking place, as I indicated a moment ago. We have those sources on high alert for keywords such as 'Volksfest' and 'RPG-7,' which of course is also true for the NSA's UNIVAC and Honeywell computers. To sum up, General," Halvorsen said, "I believe we're doing everything possible at this point in anticipation of what's likely to happen. As we get closer to the Volksfest opening, of course, I'll have more frequent updates."

Minister Calhoun spoke next. "I'm very much in favor of Major Holbrook's idea that Phil Semsch was telling us about, to have military policemen costumed as cowboys mingling as part of the crowds. I'm assuming they'd be radio-equipped"—at which Semsch and Holbrook both nodded—"to report any trouble. Captain Hines," he said, turning to the new task force member, "I assume these will be men from your MP company?"

"That's affirmative, sir. Major Holbrook has been acquiring western costumes for my men from his Volksfest suppliers and we'll be ready to go."

Semsch asked, "Charley, what do your men know about the RPG-7?"

"We don't have an exact copy of it, sir. But we do have LAWs (Light Anti-Tank Weapon) in the brigade's arms rooms and it's a somewhat similar shoulder-fired weapon. Because it's summertime and no overcoats are being worn, we're telling the men to be on the lookout for someone in a raincoat or anyone carrying a suitcase or large bag.

"The RPG weighs about 17½ pounds, so it's fairly heavy and should be easy to detect if it's being carried by someone. If it's been pre-positioned for an ambush, that will make it harder for us. Major Holbrook has briefed my men—about 18 of them—on the likely nature of an attack and indicated that it's probably going to be against the VIPs—some of you gentlemen—and very likely at the opening ribbon-cutting ceremonies.

"Major Holbrook has told us to expect Governing Mayor Brandt, you General Caraway, you Minister Calhoun, General Hay, and possibly several other VIPs at the ribbon cutting. We got word yesterday that Ambassador McGhee may be coming from Bonn. There will be hundreds of Berliners who have bought tickets at the ticket booths who will be waiting to rush into the Volksfest as soon as the ribbon is cut. That appears to be the most opportune time for the terrorist to strike with his RPG. Others of my men, who are not dressing as cowboys, will be in their regular fatigue uniforms wearing MP brassards doing crowd control, as we did at last year's

Volksfest. We've placed special emphasis on the crowd gathered at the ribbon-cutting ceremony, just in case a terrorist with a pistol might be in that crowd.

"We're not ruling out other forms of weapons either. Sniper rifles, handguns and even a small mortar, such as a 60mm, are all possibilities and we're training against those. But by and large, everything we've heard from Colonel Semsch and Major Holbrook is that the terrorists have taken pains and gone to considerable expense to acquire an RPG-7 and an attack at the Volksfest seems like the perfect opportunity to use one against us."

"Excellent report, Captain Hines," said the USCOB, which was seconded by all attendees.

Caraway ended the meeting by pointing out to all that the Volksfest opening on August 13 was only eight days away and that every effort needed to be exerted to glean additional intelligence about the terrorists' intentions and to make and implement plans to defeat them.

12 Goldfinkweg
Dahlem, Zehlendorf
West Berlin
1930 hours, 5 August 1966

Friday evening at the end of a long, stressful week. Holbrook was relaxing at home in a T-shirt and pair of sweatpants with a near-depleted bottle of Lowenbrau (his second of the evening) when his telephone rang. Probably Phil Semsch with a follow-up to the just-concluded meeting of the Volksfest task force, he assumed.

"Holbrook," he said rather brusquely into the phone. "What's up?"

"Harry?" said a somewhat hesitant feminine voice. "I'm sorry if I disturbed you."

He of the acclaimed Holbrook memory—apparently famed on both sides of the Iron Curtain—did a quick inventory of all the female voices he knew. He drew a blank.

"Harry, it's Carolyn Mattersdorf. We met at the PTA meeting, remember?"

Oh shit. He'd been entranced by the pretty brunette of the Thomas A. Roberts faculty but had never followed up, never phoned her or sent a note. Nada. Just too damn busy.

"Of course I remember, Carolyn. I was meaning to call you but we ran into some complications with the Volksfest—it opens next weekend, you know—and I lost track of time."

"No problem, Harry. The reason I called is this. *The Sound of Music* is opening tomorrow at the Outpost Theater. It won five Oscars last year, including best picture, and I've been dying to see it. I was supposed to go tomorrow night with my friend Sybil. She teaches English at TAR and she's a big Julie Andrews fan, as I am. Well … Sybil called a few minutes ago. She's under the weather and begged off for tomorrow. I'm still dying to see the movie and I was wondering if you'd like to see it with me."

Holbrook was beside himself with anticipation. "Of course I'd like to see it, Carolyn. With you, that is. Of course. I know that Rodgers and Hammerstein wrote the songs and I loved Julie Andrews in *Mary Poppins*. What about going to a matinee so we can have a meal afterward?"

"I'd like that very much, Harry. I think matinees at the Outpost are around 3 p.m., but I'll check tomorrow and call you back with confirmation."

"Great. I'll be at the office tomorrow morning, so please call me there. I gave you my number, I think."

"Yes, I have it on your calling card."

Blessed little calling card. "Can I pick you up at your quarters?" he asked.

"Certainly. I'm in the female BOQ."

"I know where it is, Carolyn. I'll wait for your call tomorrow."

"Wonderful, Harry. I'm looking forward to it," she said and hung up.

Holbrook's little heart danced with anticipation. He began humming "The hills are alive with the sound of music ..."

Site of the Fifth Annual German-American Volksfest (Deutsch-Amerikanisches Volksfest)
Clayallee and Argentinische Allee
Dahlem, Zehlendorf
West Berlin
0730 hours, 6 August 1966

Two days of steady summer rains had put construction of the Old West-style village being built for the German-American Volksfest behind schedule, with the grand opening just seven days away.

Accordingly, construction supervisor Ernst Zimmermann had ordered a full day of work on Saturday, with time-and-a-half wages. There was some grumbling among the German workers about having to work on a weekend, but fattened pay envelopes the next payday would always be welcome.

Many of the construction laborers were Turkish emigres who had come to Germany after the Wall was built in 1961. By closing off traffic between the two Berlins, the GDR had inadvertently choked off a major source of labor that supplied West Berlin with relatively low-paid, unskilled laborers to work on construction projects, while keeping East Berliners employed and well compensated.

Among these laborers was one Cemil Burakgazi, according to his citizenship and workers papers. These indicated that he had been born and raised in Sinop, Turkey, on the Black Sea coast. Sinop's only claims to fame were that it built quality wooden boats and was the birthplace of the Greek philosopher Diogenes, who had gained notoriety 300 years before the birth of Christ by supposedly scouring the civilized world with a lantern in search of an honest man. History doesn't record if Diogenes ever found such a man; perhaps there was none to be found.

In actuality, Cemil Burakgazi had never been to Sinop and wasn't Turkish. He had arrived in Germany in 1963 among several million genuine Turks who migrated there in the 1960s in search of more lucrative working conditions. Burakgazi, whose real name never became known, was in fact a Lebanese terrorist who became affiliated with the Red Army Faction. He had taken training in Libya in most of the weaponry associated with international terrorism, primarily the AK-47 assault rifle, pipe bombs, Semtex explosives, C4 plastic explosives, and the RPG-7 rocket-propelled grenade.

Burakgazi lived in West Berlin but carried papers authenticated by authorities of the GDR that his only living relative, a sister, was dying from cancer in East Berlin, which allowed him to travel frequently and without hassle from one side of the Wall to the other.

The terrorist was classified as a master carpenter and was highly regarded as such by Zimmermann and his co-developer, Werner Bauer. Burakgazi accordingly was given pretty much free rein to work on carpentry projects in the Volksfest Wild West town being constructed.

In the second story of the Deadwood Biergarten on Wyatt Earp Strasse, a few hundred meters from the Volksfest's main entrance, Burakgazi was finishing up a small two-riser flight of stairs connecting a hallway with an upstairs bedroom. Under the small staircase he had concealed a fully operational RPG-7 grenade launcher, which he had smuggled in parts onto the Volksfest site along with his personal tools.

Today he had finished concealing the weapon by boarding it up with side paneling for the staircase, held in place by some small temporary nails that could easily be removed in order to retrieve the RPG-7 when the time came to fire it.

With final checks made, the terrorist assured himself that the weapon was fully concealed until it was ready to be used in seven days. As he exited the hallway, he glanced at the open window to the rear of the building which he would use as his escape route to mingle with the Volksfest crowd of visiting Berliners.

Information Division (ID)
Headquarters, U.S. Commander Berlin
Clayallee and Saargemünder Strasse
Dahlem, Zehlendorf
West Berlin
1010 hours, 6 August 1966

"This will probably be our final meeting before the Volksfest begins a week from today, gentlemen and Frau Jochem," said Harry Holbrook as he convened his Volksfest planning group. "The rains this week cost us a couple of days, but I see, Ernst and Werner, that you've got the crews working today, even though it's a Saturday. Good thinking, which should help us catch up."

Holbrook paused, choosing his next words with care. "We've been alerted that a terrorist attack timed with our grand-opening ceremonies is a distinct possibility." He looked around the room and noted that he'd gotten the full attention of all attendees. "I can't go into details," Holbrook continued, "but headquarters has received credible reports that some terrorist groups are planning to attack our opening ceremonies. That means that Mayor Brandt, General Caraway, and all the other VIPs at the opening will be at risk unless we can prevent any kind of attack."

The group fell silent for a moment, digesting this unpalatable bit of news. "What kind of attack, Major? Small arms, gas, grenades? What are we up against?"

Holbrook pondered how much information to share. "The terrorists have apparently acquired an RPG-7 shoulder-fired weapon. They would probably also have some automatic weapons and pistols, but an RPG-7 aimed at the stand where the VIPs will be seated represents our major concern."

"What are we doing about it?" asked Paul Scholl.

"We're taking every reasonable precaution," said Holbrook. "We've got MPs patrolling the Volksfest grounds, some in uniform, some in cowboy outfits, all radio-equipped. We'll have observers watching the stands where the VIPs will be seated during the ceremonies. And I'll ask Frau Jochem to get word to all the concessionaires at the *Biergartens* to be on alert for any signs of possible trouble, without mentioning terrorists."

Holbrook turned to Ingeborg Jochem of his staff and she nodded back in agreement.

"If I get any further word before the opening," Holbrook went on, "I'll share it with you. But that's where we stand at present. Now, let's discuss all our normal arrangements. Paul, let's start with you and the media callout."

Scholl passed around the table the voluminous press kits he and his staff had prepared. Press releases in English and German announced the "Fifth Annual German-American Volksfest" opening for two weeks on August 13, reprising the Old West (*alten Westen*) theme that had proved to be immensely popular among Berliners.

Included in Scholl's press kits were photos of last year's Volksfest and movie stills from some of the John Wayne movies that would be running at the Outpost Theater. This new wrinkle that Holbrook had dreamed up was seen as a promising add-on to the array of outdoor events, such as cowboy shoot 'em ups, covered wagon rides, pony rides, bronco busting, and other features that had proven popular with the Berliners during the initial four Volksfests. The western movies also afforded an indoor alternative in the event of bad weather.

"The local press has really gotten excited," Scholl said, "about the idea of John Wayne seemingly speaking Deutsch. Although these western movies with German subtitles or dubbing have been around for years, they haven't generally been available to the German public. So, this is kind of a new slant for these old films."

Holbrook turned to Ken Silvestri, the special services manager who had located the films and made the necessary arrangements for their showing at the Volksfest. "Very nice job, Ken. If this produces a new Volksfest attraction each year, keep looking for additional films that could be shown. John Wayne movies are first priority, of course, but there are a bunch of good Randolph Scotts, Jimmy Stewarts, and Gary Coopers that might be available. Cooper's *High Noon*, for example, would go over great with many Berliners."

"There's also more recent westerns," said Scholl. "*Shane* was made in the early '50s, as I recall, and westerns don't get any better than that."

"Absolutely," said Holbrook. "So, Ken, as soon as we get this year's Volksfest wrapped up, and assuming that the crowds at the Outpost Theater prove worthwhile, please go ahead and sign us up for another round of westerns."

"Got it, Harry," said Silvestri.

"I doubt that I'll still be here next summer," said Holbrook, "since I'm pretty sure that I'll be headed to Vietnam before then, but we want to ensure that whoever takes my place gets the full benefit of the most successful ideas that you guys have come up with."

He turned to Frau Jochem. "Ingeborg, please make sure that your minutes of all our Volksfest meetings, together with the after-action reports, are placed in a separate file folder for whoever comes along to take my place. Then, as soon as the time comes around to start planning for the next Volksfest, make that file available to the new information officer."

"Yes, of course, Major Holbrook," she replied.

There was a light rap on the door of Holbrook's conference room and Frau Haupt ushered in Military Police Captain Charles Hines, commander of the Berlin Brigade's 298th MP Company.

"Sorry I'm late, sir," Hines said to Holbrook. "A little problem of shoplifting at the PX by some teenaged sons of brigade NCOs. I had to wait for the fathers to arrive and tote their kids away by their ear lobes."

"No problem, Charley. I've shared with this committee the general outline of the potential terrorist threat at the Volksfest, without getting into too many specifics. The main thing I'd like you to cover is what your MPs will be doing at the grand opening and during the two weeks that we'll be in operation."

Hines nodded, understanding from Holbrook's introduction that the RPG-7 threat wasn't to be addressed. "Got it, sir." He turned to the group. "As Major Holbrook has told you, we've received reports of a specific threat at the grand opening, and perhaps continuing throughout the entire run of the Volksfest." Hines detailed the VIPs expected to be in attendance, as well as the press and even Ambassador McGhee. "Maybe 200 to 250 people in total, I've been told. In other words," Hines continued, "our attendees at the ceremony will literally be sitting targets for any terrorist who wants to take out much of the military and civilian leadership of West Germany and West Berlin. These people will be sitting in the stands for maybe 30 or 40 minutes while speeches and remarks are being made and they'll be very vulnerable to an attack."

Hines paused to gather his thoughts before continuing, at which point Scholl interrupted his briefing.

"What kind of weapon are we worried about, Captain Hines? Are you talking about a bomb?"

Hines glanced at Holbrook to see if he should respond. Holbrook nodded a go-ahead.

"Mr. Scholl, we believe the terrorists, a Red Army Faction group, have acquired an RPG-7. That's primarily an antitank weapon but it can be awfully effective in an antipersonnel role."

Holbrook waved an arm to let Hines know he had something to add. "Please treat that last bit of information as classified and let's keep it in this room. One, we don't want anyone to overreact and be scared, and secondly, we don't want the terrorists to know what we've learned about their plans and intentions. Everyone comfortable with that?" All nodded in agreement and Holbrook signaled for Hines to continue.

"To alert us about suspicious activity of any kind," Hines said, "I've assigned about two dozen of my MPs to dress up as cowboys, sheriffs, et cetera, all in western costumes that Mr. Silvestri has been getting for us. Another two dozen will be patrolling the Volksfest grounds at all hours, dressed in their regular MP fatigue uniforms."

"Will they all be armed?" Scholl asked.

"Yes, my instructions from brigade headquarters are that—in view of the threat—all the MPs will carry their standard .45-caliber pistols with live ball ammunition, as well as billy clubs."

Hines paused at this point and Holbrook was anxious to move along to the logistics reports. "Any further questions for Captain Hines? If not, thanks for coming, Charley, and keep me in the loop if there are any problems or concerns."

"Roger that, sir," said Hines and left.

"Hines seems like a very capable young officer," said Scholl.

"I agree, Paul," said Holbrook. "If we can keep him in the Army, he has a very bright future ahead of him. All right, let's talk about beer. I hear that shipments have been delayed because of a labor shortage at the breweries and if there isn't enough beer ... well, you know how the Berliners will feel about that."

Information Division (ID)
Headquarters, U.S. Commander Berlin
Clayallee and Saargemünder Strasse
Dahlem, Zehlendorf
West Berlin
1145 hours, 6 August 1966

"Mr. Erb is on Line 1, Major Holbrook," called Frau Gertraud Haupt from the outer office.

"What's up, Hugh?" said Holbrook, picking up the receiver.

"Two things, Major, one personal, one business."

"Okay. Let's do the personal one first."

"Krista and I would like to invite you over to dinner at our house, to thank you with your help with moving my personal papers and also to thank you for serving as a pallbearer at my father's funeral at the brigade chapel. Are you free tomorrow night, say, about seven?"

"That's very nice, Hugh. It isn't every day that a bureau chief and his arch enemy, the public information officer, sit down to break bread together, but I'd be happy to accept. Can I bring anything?'

"Maybe just a bottle of wine from the Class VI store. Will you be bringing a date?"

Holbrook thought for a moment. He had a movie and dinner date with Carolyn Mattersdorf on for that evening and he wondered if it might be overdoing and rushing things to invite her for a second consecutive evening out. "Let me ask a young lady I know if she might be interested, Hugh. Can I get back to you tomorrow morning?"

"No problem. Krista will have enough *Wienerschnitzel* either way. Just let me know so I can set the table correctly."

"What's the business item, Hugh?"

"Your Volksfest will be opening a week from today for a two-week run. Is that correct?"

"Yes, that's right."

"Do you have any security concerns?" Erb asked.

Uh oh. Holbrook was quickly on guard. The newsman had heard something about the terrorist threat and was probing for confirmation. No way was Holbrook going to give the AP's Berlin bureau chief a heads-up about the Red Army Faction's suspected RPG-7. If Erb wrote about the threat and his story was picked up by German language newspapers in West Berlin, Volksfest attendance might drop by half.

"Hugh, we always have security concerns. We had almost 300,000 visitors at last year's Volksfest and there are always going to be some drunken incidents, a fight or two, maybe a pickpocketing. We'll have the brigade's MPs plus some civilian contract personnel roaming throughout the grounds at all hours. We pretty much know what to expect."

"Okay, but what's this I hear that your German contractors have been procuring cowboy uniforms for your MPs? Are you going undercover against some form of threat?"

Holbrook had to watch every word he'd say in reply. Dinner host or not, Hugh Erb was the most significant newsman in West Berlin and Holbrook needed to deflect Erb's inquiry.

"As I said, Hugh, we always have MPs and paid German rent-a-cops patrolling the grounds. This year we thought it might be advantageous to dress up some of the MPs in western gear so they'd blend in more readily with the crowd. The Berliners will be wearing cowboy costumes, along with their children, and some of them like to wear Native American clothing and headdresses. So it's basically a way to blend in and be less conspicuous than they'd be in their uniforms. Kind of heading off trouble at the pass, as they used to say in the old John Ford oaters."

While Erb digested this bit of information, Holbrook tried to change the focus of the conversation a bit. "Speaking of old western movies, have you heard what we're doing at the Outpost Theater?"

"No, what's up there?"

"We've arranged to show some old John Wayne westerns with German titles or dubbing. The Outpost will be open to Berliners and their kids for one mark, something we've never done before. I don't think these movies—we've got *She Wore A Yellow Ribbon and The Searchers,* and a couple more—have ever been available in Berlin in the German language."

"That's a nice touch, Major. In other words, if families get tired of the beer and fireworks, they can wander over to the Outpost and watch a John Wayne movie. First time you've done this?"

"First time," Holbrook confirmed.

"I might write something about it. Who's got the details?'

"Ken Silvestri, our special services officer. Ken put it all together. I'll give him a call and tell him to update you. How much longer are you going to be in the office on a Saturday morning?"

"It's getting a little late and I promised Krista and Klaus that I'd take them shopping. Why don't you have him call me Monday morning around 9:30? Would you spell his last name for me? And you'll call to let us know if you're bringing a date tomorrow, right?"

"I will," said Holbrook, making a note on his desk calendar.

"Gertie," he called out, "please get Ken Silvestri on the phone."

Holbrook relaxed a bit, apparently having gotten Erb off the scent of a terrorist threat at the Volksfest opening. It was time to go home, have a quick lunch, then shower, shave, and change out of uniform for his movie and dinner date with Carolyn Mattersdorf.

Drei Bären Café
Kurfürstendamm
West Berlin
1800 hours, 6 August 1966

"This is really a very nice drink, Harry," said Carolyn Mattersdorf.

They were sitting outdoors at the Drei Bären (Three Bears) Café on the KuDamm, West Berlin's most glamorous street, essentially a long, wide boulevard filled with upscale shops, hotels, and swanky restaurants. Some visitors felt that the Kurfürstendamm's vibrancy was comparable to that of the Champs Elysees in Paris.

Holbrook had ordered Berliner Weisses for the two of them, since Carolyn had deferred to his suggestion. The drink was a low-alcohol beer flavored with raspberry syrup and served in a large bowl-shaped glass. A century ago, Holbrook told her, it had been the most popular alcoholic drink in Berlin, with 700 breweries producing the beer, but modern tastes had shifted to other beverages.

Nevertheless, Holbrook told Carolyn, it was one of his favorites, and on a warm, cloudless summer evening such as this it was truly refreshing, he said.

He had dressed casually for this important first date and chose a navy blue blazer with chino trousers and a button-down light blue dress shirt, open at the collar. For the first time, he was wearing the pair of brown tasseled loafers he had come home with after his second visit to the KaDeWe department store.

Carolyn's yellow sleeveless summer dress highlighted her summer tan. With school out of session for the summer, she had spent time sunning outside the female BOQ (bachelor officer quarters) that TAR female schoolteachers shared with women officers of the USCOB and brigade staffs.

"So, what did you think of the movie, Harry?" she asked. They had taken in the matinee showing of *The Sound of Music* at the Outpost Theater and were now relaxing, enjoying each other's company while watching the Saturday evening strollers up and down the KuDamm.

"I loved it, I really did. I knew that it was a big success on Broadway but the movie really capitalizes on the Alps and the beautiful green valleys. And the music by Rodgers and Hammerstein is just unforgettable.

"The song 'Edelweiss,'" Holbrook continued, "was actually the last thing Hammerstein wrote before he passed away in 1960, I believe. Many people who have listened to the LP recordings of the show have assumed that it's a traditional German folksong, when in fact it came out of the pens of Richard Rodgers and Oscar Hammerstein.

"I suppose you could say," Holbrook the erudite theater critic continued, "that the movie is very schmaltzy, full of old-fashioned corniness and sentimentality. But it won Oscars this year for best picture, best musical score, best editing, and best directing, so I guess you could say that it was a huge success. And audiences loved it. Look at how the crowd at the Outpost, including lots of children, cheered as the movie ended."

Carolyn was looking intently at her date, taking it all in. She was 27, a full seven years younger than Holbrook, and appeared suitably impressed with his worldliness. (At this point she was still unaware of his legendary memory, especially since he had apparently forgotten to phone her after their first encounter at the Thomas A. Roberts PTA meeting.)

They exchanged informal CVs, as first-daters do. Holbrook explained that he'd been headed toward a career in the ministry, much like his father, but had become interested in the Army via the ROTC program at Penn State. He added that he was divorced, with two young children living with their mother in Pennsylvania.

Carolyn came from a very conservative family background in Rockford, Illinois. Her father was an electrical engineer at Sundstrand, a large manufacturer of aerospace and industrial products in Rockford. Her dad had a master's degree in engineering from the University of Illinois and was an elder at their church in Rockford.

"What about your mother?" Holbrook asked.

"A homemaker. She earned a degree in early childhood education but then my older brother came along, then me, and then my little sister Peggy, so she really never was able to fulfill her career as a teacher."

Holbrook thought long and hard about wording his next question. "What about boyfriends, Carolyn? Are you seeing anyone on a steady basis, either here in Berlin or back home in Rockford?"

"Not really, Harry. This is the first date I've been on in maybe six months and there was really no one back home who really interested me. I guess you could say that I'm a very old-fashioned girl and that I choose my dating partners very carefully. I took a liking to you at the PTA meeting and this has been a very nice day so far."

Holbrook got the message. Carolyn Mattersdorf was very much a virgin and was committed to saving herself for the one man who might fulfill her expectations. Any hopes he had entertained of getting laid that night (he had even placed a condom inside his wallet) suddenly went *kaput*, as their German acquaintances might say.

Oh well, there were other fish in the sea. But Holbrook had a thought.

"Carolyn, I had an invitation from an American reporter to have dinner tomorrow night at his home. He's an American of German descent and has a wife who's a Berliner. They have a son who's about five or six, I think. They've asked if I wanted to bring along a ... guest"—on the spot he'd decided against using the word "date," since that might be perceived by Carolyn as rushing things—"and I wonder if you might be interested in meeting them."

As Carolyn swished the Berliner Weisse around in her glass, weighing her options and pondering whether she wanted to see this interesting, somewhat unsettling, Army major two nights in a row, Holbrook filled in the silence.

"Hugh Erb is head of the Associated Press news bureau in Berlin. He's probably the most important newsman that I deal with. The AP is a wire service that feeds news and information to newspapers, radio, and TV stations all across America and much of the world. When AP reports something, it usually has clout. It's very unusual for a spokesman like me to be invited for dinner at the home of a major news person, since by definition we work on opposite sides of the street."

Carolyn considered this. "Why do you think he invited you, Harry?"

"I'm not completely sure. A while back I did a favor for him and I suppose that may have been a factor."

She leaned forward. "What kind of favor?"

"No big deal, really. He needed help in moving some personal papers from here to the Zone and I was able to assist him."

Carolyn's raised eyebrows suggested she intuitively knew that this was only part of the story. She decided to learn more tomorrow in hopes of finding out more about Harry Holbrook. "I'd love to go, Harry. What time?"

"I'll pick you up at the BOQ at 6:30. I'll phone Hugh tomorrow morning to tell him that you're coming. It's just Hugh—his full name is Hubert, by the way—Krista, and little Klaus, or Klausi as I call him. Dress casually, slacks or jeans would be fine."

That taken care of, they ordered dinners of *Sauerbraten*, along with a second Berliner Weisse. Holbrook had her home at her BOQ by 10:30. They parted by shaking hands outside Holbrook's car, together with a very chaste kiss.

So much for first dates, reflected the peerless warrior on his drive home to Goldfinkweg. Maybe tomorrow might be a little livelier.

Erb Residence
Theklastrasse 35
Dahlem, Zehlendorf
West Berlin
1950 hours, 6 August 1966

Hugh Erb, having opened the bottle of Riesling that Holbrook had brought, poured glasses for the four adults and opened a green glass bottle of Coca-Cola for Klaus, pouring some into a glass.

"Here's a toast to the success of your Volksfest next week, Major."
Glasses clinked all around.

"Hugh, just for tonight, can you bring yourself to call me Harry?"

"Certainly, Major," Hugh joked. He asked Carolyn about her background and she told Erb essentially what she had imparted to Holbrook the previous night. German-born Krista Erb, a beautiful Nordic blonde in her mid-to late-thirties, studied Carolyn intently, apparently guessing what the schoolteacher and the infantry major might have in common. On the surface very little, she concluded.

Carolyn accepted a second glass of the dry white wine from her host. It loosened her up a bit. "Hugh, what's the connection that brings Harry as a guest into your home? You two are supposed to be sworn enemies, I understand."

Erb glanced over his wine glass at Holbrook, then took a long sip. "Can you keep a secret, Carolyn?"

"Of course I can."

"Okay, I'll spill the beans. My father—God rest his soul—passed away back in June. The Erb family has a number of burial plots in a Catholic cemetery near Cologne, which is where I was born and raised until my parents moved to the U.S. So my father—Grandpa Erb, God rest his soul—wanted to be buried there and I promised him that I'd take care of it. He's been living with Krista, Klaus, and me for the past five or six years, ever since he became too frail to live by himself."

Erb paused, gathering his thoughts and sentiments. He poured himself another glass of wine after offering some to his guests, who each declined. Carolyn leaned forward, wondering where this was heading. Holbrook leaned back, knowing that he had violated four-power regulations and that he could still get burned for it.

"To get my father's coffin from Berlin to Cologne, it would have to transit the 110 miles from Berlin to Helmstedt in the Zone. There was no way to fly the coffin to the West and if I shipped it by a hearse, the … Vopos"—here Erb had to stifle a curse with Klaus present—"would search the coffin and violate his body."

"So what did you do?" Carolyn asked, clearly engrossed in the saga.

Erb took a sip of the Riesling. "I went to the good major here and laid it out for him, everything upfront and on the line. I asked him to ship it on the Army's duty train because that's untouchable as far as the Vopos and Russians are concerned."

"And what did Harry say?" she asked, shifting her gaze between the two men, one seated next to her and the other across the table.

"He told me, as I knew he would, that Army regulations and the four-power agreements among the occupying powers here in Berlin strictly prohibited shipping the coffin of a man who was essentially a German national."

"And that's how it ended?"

"Not exactly. I told Major Holbrook—I mean Harry—that I was aware that he'd recently authorized a shipment on the duty train of some professional papers for the NBC guy in Berlin. I told Harry that I also had professional papers to ship."

Carolyn was intrigued. "So he went to the general and got approval to ship them?"

"Not exactly, Carolyn. He knows that Caraway is a nincompoop. He knew that going to the USCOB would be a total dead end and would result in instant disapproval."

"So what did Harry do?"

"He signed the papers to authorize the shipment, then went with me to the *Bahnhof* to make sure that the hard-nosed Russian captain there didn't gum things up."

"But Harry could have gotten into real trouble, couldn't he?"

Erb took another swallow of his wine. "Probably a career ender. For sure he'd never get promoted to light colonel and he'd probably spend the rest of his derailed career supervising latrine construction in Vietnam."

Carolyn turned to her date for the evening, appraising him in a new light. "Harry, didn't you realize that by helping Hugh you were jeopardizing your own future, your own career?"

Harry, fresh from his recent discussions with Erb about John Wayne movies, had a fleeting inclination to quote The Duke and say, "A man's gotta do what a man's gotta do," but he was rational enough to stifle that stupid thought.

"I did what was right, Carolyn. I knew Grandpa Erb, used to greet him on his evening walks through the neighborhood, often with Klausi at his side. It was really no big deal to give Hugh the authorization he needed."

Erb responded. "Not exactly true, Carolyn. It was a very big deal for Grandpa Erb and for Krista, Klausi, and me. Did you know that I asked the major to be a pallbearer at the funeral, after I asked him for permission to hold the funeral services at the brigade chapel?"

"No, Hugh," Carolyn stammered, thoroughly taken aback by all these revelations. "I had no idea that Harry was involved in so many things."

Krista Erb entered the conversation for the first time. "In many ways," she said in her accented English, "Major Holbrook is not a bad man, all things considered," and she smiled at them both.

Carolyn was quiet on the drive back to the female BOQ, thinking through the evening's developments and reprising them in her own mind. "Harry, are you always such a risk-taker?"

"There really wasn't that much of a risk. What I did just made good sense."

"You say that you're headed to Vietnam in a few months. Will you be taking big risks over there, like you did for Hugh and his family?"

Harry's car was approaching Carolyn's BOQ and he turned to look at her as he parked it at the curb. "I'm not much of a risk-taker, Carolyn," he said. "I just do what needs to be done, hopefully when it needs doing."

She leaned forward, kissed him deeply on the lips, and ran into the building.

11

Bleachers opposite the main Volksfest gate were filling up quickly with Berliners anxious to attend the opening ceremonies and then gain early admission to the festivities on a beautiful sunlit summer day.

The U.S. ambassador to the Federal Republic of Germany (West Germany), George C. McGhee, had decided at the last moment to take in the Volksfest. He and his wife Cecilia (whom he had once described as the "most beautiful and richest girl in Texas") were flying in from Bonn in a small State Department airplane. General Caraway and Minister Calhoun had gone to Tempelhof Airport to await the arrival of "Big George" McGhee.

General Hay, Caraway's second in command, had tightened security precautions, not only because of the McGhees' presence but also because West Berlin's governing mayor, Willy Brandt, would be

147

present in the stands and some Berliners were fervently opposed to Brandt's leadership of the Divided City.

West Berlin *Polizei* were visible everywhere in their blue-gray uniforms, doing traffic control, organizing queues of attendees, and watching for possible trouble. They performed this duty each August but had been instructed to be especially watchful this year for unspecified reasons.

Harry Holbrook was at work in the press section of the bleachers, overseeing his staffers, who were passing out press kits and answering questions from the media. He did some hobnobbing with the press and then left the bleacher area, heading for the Volksfest main gate.

At 10 a.m.—one hour before opening—the 298th Army Band began to play a medley of German and American popular tunes, including some Sousa marches and themes from western movies such as *High Noon* and *Shane*, along with some familiar German oompah numbers with their heavy brass component.

Just inside the main gate, Holbrook linked up with Captain Hines. "You've got radios for both of us, Charley?"

"Roger that, Major," said Hines, handing Holbrook a small hand-held olive drab field radio.

"And you've got your .45?"

Hines gestured to his brown leather holster.

"Ammo?"

"Locked and loaded, sir."

"Good. Let's make a brief tour and see that all your MPs—both those in uniform and those in cowboy outfits—are in place."

Holbrook and Hines began a walking tour of the Volksfest grounds, questioning MPs as they went as to whether they had seen anything unusual. Negative reports from everyone.

"How long did you say an RPG-7 was, Charley?" asked Holbrook.

"About 37 inches, sir. A little over a yard."

"I don't see how anyone could get through that gate smuggling a yard-long missile launcher, plus a grenade for it, do you?"

"I doubt it, sir. If this was a rainy day and people were wearing raincoats, I'd say it might be possible to sneak a weapon through. But all the Berliners I've seen so far are wearing T-shirts or short-sleeved shirts, along with skirts, short pants or lederhosen. There are lots of cowboy hats and some are decked out with leather chaps, but I sure don't see any way someone could manage to smuggle an RPG past the gate."

"I agree, Charley," said Holbrook. "It's probably another scare tactic by the terrorists, designed to keep us guessing about possible strikes against us. But keep your MPs on high alert until it's all over, OK?"

"Right, sir," and Hines spoke into his handset.

Site of the Fifth Annual German-American Volksfest
Clayallee and Argentinische Allee
Dahlem, Zehlendorf
West Berlin
0945 hours, 13 August 1966

Near the main gate, master carpenter Cemil Burakgazi, supposedly a Turkish émigré, was talking animatedly with construction supervisor Ernst Zimmermann. They were conversing in German, handicapped by the Turk's limited fluency in the language.

"There is no need to go back in," Zimmermann was arguing.

"But I accidentally left behind upstairs in the Deadwood Biergarten a very expensive measuring device which is your property," Burakgazi argued. "First of all is that it has value and additionally a child could be hurt if he sticks a finger in the device.

I can be in and out of the Volksfest grounds well before the first visitors come through the gates."

Zimmermann weighed the pros and cons. The Turk had been a solid, dependable worker, always ready to do what was asked of him and always doing it well. Even though Captain Hines had made it clear that no one was to be admitted to the grounds until all his MPs had radioed in that they were in position, Zimmermann was inclined to take a chance with his master carpenter. And the measuring device was worth several hundred marks.

"All right, Cemil, five minutes. *Fünf Minuten!* I want you back here in five minutes or less or we'll both be in hot water with the MPs. *Verstanden?* You got it?"

"Yes sir. Five minutes. I'll be back with the instrument." Showing the worker's pass hung around his neck, Burakgazi walked past the row of uniformed MPs and West Berlin *Polizei* manning the still-closed admittance gates, heading for the Deadwood Biergarten, where he had supposedly left his device but where actually he had concealed an RPG-7 and a grenade for it.

Reviewing Stand
Site of the Fifth Annual German-American Volksfest
Clayallee and Argentinische Allee
Dahlem, Zehlendorf
West Berlin
1045 hours, 13 August 1966

With 15 minutes to go until the start of ceremonies, almost everything was in place at the reviewing stand on Clayallee, adjacent to the Volksfest grounds.

Ambassador McGhee and his oil-heiress wife Cecilia were shaking hands all around with invited guests representing the three Allied nations still occupying West Berlin, along with officials from the West Berlin Senat and district mayors.

General Caraway and Minister Calhoun, having driven with the McGhees from Tempelhof to the Volksfest site, stood by, making introductions as guests jostled among themselves to shake hands with the American ambassador. Calhoun led Governing Mayor Willy Brandt forward for a hand-shaking photo with McGhee.

Brigadier Graham Huddleston, who commanded the British Berlin Infantry Brigade, and Général de Brigade François Binoche, commander of *Forces Françaises à Berlin*, the French occupation force in Berlin, both came forward to greet McGhee and shake hands with Brandt, in a neat little photo op that Holbrook had arranged for U.S. and West European television audiences. Binoche, who had lost his right arm fighting the Nazis in World War II, saluted McGhee with his left hand.

The photos and video footage, Holbrook had felt, were nice symbols of Allied cooperation and shared responsibilities in keeping West Berlin out of the Soviets' grasp, even though the city lay deep behind the Iron Curtain.

Sitting in the bleachers by himself, dressed in a typical German business suit with a tie, sat a special invited guest of Holbrook's, Colonel Dmitri Lazarev of Spandau Prison. In another row, wearing his yarmulke, sat Rabbi Ernst Halbfinger, accompanied by his good friend Meier Grossmann, both guests of Holbrook.

At 1100 hours, the band stopped playing and the crowd hushed as everyone sensed that the opening ceremony was about to begin. General Caraway asked the VIPs to take their seats—each labelled with names and titles—and strode to the lectern to welcome everyone.

Using for the most part a speech drafted by Holbrook and Paul Scholl, Caraway began to speak.

Loudspeakers and amplifiers boomed his remarks across the reviewing stands and all across the Volksfest grounds, where Holbrook and Hines could hear every word.

"Governing Mayor Brandt, Ambassador McGhee, Brigadier Huddleston, General Binoche, invited guests, and Berliners of all ages, welcome to the Fifth Annual German-American Volksfest!"

As Caraway's voice rose for his welcoming words, the crowd broke out in a cheer. None among the Berliners doubted that—except for the presence of the three occupying powers, but especially the 6,000-man American force—they would all be living under Soviet control, much like their friends, and in some cases families, in East Berlin. After all, hadn't the youthful American President—since shot down by an assassin's bullet—stood among them five years earlier and proclaimed "*Ich bin ein Berliner!*"

Many in the crowd spoke little English and couldn't grasp the meaning of Caraway's words. But they noted the enthusiasm of the English speakers in the stands and echoed their fervor.

As Caraway finished his remarks and asked everyone to rise for the national anthems of the Federal Republic of Germany, followed by the anthems of Great Britain, France, and the hosting nation, the United States, everyone stood. Many placed their hands over their hearts, while those in uniform, including West Berlin *Polizei*, saluted.

The 298th Army Band struck up the opening strains of the West German anthem, officially called "*Das Lied der Deutschen.*" Most of the Berliners raised their voices in song as the first of four national anthems began to play, with trumpets, trombones and snare drums parading the melodies for miles around.

Holbrook and Captain Hines had been patrolling the Volksfest grounds as the band struck up. It suddenly dawned on Holbrook that this was the moment of maximum exposure for all the VIPs and attendees in the reviewing stand.

In a flash, the terrorist's plan came to him: fire the missile under cover of the band's loud music and then disappear as the crowd of visitors swarmed over the Volksfest grounds.

Holbrook's voice rose a notch as he realized how much was at stake.

"Charley," Holbrook said, "the audience will be standing for several minutes while the national anthems are being played. If there's going to be an attack, it's going to come at any moment."

"Roger, sir," said Hines. "I've got every MP on our highest alert status."

"If you had an RPG and wanted to take out a bunch of important people at one clip, where would you position yourself?"

Hines looked around, doing a swift 360-degree reconnaissance. The attacker needed to be closer to the reviewing stand, he felt certain, and would require a higher altitude than ground level.

Hines began scanning the newly constructed buildings closer to the main gate. His eyes swept through the possible attack sites and kept returning to a two-story building about 500 yards inside the Volksfest grounds: the Deadwood Biergarten.

"The saloon, sir! Deadwood! Upstairs, second floor!"

Instinctively, the two Army officers began to run toward the beer garden. Holbrook was in his summer tan uniform while Hines was wearing fatigues with an MP brassard on his arm. Hines' .45 pistol kept thumping against his side as they ran.

Moving as quietly as possible, Holbrook and Hines entered the Deadwood Biergarten through its swinging brown saloon doors. In a very few minutes, the dance hall girls and ladies of the evening would be arriving at the Deadwood to take up their assigned positions. If there was in fact a terrorist at an upstairs window, he needed to be neutralized immediately.

"Get your pistol ready, Charley," said Holbrook as they crept up a flight of newly built wooden stairs. Hines withdrew the weapon from its holster and held it in an upright position as the two officers took the stairs one by one, moving on tiptoe.

At an upstairs window opening overlooking the reviewing stand on Clayallee, Cemil Burakgazi had finished assembling his RPG-7 and was in process of loading an armed high-explosive antipersonnel grenade into its muzzle. The 85mm rocket-assisted grenade fit snuggly into the smoothbore launcher tube.

Burakgazi had used the cover of the band's music to remove the weapon from its hiding place under the small flight of stairs and assemble it. He would now use that same band cover, while national anthems were being played, to fire his weapon, eliminate most of the dignitaries in the stands, and jump from the second-story window opening just as the crowd swarmed onto the Volksfest grounds, joining them as one of the visitors.

The closed door behind Burakgazi suddenly burst open and he turned to see two American Army officers in uniform. Without flinching, he quickly returned to his weapon's telescopic sight and began his trigger squeeze as he sighted in on the reviewing stand.

"Now, Charley!" screamed Holbrook. "Two in the head!"

Hines was startled. He was expecting to grab the terrorist to neutralize him but quickly realized that Holbrook was right. There was no time for prisoner-taking.

Hines fired two shots into the back of Cemil Burakgazi's skull, which exploded like a ripe watermelon. The grenade launcher, still armed, fell harmlessly from his shoulder and clattered to the wooden floor.

Holbrook heard the muffled chatter of the dance hall girls and the saloon's piano player as they arrived at the *Biergarten*. "Nobody comes upstairs yet," he called down the flight of stairs. "We've got a broken step up here and it's dangerous."

"Charley, radio some MPs to close the Deadwood off to the crowd for now. Then get Colonel Semsch on the horn for me."

Hines summoned four of his MPs to the Deadwood and then radioed Semsch, who had been equipped with a radio and was on the MPs' frequency. When Semsch came on, Hines handed the radio to Holbrook.

Before Holbrook spoke to Semsch, he told Hines to get a body bag for the dead terrorist and a plastic casing for the weapon. "Eagle 2, this is Eagle 6. Do you copy?" he said into the radio's mouthpiece.

"That's affirmative," Semsch replied. "What's your situation, Eagle 6?"

"There was a problem with that tube we've been talking about, but it's all over. Repeat, no longer a problem."

Semsch swallowed hard. Near disaster averted. "Where are you, Eagle 6?"

"Deadwood saloon, second floor. I have one tube and one indisposed construction worker who needs removal."

"Roger that, Eagle 6, I'm on the way," said Semsch.

1 2

Office of the U.S. Commander Berlin
Clayallee and Saargemünder Strasse
Dahlem, Zehlendorf
West Berlin, West Germany
0840 hours, 14 August 1966

Once again Major Harrison Holbrook Jr. was standing in a position of near-attention on the carpet of the U.S. Commander Berlin, waiting for the axe to fall on his hapless head.

"By whose authority, Holbrook, did you presume to order Captain Hines to 'take out' the terrorist yesterday, despite standing provost marshal instructions to 'neutralize and take into custody' such suspects?" The USCOB's ever-glowing bourbon-colored proboscis was aflame with rage.

Holbrook for once had no one to cover his back. There was no longer a Colonel Hill in USAREUR to cover his ass this time around. The only excuse for his actions that he could cite was that the terrorist had to be eliminated the very instant his finger moved toward the RPG's triggering device. There was simply no room for negotiations with lives at risk.

It was time to grovel a little. "Sir," Holbrook began, "I had to react instantaneously to what I thought was an emergency situa—"

The door to the USCOB's office suddenly opened. "I said no—repeat no—interruptions!" Caraway thundered as his secretary's head appeared in the open doorway.

"Sir," she stammered, "it's General O'Meara, holding for you on the secure line from Heidelberg."

The USCOB rose in his seat in some form of sitting at attention. He groped for the red phone, at the other end of which the four-star commander of all U.S. Army forces in Europe was waiting, apparently ready to tear him a new asshole for yesterday's debacle at the Volksfest opening ceremony.

"Caraway here, sir," he said in a shrunken voice.

"John," said General Andrew Pick O'Meara, commander of the most powerful peacetime Army the United States had ever assembled, the Army protecting Europe against a Soviet incursion. "That was brilliant work yesterday, simply brilliant!"

In Berlin, General Caraway swallowed hard in disbelief. "Thank you, General," was all he could say.

"John, most of my generals would have settled for taking that terrorist son of a bitch as a prisoner and then waiting for some court a couple of years from now to sentence him to Leavenworth or some such. It takes a leader with real balls like yours to realize that if we're ever going to purge these vermin from the face of the earth it's going to take decisive action. Yes sir," the CINCUSAREUR repeated, "decisive action."

As Caraway was still gathering his wits, uncertain how to respond, O'Meara continued, "General, I plan to visit you in Berlin the day after tomorrow. I want to see this Volksfest I've heard so many good things about and I'm bringing a Legion of Merit for you and an ARCOM for your outstanding MP captain. The work the two of you did yesterday deserves to be rewarded on the spot and I'm going to take care of it! Well done, General!"

"Thank you, sir," said Caraway, but O'Meara had already hung up.

Standing in front of the USCOB's desk, Harry Holbrook had heard every word on both sides of the conversation. He looked at Caraway as the general realized that Holbrook was still standing before him, waiting to be crucified. For once, the USCOB was speechless, uncertain what to say next.

Holbrook decided to help him out. "Sir, I'd better alert the brigade that we're going to have an honors ceremony Friday. I'll get a press advisory out this afternoon that General O'Meara will be flying in to present the awards and tour the Volksfest. Will that be acceptable?"

General Caraway was still in shock. He kept rubbing his right hand over his thick eyebrows as if trying to clear his line of vision over what had just happened.

"Yes, yes, Holbrook, that will be fine."

"And I think we ought to trot out the 298th Band for the occasion, don't you think so, sir?"

"Yes, yes, Holbrook, that will be good."

"Thank you, sir. I'll make the necessary arrangements and coordination. Will there be anything else, General?"

"No, no, Holbrook. You may go now," the USCOB said in a state of near-collapse.

Holbrook saluted, but the general was looking down at his desk blotter and didn't return the salute. Holbrook left quietly, almost on tiptoe.

13

Four-star general Andrew P. O'Meara, commander of the 250,000 soldiers of U.S. Army Europe, was ready to troop the line with Generals Caraway and Hay.

O'Meara had risen early at his quarters in Heidelberg to fly with his small entourage into Tempelhof Airport. There he had been welcomed by Caraway, who explained that Hay was busy getting the Berlin Brigade assembled for the awards ceremony.

O'Meara commanded a powerful fighting force, consisting of his soldiers, tanks, artillery, and tactical nuclear weapons, all designed to prevent or at least slow down a potential Soviet incursion across the continent of Europe. But if hostilities were ever to begin, West Berlin was the flashpoint and the most vulnerable of O'Meara's bastions.

The CINCUSAREUR had arrived with a spring in his step, Caraway noticed. O'Meara's good mood during his congratulatory phone call two days earlier was still evident, the USCOB noted with considerable satisfaction. Perhaps the powers that be in the White House and Pentagon had acquiesced in the rash decision by that unpredictable major to eliminate the terrorist.

Escorted by West Berlin motorcycle *Polizei*, Caraway's olive drab sedan—sporting a pair of metallic red and white small flags with four stars on two front fenders—drove through the streets of West Berlin toward McNair Barracks, home of the 6,000-man Berlin Brigade.

The barracks, which had served in World War II as home to AEG Telefunken, where military equipment was developed and produced, including an important radar-guided flak system, had been named for Lieutenant General Leslie J. McNair, tragically killed by friendly fire in Normandy a few weeks after D-Day in 1944.

O'Meara, carrying a small walking stick in his left hand, saluted the colors as he trooped the line, with Hay on his left as escort and Caraway a step behind. They were all dressed in the summer tan uniform with blouses and trousers, while the troops, on a beautiful mid-August morning, were clad in starched khaki uniforms with short-sleeve shirts.

The tradition of trooping the line consisted of a ceremonial inspection of the formation first from the front, then going around to the rear. Soldiers of the brigade stood at rigid attention as the inspecting party passed in front of and then around them.

O'Meara couldn't help but note that most of the brigade's rifle companies were commanded by first lieutenants, rather than the prescribed captains. He knew the explanation: "Captains gone off to Vietnam, Hay?"

"Yes sir," replied the brigade's commander. "Or else sent to training bases in the States."

"Well, your first lieutenants seem to be doing a fine job, General. These are alert, good-looking troops." Turning over his left shoulder to Caraway, he said, "John, I'm impressed with the job the two of you are doing under very difficult circumstances. Please keep it up."

Both his escorts nodded in satisfaction. The inspection finished, O'Meara and Caraway moved toward a microphone that had been set up at the formation's front and center. O'Meara's aide-de-camp and a female major were waiting there as Hay took his place at the head of the formation. Captain Charles A. Hines stood facing the aide and Caraway took his place next to Hines, since they would be the two award recipients.

The aide, a sharp-looking lieutenant colonel with several rows of combat decorations from Vietnam, stood at attention, holding a pair of medals, as Major Lillian Baker of USAREUR's G-1 (Personnel) section began to read the citations.

"The Legion of Merit (First Oak Leaf Cluster) is hereby awarded to Major General John S. Caraway for outstanding leadership in the disruption of a major terrorist plot against the leadership of West Berlin and the occupying powers. General Caraway provided the guidance and strategic initiatives that helped defeat the terrorist attack."

The aide, wearing a black and white nameplate that read "Boggs," handed a crimson Legion of Merit ribbon and medal to O'Meara, who pinned it above Caraway's left breast pocket, above Caraway's previous decorations.

"Well done, General," said the commander-in-chief.

Major Baker then read the citation for Captain Hines. "The Army Commendation Medal is hereby awarded to Captain Charles A. Hines, Military Police Corps, for conspicuous bravery in defusing a terrorist attack against the leadership of West Berlin and the occupying powers. Captain Hines' devotion to duty under dangerous conditions are in the finest traditions of the officer corps."

As O'Meara pinned the green ARCOM ribbon and medal on Hines' khaki shirt, he said, "Great work, Captain. You make us all proud."

"Thank you, sir," said Charley Hines.

The brigade, led by General Hay, then passed in review, each soldier carrying his M14 rifle at right shoulder arms. Each company's guidon was dipped as it passed the reviewing stand and as its company commander saluted while his men executed "eyes right."

"A fine performance, generals," said O'Meara as the final unit passed the reviewing platform. "Very well done. I'm highly impressed with the work you two are doing here. But now let's haul ass for your Volksfest that I've heard so much about," he said, as a pair of sedans drove up and the German police motorcyclists prepared to lead. "I want to get there before the crowd does."

Main Gate, Fifth Annual German-American Volksfest
Dahlem, Zehlendorf
West Berlin
1030 hours, 15 August 1966

Harry Holbrook paced a little nervously at the Volksfest's front gate, awaiting the arrival of CINCUSAREUR and his party. Holbrook hadn't been involved in the awards ceremony at McNair and had instead used the time to make sure everything was in readiness for O'Meara's visit.

As O'Meara's sedan drove up, Holbrook rushed to meet it and saluted. "Major Holbrook reporting, sir," he said.

O'Meara seemed anxious to exit the car. "Dale," he said to his aide, "try to slow the people in the other car down a little. Comment about the fine ceremony and tell them how impressed I was. I want to spend a few minutes alone with Holbrook," he said, eyeing the major's nameplate on his khaki uniform.

"Roger, sir," said Colonel Boggs.

"Lead the way, Major," said the commander-in-chief.

The two of them passed through the main gate, which had been opened just for them and which quickly closed behind them.

"Talk me through the complete sequence of events, Holbrook," O'Meara said. "I've read Semsch's very fine report but I want to get it straight from the horse's mouth."

"I understand, sir."

"First off," said O'Meara, "you're a PIO. What the hell are you doing in the counterterrorism business? Weren't you also involved in the Russian pilot's defection? And earlier in that gun-pointing incident at the train station? How do you keep getting involved in all this shit when you're supposed to be passing out press releases?"

Holbrook fingered the bridge of his glasses. "I don't have any explanation, sir. Of course, the Volksfest is one of my main responsibilities each year, so security here certainly falls within my bailiwick."

"So why didn't Caraway put you in for a medal too, at least an ARCOM?"

"Sir, I have no idea. Maybe it's because I tend to stick my nose into other people's business."

"Maybe so, but more often than not you're right," said O'Meara. "Show me where the terrorist was."

They were approaching the Deadwood Biergarten. "He was upstairs at a second-floor window, sir. He'd been posing as a master carpenter, which he really was, and he used that as a pretext to enter the grounds and prepare the RPG-7 he'd previously hidden here. Watch your step as we go up these risers, sir," he said, just as Boggs, the general's aide, joined them.

"I held the others up for a few minutes, sir," Boggs reported. "They'll be along shortly."

At the upper level, Holbrook pointed out where the terrorist had stood, weapon mounted on his shoulder, ready to be fired. "As Captain Hines and I ran through this door, sir, he took a quick look

163

at us and then decided to complete his mission even though he'd been burned. He refocused on his gunsight and moved his finger to the trigger."

"Then what?" asked O'Meara.

"Sir, he was a moment away from firing the damn thing. There was simply no time for Charley or me to warn him or scare him off. He had to be eliminated at that very moment."

O'Meara nodded in agreement. "Dale," he said, turning to the aide. "You're familiar with the RPG-7 from Vietnam, I believe. What kind of damage could the son of a bitch have done from here?"

Boggs moved past the general, leaned forward and squinted through the window opening. "He had a direct line of sight toward the VIP bleachers, sir. From this range and altitude a direct hit would have wiped out or seriously wounded just about everyone in the bleachers."

O'Meara nodded in agreement. "You did good, Holbrook. Colonel Boggs is just back from Vietnam. He commanded a battalion in the 1st Cavalry Division and was involved in the heavy fighting in the A Shau Valley last November."

Eyeballing Major Holbrook's slim array of awards and decorations—an Army Commendation Medal with an oak leaf cluster denoting a second award and not much else—O'Meara said, "You haven't been to Vietnam yet, I see."

"No sir. General Caraway has me on a list that's protected from the drawdown. I can't leave for Vietnam until he gets a suitable replacement."

"I see. Your replacement presumably has to be a school-trained PIO?"

"That's correct, sir. I was sent through DINFOS (Defense Information School) before being assigned to Berlin."

"Where did you finish in your class?'

"Sir, I was honor graduate," Holbrook admitted.

O'Meara wasn't surprised. "Dale," he said, "make a note for when we get back to the office. Remind me to call DSCPER (deputy chief of staff for personnel) in the Pentagon and see if we can get a replacement for Holbrook in the pipeline as quickly as possible."

Turning to Holbrook, he said, "You have any preference for what unit you go to in U.S. Army Vietnam?"

Holbrook nodded at the large yellow and black horse's head unit insignia that the general's aide wore on the right shoulder sleeve of his uniform blouse, indicating service in combat with that unit. "I'd like to go to the 1st Cav, sir," said Holbrook, "same as Colonel Boggs."

"Dale, you still have some contacts with people serving in the Cav over there?" asked O'Meara.

"Yes sir, I'm sure I do."

"Make a note to get in touch with them and see if they can use Major Holbrook. I take it," he said to Holbrook, "that you don't intend to be a PIO in Vietnam?"

"Not if I can help it, sir," said Holbrook with a grin.

They descended the steps from the saloon's upper level just as Caraway, Hay, and Major Lillian Baker arrived. Holbrook's jaw dropped when he saw Baker.

"Lil ... I mean Major Baker ... I had no idea you were in Berlin," he stammered.

"The general brought me along to read the citations, Major Holbrook," she said. "It's nice to see you again."

"Let's finish the tour, Holbrook," said the CINC. "Tell me about those horses over there."

"That's the O.K. Corral, sir. The Earps and the Clantons have a gunfight there every afternoon at 1400 and 1930 at night. The Berliners love it."

O'Meara toured the entire Volksfest grounds. By then, MPs in uniform and costume were taking their places and the CINC quizzed a couple of them, seemingly satisfied with their responses. Dance hall girls in costume began arriving and went to their assigned saloons and *Biergartens.*

O'Meara glanced at his watch. "I really need to be getting back to Heidelberg," he said to Caraway. "Thanks, Holbrook, for a good tour and good work the other day with the terrorist. Sorry I can't be leaving Major Baker with you"—the sly O'Meara had noted the interplay between Baker and Holbrook when Harry saw her—"but maybe another time. General Caraway, General Hay, Major Holbrook," CINCUSAREUR summed up, "very fine visit. Everyone here seems on top of things. Good job by all."

Lil Baker waved goodbye to Harry as she entered a sedan with O'Meara and Boggs, waiting to be escorted back to Tempelhof by the *Polizei* motorcyclists. Holbrook waved back. They'd shared some good times together. *Very* good times, in fact. Just hadn't worked out. Maybe it wasn't meant to work out, he reflected.

14

Teachers' Lounge
Thomas A. Roberts Elementary School
Hüttenberg 40
Dahlem, Zehlendorf
West Berlin
1845 hours, 8 September 1966

Carolyn Mattersdorf had asked Harry to arrive a few minutes early for Miss Barbara Drew's first PTA meeting of the new school year. He'd wondered why, but realized as he was being introduced to half a dozen of the young women on the school's faculty that he was being paraded for her friends as "Carolyn's new fella."

He'd worn jeans and a long-sleeve western-style shirt for this meeting, since there didn't seem to be a need to wear his uniform a second time. Perhaps he should have dressed up a little more, he wondered, as he shook hands and mingled with Carolyn's colleagues.

Promptly at 7 p.m., Miss Drew blew the referee's whistle hanging from her neck and ordered everyone to be seated. *I knew it*, thought the ever-watchful Holbrook, who had suspected at his initial PTA meeting that she employed a shrill ref's whistle to demand attention from her students.

Holbrook sat next to Carolyn in a seat she pointed to. It was clear that she was proud of her new beau and was showing him off. In recent weeks they'd shared a couple of lunches and dinners and had taken in some movies at the Outpost Theater, but had never gone beyond some kisses and embraces. Harry felt that sex wasn't in Carolyn's script just yet and he was careful to comply with her very deliberate, old-fashioned timetable.

Miss Drew began the meeting, welcoming everyone to the new school year. There were some new faces among the parents, of course, and she introduced the faculty members to them, after asking each set of parents to identify their student at the school.

Several of the teachers present had the new students in their classes and whispered to the parents to come chat with them when the meeting finished.

Miss Drew called for reports from her several committees, after the last of which Harry Holbrook raised his hand to speak.

"Major Holbrook," she called out for the benefit of the new attendees, "is a member of the staff of the U.S. Commander Berlin and is always a welcome guest at these meetings." She smiled as she saw Carolyn Mattersdorf's eyes travel to Holbrook. Not much went on at TAR that Barbara Drew didn't know about.

"Major Holbrook," she said, "would you like to say something?"

Holbrook rose from the confines of his small student's chair. "Yes, Miss Drew, if you please. We had a very successful Volksfest last month and I'm certain that some of you attended."

Heads nodded. "Well, the weather was perfect and we sold a lot of beer and souvenirs. But for the first time we showed John Wayne movies in the German language at the Outpost Theater, and quite frankly, we made a bundle from that enterprise. Volksfest proceeds were all given to the Berlin Senat for distribution to the West Berlin schools, but there's one school that I wanted to personally recognize. Miss Drew," he said, moving forward from his seat to where the principal stood, "here's a check from the Volksfest to put into your PTA fund to help buy school supplies for your students and teachers."

Miss Drew opened the business-letter-size envelope, donned the eyeglasses that hung from her neck next to the referee's whistle, and examined the check.

"Oh, my goodness!" she exclaimed. "Four hundred seventy-three dollars and 29 cents! Goodness gracious! We've never had that kind of money in our PTA account. Thank you so much, Major Holbrook, and thanks to the Berlin Command. Miss Mattersdorf, as treasurer of the PTA fund, will you please see that this check is deposited in our bank account and thank Major Holbrook in person for this largesse."

All the faculty present knew what their principal was alluding to and they smiled. Carolyn blushed, while Holbrook, as usual, missed the *entendre*.

The meeting over, Carolyn and Holbrook walked to the separate cars in which they'd traveled to the school. "You kept that check as a surprise from me," she said, giving him a gentle jab in the arm. "Thanks for coming and for meeting all my friends, Harry. A few of them went with me to take in your Volksfest. It was a lot of fun. Did everything go well there?"

"Carolyn, it all came together perfectly. General O'Meara stopped by a couple of weeks ago and complimented us all. It couldn't have gone better," he told her, omitting mention of one salient incident.

12 Goldfinkweg
Dahlem, Zehlendorf
West Berlin
0246 hours, 14 September 1966

The phone next to Holbrook's bed was ringing insistently.

He glanced at the clock next to the phone on his bedside quartermaster-furnished end table.

It's 2:46 in the morning! he thought to himself! *What the hell is going on?* Suddenly he remembered that the brigade hadn't held a disaster response drill in quite some time. Maybe a year. It just might be time for one. Unless, of course, this was the real thing and the Russians were mounting their long-dreaded attack against West Berlin, an island of freedom and a thorn in Moscow's side ever since the Potsdam Agreement divided the city back in 1945.

He picked up the phone and listened to the recorded message. "This is a disaster response drill. Repeat, this is a drill but all participants are directed to proceed immediately to their assigned duty stations with full combat loads. Repeat: This is a ..."

Holbrook was already on the move. From his metal wall locker he grabbed a set of fatigues, rather than the khaki uniform he'd laid out before turning in last night. That is, turning in just a few hours ago, he corrected himself.

There was no time for a shave. He swished some Listerine around in his mouth to get rid of the night taste, did a quick pee and then was dressing. From the wall locker he drew his steel helmet and cartridge belt with his .45 pistol and first aid packet affixed to it. Ammo for the pistol wasn't authorized to be kept at home but would be distributed at the rally point.

Whoops. He'd almost forgotten the manila folder containing his required actions at the rally point. For the most part, he was responsible for making telephone contacts with news people across the Free World, notifying them that West Berlin was under attack by the Group of Soviet Forces in Germany. The folder contained a listing of agencies to be contacted in the order of importance, phone numbers, etc. Hugh Erb's Associated Press Berlin bureau, with its worldwide clout, was at the top of Holbrook's callout list, although he reasoned that once Erb had heard the Soviet artillery crashing through West Berlin targeting Allied military installations, he most certainly would have deduced what was taking place.

170

As he ran to his POV, he could see that MP jeeps with flashing lights were already patrolling the housing areas, looking for vehicles in driveways that were guilty of not being parked facing the street. Dependents weren't required to participate in these alerts but all knew that their evacuation via the Autobahn to Helmstedt in West Germany was the command's first and highest priority.

Captain Hines had instructed his MPs to rouse the occupants of every tenth set of government quarters to have soldiers come to their cars in pajamas and turn on ignition switches, to ensure that gas tanks were at least half full. Noncompliant personnel were subject to non-judicial punishment and usually a fine of $150 or more.

Holbrook climbed into his '61 Chevy Impala, noting with satisfaction that his gas tank was about seven-eighths full. He began to accelerate through the nearly deserted early morning streets of West Berlin.

The three Allied forces occupying the divided city were keenly aware that a Soviet attack on West Berlin—involving tanks, artillery, warplanes, and hundreds of thousands of soldiers—couldn't possibly be repulsed by the 11,000 or so American, British, and French soldiers garrisoning their respective zones of occupation, with the French to the north, the Brits in the center, and the Americans in the southern sectors of the city.

The hope was that the defenders of West Berlin could delay the Soviet onslaught by at least a day, since an attack on Berlin was clearly the forerunner to an assault against all of West Germany, and perhaps even further westward.

By buying time, the Berlin Command might be able to allow Allied soldiers and airmen in West Germany to move into their prescribed blocking positions, such as defending the historic Fulda Gap in central Germany that constituted a pathway to the Rhine River. Delaying the Soviets in Berlin would allow Allied aircraft to commence operations, permit artillery units to deploy to preassigned firing positions, and allow for tactical nuclear weapons—"suitcase bombs"—to be positioned along major road arteries, bridges, and tunnels to impede the Soviet advance.

By the time all this had been accomplished, not much would presumably be left of the defenders of West Berlin. But their mission was to buy as much time as possible before succumbing to the Russian onslaught.

To defend their assigned portion of the city, USCOB and the Berlin Brigade's headquarters had chosen to direct operations from the Olympiastadion, the historic 100,000-seat stadium that Adolf Hitler had built to house the 1936 Summer Olympic Games.

Berlin had been chosen by the International Olympic Committee in 1931 to host the XI Summer Olympic Games. When Hitler and his Nazi Party ascended to power in Germany beginning in 1933, it seemed an opportunity to propagandize to the world the values of National Socialism (Naziism) and of Aryanism. Accordingly, Hitler had ordered construction of a massive sports complex in the Grunewald, encompassing 330 acres. The *Stadion* was constructed atop the foundation of a prior sports complex, so that its lower half was recessed a full 39 feet below ground level.

Unfortunately for Hitler, his plans to foster Aryanism took a tumble when 22-year-old American track and field star Jesse Owens, an African American athlete from Ohio State University, ran off with four gold medals, highly embarrassing Der Führer.

Deep within the stadium's underground confines, Generals Caraway and Hay would direct their respective operations, sending the brigade's M48 tanks to the Wall in an attempt to seal it off at Checkpoint Charlie and committing its infantrymen to designated buildings, as well as fighting positions in the Grunewald to slow down the Russian attackers.

Holbrook parked his POV near the gate that led downward into the stadium's bowels, having participated in these exercises twice before. He went to his "office" and began to ensure that he had phone contact if he needed to begin an actual media callout. The phones worked and he hung up without making any calls.

All around him, other elements of the USCOB headquarters were making similar tests and checks. After almost an hour below ground, word was passed that the exercise had been successful and all personnel were to return home or to their regular nighttime duty stations.

For Holbrook, he couldn't get home fast enough or back into bed without a moment to lose. This was even worse than Phil Semsch's "shit-list" Wall tours, he decided.

12 Goldfinkweg
Dahlem, Zehlendorf
West Berlin
0633, 14 September 1966

He'd been asleep less than an hour when the stupid phone rang again. Groggily, he picked up the handset and mumbled "Holbrook."

"Major, it's Hugh Erb," said the voice at the other end of the phone line. "I hate to disturb you, but I figured you're wide awake. I heard your brigade tanks rumbling down Clayallee a couple of hours ago and I'm wondering what the hell is going on? Have the Russians attacked us?"

"Afraid not, Hugh. Not much of a scoop for you. The Army does an unannounced disaster response drill once or twice each year and apparently it was time for the command to hold one. It's always unannounced and designed to catch us by surprise, which would be the case, of course, if the Russians attacked."

Erb digested this information. "I saw MPs checking private cars in my neighborhood. What was that all about?" Holbrook explained the requirement that cars be parked facing the street and with adequate gas in the tank.

"Were you part of the alert, Harry?" Erb asked, remembering Holbrook's insistence that Erb call him by his first name even though this was an official discussion between a newsman and an information officer.

"Yep, they woke me up a little before 3 a.m. with a recorded message telling me to report to my duty station."

"And where would that be, Harry?"

Holbrook paused a moment, pondering whether he should disclose to the Associated Press's Berlin bureau chief the location of USCOB's alternate headquarters in the event of a Soviet attack. *What the heck*, he concluded. The Russians sure as hell knew from their numerous agents in West Berlin where all the USCOB and brigade trucks and wheeled vehicles had been headed.

"Hugh," Holbrook answered, "in the event of an attack we deploy to the Olympic Stadium. Deep down underneath it—it's an old series of locker rooms and exercise rooms—is where we'll make our last stand."

"Sounds like the Alamo," said Erb. "In other words, if the Russians attack us, you guys just have to hold out until reinforcements arrive, knowing that there's no way troops from the Zone can get here in time."

"I guess you could put it that way," Holbrook agreed. "But just remember that an attack against us and our allies in West Berlin constitutes an attack against the United States itself. The Russians can wipe us out but then they'll have World War III on their hands."

"I think I might like to write something about it," said Erb. "Any chance I could get access to your underground bunker?"

"I'm not sure, Hugh, but I'll look into it." Privately, Holbrook was skeptical that such a request could be granted.

"Thanks, Harry. You sound as if you could use a little more sleep."

Holbrook totally agreed. He was sound asleep moments after hanging up the phone.

15

The USCOB headquarters traditionally held a formal dinner dance at the Harnack House each September to celebrate the arrival of the fall season. Holbrook was proud to bring Carolyn as his date, since he had come stag the previous year.

She looked radiant in a gold brocade sheath dress with matching shoes, and Holbrook beamed with pride as he introduced her to his colleagues on the USCOB staff. Alicia Semsch, wife of Harry's friend and colleague Phil Semsch, looked Carolyn over with a practiced eye, wondering if this new interest of Harry's might lead somewhere.

"That's a beautiful dress, Carolyn," Holbrook said. "Is it new?"

"Yes, Harry. I bought it just for this occasion. I found it at KaDeWe, the big German department store. Have you been there?"

"Yes. As a matter of fact, the loafers I wore on our first date at the Drei Baren came from KaDeWe."

"I must have spent a month's salary," Carolyn said, "on this dress and the matching shoes," she said showing a pretty ankle to Harry.

Compliment her on the shoes, fool, Holbrook's inner voice told him. *Women love to be complimented on their shoes.* How did he know that? No idea. "Those are lovely shoes, too," he said. It worked! Carolyn beamed at the compliment.

The roast beef dinner was better than the Harnack House usually offered, and after dessert and an after-dinner wine the sated Holbrook was ready to find a quiet alcove for napping when General Caraway tapped his wine glass with a spoon.

Oh shit, thought Holbrook, sitting up. *Here comes a speech.* Caraway spoke at some length about all that the Berlin Command—here he nodded at General and Mrs. Hay sitting nearby at the head table—had accomplished the past year despite being handicapped by the USAREUR-wide drawdown that had stripped the command of so many of its experienced officers.

Holbrook, glancing furtively around the room, confirmed for himself that he was the only infantry major present, and he knew there were none left in the brigade either. He was fast being left behind in career progression without service in Vietnam. Maybe General O'Meara had been sincere in helping unearth a replacement for him as the USCOB information officer.

When Caraway had finished his remarks, a small combo of brigade soldiers moonlighting for some extra spending money began to play music for dancing. They did a nice job, Holbrook felt, with standards from Cole Porter, Irving Berlin, and Rodgers and Hammerstein. When they began to play "Getting to Know You" from Rodgers and Hammerstein's *The King and I,* Carolyn gave the inert Holbrook a nudge and indicated that she'd like to head for the dance floor.

Ballroom dancing was not one of Harry Holbrook's greater accomplishments. He made do of a sort, trying to avoid crushing her beautiful gold-colored shoes. He was aware that many of his colleagues were sporting the dressier blue mess dinner jackets over their yellow-striped blue uniform trousers, while he had to settle budget-wise for the less dressy regular blue jacket.

Major Robert Poydasheff, the command's staff judge advocate, was dancing with Mrs. Caraway, Holbrook noted, as he tried keeping his eyes off his own fallible feet. Matter of fact, the suave, urbane Poydasheff was clutching Mrs. Caraway—a very handsome, well-proportioned woman of about 50—kind of closely, a circumstance that hadn't been lost on her two-star husband who was puffing a cigar, sipping his favorite Wild Turkey bourbon that the Officers' Club stocked at his insistence, and apparently plotting which circle of hell his command's lawyer should be consigned to.

As Carolyn and he danced, Holbrook wondered how a beautiful woman such as Mrs. Caraway—Belinda, he believed, was her given name—could have married a toad such as the general. It was ironic, he felt, that so very often the world's most gorgeous women married some of its ugliest-looking men. *Look at Carolyn and me,* he thought, narrowly missing her left foot with his out-of-sync right, *and then try to figure out why this beautiful young woman seems to be attracted to me.*

Needing a break from his dancing exertions, Holbrook suggested to Carolyn that they sit out a number or two. To his horror, striding confidently across the dining area to his table was the oleaginous Major Poydasheff, his eyes glinting with evil intent.

"Harry, my boy," he exclaimed in his greasiest manner, "you haven't introduced me to your date!"

Holbrook wanted to say, "Yer durn tootin' I didn't, you miserable woman rustler," but restrained himself. But Carolyn responded. "I'm Carolyn Mattersdorf," she said to Poydasheff. "I teach at Thomas A. Roberts and I think I must have your daughter Diana in my sixth-grade math class."

"And so you do, my dear," said the command's lawyer. "Would you allow me to trip the light fantastic with you for this next number? Okay with you, Harry?"

Harry glowered. He put on a false front and agreed. "No problem, Bob," he said, inwardly seething as Carolyn acquiesced and Poydasheff led her to the dance floor.

The band played a couple of Cole Porter's most danceable classics, "Night and Day" and "True Love." The smarmy attorney swept Carolyn Mattersdorf around the dance floor as Holbrook writhed with jealousy. For once he could identify with General Caraway, he thought, in wishing ill for the lawyer.

The number ended, Poydasheff led Carolyn back to her chair next to Harry's, thanking her for the dance and giving Holbrook a sly wink of approval. Harry shuddered.

Carolyn was enthused. "Harry, Major Poydasheff is such a wonderful dancer you wouldn't believe it! He knows all the intricate moves. I'll bet he's taken lessons somewhere, probably at an Arthur Murray studio. Harry, are you feeling all right?"

She looked closely at her date, who looked somewhat peaked, green at the gills perhaps.

"I'm thinking that perhaps there was something in the salad dressing that didn't agree with me," Holbrook explained lamely.

"Well, let's get you home right away," Carolyn insisted. "Let me have the car keys." They said their goodbyes as they left, explaining that Holbrook was somewhat under the weather.

She drove him home to 12 Goldfinkweg, skillfully backing the Impala into its prescribed position facing outward, and then led him into the house. She maneuvered him upstairs and told him to undress and get into bed, which he did, falling asleep immediately. Later, she stuck her head in the bedroom door, checking on his well-being. He snores a little, she concluded from the available evidence, and closed the door.

Holbrook awoke with a start. He could swear he smelled bacon frying downstairs. And how had he gotten into his pajamas?

He donned his well-worn bathrobe and headed downstairs. In the kitchen, wearing one of his long T-shirts under an apron, Carolyn Mattersdorf was grilling bacon and preparing to fry some eggs. Her brocade dress of the night before was folded neatly on the arm of the couch where, Harry surmised, she must have slept.

She looked up at him. "I hope you're feeling better, Harry," she said. "You didn't look well at all when I put you to bed."

"Nothing serious, just something at the party that didn't agree with me," he explained, pleased at his clever choice of words.

"Are you well enough to go to chapel with me?" she asked.

"What time is the service?" Holbrook was far from a regular at the Berlin Command's nondenominational church services.

"It's at 10:30. Let's eat, then I'll take your car and run home to freshen up and change clothes, then come back and pick you up. Will that be okay?"

Holbrook, despite his upbringing as the son of a Methodist minister and his one-time flirtation with entering the ministry, had been absent from church services for the past several years. He and ex-wife Holly had taken their young children to Sunday services on a regular basis wherever they'd been stationed, but he'd lost the church-going habit in recent years.

As they ate their bacon and eggs, Carolyn remembered something. "Harry, there was an envelope on the floor at the front hallway. It must have come through the mail slot," and she got up to get it from the hallway table. As she rose from her chair,

Holbrook couldn't help but admire her long, slender legs emerging from his T-shirt.

"Here it is, Harry," she said, handing him the envelope. "Sure smells nice."

Holbrook knew instinctively what the envelope contained: another note from Frau Bausch. He needed to explain the circumstances to Carolyn, concerned that she might conclude there was another girlfriend out there.

"It's from the woman who owns Bausch Porzellan," he explained. "I've been in touch with her about the KPM china over there in the cabinet."

Carolyn accepted the explanation gracefully. "Harry, are you well enough to clean up the dishes while I get dressed and head home?"

"Of course. I'm feeling fine this morning. Thanks for taking care of me."

Carolyn smiled, picked up her party dress and shoes, and headed for the bathroom.

Holbrook opened the scented envelope. Inside, in the same expensive stationery as last time, was a handwritten note:

> *Major Holbrook, please be at the store at 5:45 p.m.*
> *next Monday, September 26. I have important news.*
> *Angelika Bausch.*

Berlin Brigade Chapel
Clayallee
Dahlem, Zehlendorf
West Berlin
1020 hours, 25 September 1966

Carolyn had changed into a simple summer dress and Holbrook was wearing his standard navy blue blazer with chino slacks combination as they approached the brigade chapel.

Father Mulcahy, the brigade chaplain, stood outside the church entrance, welcoming attendees. "Carolyn, very nice to see you again," he remarked. "And Harry, I guess I haven't seen you since the Erb funeral back in June."

"I suspect you're correct, Father," Holbrook replied. "I haven't been very devout lately, I'm afraid."

"Well, we can pray that Carolyn brings you back into the fold. Please get seated; we'll be starting very soon."

Mulcahy, a Roman Catholic career Army chaplain with the rank of major, delivered a very good sermon on the topic of becoming familiar with the holy bible.

Carolyn, glancing over at Holbrook beside her, could tell that he was engrossed in the sermon, perhaps learning from it. As the priest summed up an admonition that frequent readings of the bible could make us all better human beings, Holbrook nodded in agreement.

Leaving the church, he told Mulcahy that he had enjoyed the sermon and had learned from it.

"Then come on back, boyo," said the brigade chaplain. "You don't know the half of what you can learn in a house of worship."

Carolyn suggested that they eat lunch at the KaDeWe department store, since she needed a new pair of bedroom slippers. They both enjoyed a very nice shrimp salad in the store's restaurant, after which Carolyn found bedroom slippers she liked, while Holbrook decided to invest in a new bathrobe, having been somewhat embarrassed by the threadbare condition of the one in which he had come downstairs that morning. He avoided the men's shoe department.

Unconsciously, it seemed, they walked hand-in-hand through the many KaDeWe departments, enjoying each other's company and taking in the displays of high-quality upscale merchandise.

By 2 p.m., each realized they had chores to perform ahead of Monday's return to work. Carolyn said she had laundry to be taken care of, while Holbrook—who strove each weekend to write a letter to each of his children, now seven and five—had that task still ahead of him, as well as getting his uniform ready for tomorrow and spit-polishing his low-quarter shoes.

They kissed as he dropped her off at her BOQ after making plans for the coming weekend.

"Thank you for a wonderful time, Harry," Carolyn said. "I'm so sorry you became sick at the USCOB dinner." *Not really sick*, he thought to himself, *just sick with envy about that low-life lawyer dancing with my girl and holding her close.*

I guess I'm very much smitten with Carolyn Mattersdorf, Holbrook concluded. *I wonder where this might be heading.*

16

Bausch Porzellan
Platz der Luftbrücke
Adjacent to Tempelhof International Airport
Boroughs of Tempelhof and Kreuzberg
West Berlin
1755 hours, 26 September 1966

"You are aware, are you not, Major Holbrook, of what is taking place next weekend?" said Frau Bausch as she admitted him to her just-closed porcelain store.

Holbrook searched his memory. Nothing came up at first. Then it dawned on him what she was alluding to.

"The prison. Spandau," he said aloud. "Next weekend they'll be releasing Speer and von Schirach."

"That is correct," she confirmed. "And there is likely to be trouble."

Holbrook was well aware of the pending release from Spandau Prison of two of the three remaining convicted Nazi war criminals. But Frau Bausch's use of the word "trouble" got his undivided attention.

"What kind of trouble, Frau Bausch?"

"Do you remember that formidable-looking young man you met at the rabbi's office in the New Synagogue?"

"Yes, Samuel or Schmuel. Why?"

"My understanding is that he is an agent of the Mossad, the Israeli intelligence organization."

Holbrook had concluded much the same. "But he was here in connection with the Volksfest attack, I thought," he said.

"That is correct, Major. But I am told that he had a secondary purpose."

"And what was that?"

"He was instructed to find firing positions for assassinating the two Nazi prisoners upon their release from Spandau Prison."

Oh shit, thought Holbrook.

Office of the Intelligence Officer
Headquarters, U.S. Commander Berlin
Clayallee and Saargemünder Strasse
Dahlem, Zehlendorf
West Berlin
0915 hours, 26 September 1966

"What do you make of it, Phil?" Holbrook inquired of Colonel Semsch after he had completed briefing the intelligence officer on Frau Bausch's revelation of the night before.

"I'm thinking about it, Harry, and what our options are. The prison, of course, is in the British sector, so the logical first step would be to alert Huddleston's people and provide any further intelligence assistance we can muster.

"The problem with that approach," Semsch continued, "is that it opens us up to all kinds of questions about where we got our intel, whether it's been confirmed or not, and so on. I'm not sure that we want to share our sources with anyone, even the Brits.

"You and Hellerstein got to eyeball this Samuel, right?" Semsch asked.

"Yes. He came into Rabbi Halbfinger's office, a little bit late for the meeting at the synagogue about the Volksfest threat. The rabbi introduced him as a 'visitor from the east' and Hellerstein and I both got the same impression that he was Mossad."

"Only the Volksfest and the RPG-7 were discussed, right?"

"That's correct. He confirmed that the Red Army Faction had been successful in acquiring an RPG-7 from a Czech arms dealer and that the intent was to use it against VIPs at the Volksfest opening."

"And no mention of Spandau, Harry?"

"Not while we were there. Norm and I left immediately after that conversation to complete our Wall patrol and to write the memos we gave you the next morning. Everything we learned from Samuel is in those memos."

Semsch leaned back in his office chair, steepling his fingers. He needed more information before making a decision. In other words, actionable intelligence.

"Describe this Samuel or Schmuel, Harry."

The Holbrook memory kicked in. "He's about 5 foot 10 in height, strong, muscular build, weighs about 180 pounds. Probably mid-thirties in age. Dark-complected, long sideburns, full head of hair. No facial hair, no visible tattoos. Very intimidating presence. He moves very forcefully, very deliberately. I wouldn't be surprised if he's some kind of specialist in assassinations."

Semsch nodded in agreement. "Kidon," he said.

"Pardon?" said Holbrook.

"Kidon," Semsch replied and spelled out the word. "It's Hebrew for 'tip of the spear.' It's Mossad's assassination unit, an elite small force of trained assassins, most of them former soldiers from the Israeli Defense Force's special forces unit. Very nasty people, I'm told."

"So what are you going to do?" Harry asked.

"I'm not sure. This is a ticklish one. If I tell the Old Man, he'll go ape and run to the Brits with it. Then whatever rapport Norm and you have established with the Jewish people in East Berlin will suddenly disappear. And that rapport helped save a bunch of very important skins at the Volksfest opening, you'll recall."

Holbrook had no problem remembering what had taken place at the Volksfest opening.

Semsch rose from his desk, opened his door slightly, and stuck his head out. "Grace," he said to his assistant, "please track Norm Hellerstein down and get him in here pronto."

"Yes sir," said Mrs. Wertman. Four minutes later, Sergeant Hellerstein knocked on Semsch's door.

"Come in, Norm," the USCOB G-2 said. "Harry, please repeat for Norm everything you just told me. Maybe if I hear it a second time, I might be able to figure out what to do."

Holbrook repeated his report verbatim, omitting nothing.

"What do you think, Sergeant?" asked Semsch.

"He was very definitely a formidable-looking presence, sir. I agree *en toto* with Major Holbrook's assessment."

"Spoken like a true lawyer-in-the-making, Norm," joked Semsch. "So, what do we do now?" He glanced at his desk calendar. "Today is Monday, September 26. The prisoners will both be released from Spandau at midnight, October 1, which is Friday night, Saturday morning. I'm very skeptical that we have time to formulate a plan of action between now and then and get it cleared by our people and the British."

Semsch continued with his musing. "Let's see. We can sympathize with the Israelis' motivation for wanting Speer and von Schirach dead. Together, those two are responsible for the imprisonment and deaths of hundreds of thousands of the Jewish people. Auschwitz and Birkenau together killed a million Jews, Treblinka another 900,000. Speer provided Jewish slave labor for Nazi construction projects and made a personal fortune from it, while von Schirach sent the Jews from Vienna—maybe 60,000 or more of them—into the concentration camps.

"So on the one hand," Semsch continued his thinking out loud, "we can sympathize somewhat with the Israelis' thirst for revenge. But on the other hand, the assassinations of these two Nazis would open up multiple cans of worms that would upset the balance of power here in Germany and perhaps in much of Europe. There would be massive protests here in West Berlin, with people claiming that these two old men have served their time and deserve to die normal deaths."

Semsch had talked himself into a decision. "So we handle it ourselves," he said. "You two are the only ones on our side who know what Samuel looks like, right?"

Holbrook and Hellerstein nodded in agreement.

"Okay," said Semsch. "Stop him. Whatever it takes, do it. Whatever it takes," he repeated, so that his intent was 100 percent clear to them. They nodded.

17

Holbrook was behind the wheel of his '61 Chevy as he and Hellerstein, both wearing casual civilian clothes, drove through the British sector of West Berlin, heading toward the prison from which the two prisoners would be released in another hundred hours or so.

They had stopped off at the Bausch porcelain store to see if anything new had been learned, but Frau Bausch told them there was nothing additional to report.

"What we're looking for, Norm," said Holbrook, "are firing positions—vantage points from which a sniper at night can observe the prison's front gate, fire two well-aimed shots, and then escape. Let's think it through, using the Army's asswards-backwards planning sequence. How does he escape after making his kills?"

"Privately owned vehicle, sir. Inconspicuous car, something like an Opel Kadett, a small family car. Neutral color, white, maybe gray."

"Good. Where does he drive it to? Not back to East Berlin, I assume?"

188

"Agreed. No way he can put the rabbi and the people in the synagogue at risk if he's being chased. No, he's got to head away from East Berlin."

"Does he chance taking the Autobahn to Helmstedt?" asked Holbrook, raising cogent questions much as Socrates himself might have done.

"No way, sir. He's a sitting pigeon on the Autobahn, with Vopos guard posts and patrols all along the corridor. He needs to avoid any form of constriction, of being hemmed in."

"How about an East German train to the West?"

"Same problem for him. He's too confined. A railroad track is a confinement by its very definition. If he's caught and flees from the train, he's a dead duck. The Vopos will chase him down and kill him on the spot."

"So how does he get out of here, Norm? Let's assume he wants to get back to Tel Aviv as quickly as possible to make a report to his superiors."

"That'll be General Meier Amit, sir, the Mossad director general. It's more than likely that Amit is personally coordinating this activity because of the global repercussions that are likely to take place. My guess is that Samuel is working directly for Amit."

"Okay, so how does Samuel get back to Tel Aviv safely and quickly?"

Both men saw the answer simultaneously. "A Mossad small private jet," said Holbrook.

"That's exactly right, sir!" agreed Hellerstein.

"And where's the likeliest airport?" asked Holbrook.

"Tegel," they said in unison. The airport in the French sector used primarily by Pan American and British European Airways also serviced the light aircraft of the French brigade in Berlin. A small jet posing as an important business executive's private transport would blend in very inconspicuously with the routine comings and goings at Tegel.

Holbrook continued with that narrative. "So he arrives in a Mossad-operated jet at Tegel, bringing his weapon with him. He picks up an Opel Kadett that his buddies will have rented for him from Avis or Hertz, drives to the place where he'll make the kills, parks the car close by, and sets up position waiting for midnight and the prisoner release. Then back to Tegel, turn in the rental car, hop aboard the Mossad plane, and take off for Tel Aviv."

"It's the most probable sequence of events, sir," Hellerstein said.

"So, Norm," Holbrook said, "Colonel Semsch needs to use his sources at the air safety center to quietly find out if and when a small Israeli commercial jet will be inbound to Tegel and what its departure date and time are. We good so far?"

"Roger, sir," said Hellerstein.

"Okay, now let's figure out where he's going to shoot from."

The neighborhood across from Spandau Prison consisted primarily of commercial warehouses, some of which had been leveled by bombers of the United States and Royal Air Forces during World War II. Some of the warehouses had been rebuilt, while others had been razed and their replacements were currently under construction.

Holbrook had brought with him from his office the Pacemaker Speed Graphic Camera widely used by members of the news media for photographing events. His intent was to photograph the most logical sniper-shooting locations and then consult with Phil Semsch about the likelihood of each one.

He and Hellerstein made their way through some wreckage, kneeling or lying down to simulate the sniper's likely use of a bipod, firing from the prone position. But lying down and simulating taking aim at the prison's main gate and front courtyard made them realize that it was a substandard firing location. The prison courtyard would be well lighted so that the news media could take pictures and report on the events, and allow members of the public—held behind police barriers—to observe the historic moment. So the

190

sniper would have adequate lighting to observe his targets, but he needed a better firing position than this.

"We're too low, Norm," Holbrook concluded. "He needs to be up higher."

Both men glanced upward at the construction girders framing the nine- or ten-story office or apartment building being built next door. They left the wreckage and trudged over to the new building.

The fence around the site had an unlocked gate and they passed through it. There were no workmen in evidence, so they began climbing the concrete stairs that had already been constructed. Holbrook paused at the second floor and began taking pictures from the point of the building that was closest to the prison's gate.

"About a thousand, maybe eleven hundred yards from here to the prisoner release point, I estimate," Holbrook said.

"That's about right, sir. An experienced sniper with a good weapon and telescopic sight should have no trouble killing his targets from this position."

They both lay down in the prone firing position, simulating where the assassin might locate himself and his weapon. "Take the camera, Norm," said Holbrook, "and snap some pictures of me as I pretend to be firing a rifle mounted on a bipod."

That done, Holbrook wondered where the sniper would park his getaway vehicle if their assumptions were valid. They found a narrow driveway just behind the building being constructed and concluded that it was a logical parking space, convenient to the killer as he made his getaway and sped to Tegel Airport.

"All right, Norm," said Holbrook, "let's get out of here before we attract any attention." They walked the hundred yards or so to where Holbrook had parked his Chevy POV and began the drive back to the USCOB head shed.

"I'll get these pictures developed in my office photo lab, Norm. You get with Colonel Semsch, brief him on what we think is going to take place, ask him to establish liaison with the air safety center so that we learn if an Israeli small jet is inbound in the next few days, and then ask him to fill us in on the possible sniper rifles that Samuel is likely to use."

"Got it, sir. What's your plan if we confront the sniper? Do we apprehend him, do we shoot him on the spot, do we turn him over to the Berlin police, or what?"

"Good questions, Norm. I'll remember them and I'll ask your boss when I meet with him. I'll have the photos ready by midday tomorrow, so see if he can meet with us tomorrow afternoon."

Office of the Intelligence Officer
Headquarters, U.S. Commander Berlin
Clayallee and Saargemünder Strasse
Dahlem, Zehlendorf
West Berlin
1414 hours, 28 September 1966

"We think that that location—me in the prone firing position in that corner of the incomplete building—is where he's most likely to set up," said Holbrook.

Spread out before Semsch on his conference table were the two dozen or so photos that Holbrook's Speed Graphic had snapped. Semsch studied each carefully as he walked around the photo display.

"No one saw you?" he asked.

Holbrook and Hellerstein both shook their heads. "No one was around," Holbrook said. "My guess is that work was at a halt pending delivery of more materials," said Hellerstein.

"Good thought, Norm," said Semsch. "I've been in touch with my contact at the air safety center. He's one of Halvorsen's CIA guys, so I had to brief Roger on what we're doing and I told him to keep his nose out of it, that we had it under control. As of now, there are no

Israeli flights inbound to Tegel, but that's not surprising since the prison release is still three days away.

"I have some people acquiring data on what sniper rifle the Israelis are planning to use. I'll have their thoughts tomorrow or the next day. That brings us to," Semsch said with a furrowed brow, "what do we do with Samuel when we shit on his mission, to coin a phrase. What do we do with him? Your thoughts, Harry?"

"To begin with, Norm and I both need to be armed. Forty-fives with live ammo, agreed?" Semsch nodded in concurrence. "If we're unable to stop him, Norm and I need to take him out, just like we did with the Volksfest guy." Again Semsch nodded in agreement, withholding a comment that the "taking out" of terrorist Cemil Burakgazi was Holbrook's idea and no one else's. The only viable action under the circumstances, but not a consensus decision by any means.

"If we're forced to take him out," Holbrook continued, "there are likely to be repercussions. The Israelis will wonder what became of their boy. Are we going to return the body to them or would we dump it in the Havel River, which is close by?"

"If we kill him, Colonel," said Hellerstein, "all the contacts I've developed in East Berlin will go poof. They'll just dry up and disappear. I realize that we can't allow him to murder the two Nazis but killing the sniper should be used only as a last resort."

"Well spoken, Judge Hellerstein," said Semsch with a grin. "You've already got the wisdom of Solomon and you're not even in law school yet."

"All right, here's what we'll do," said Semsch. "Let's adjourn for today and sleep on the matter. By tomorrow I hope to have more info on sniper rifles that are likely to be used and maybe an update from the CIA guy at the air safety center about the arrival of Israeli aircraft. Meanwhile, I'd like the two of you to revisit the likely firing site and verify for yourselves that it's the most plausible. Come up with a Plan B, just in case. We in agreement on everything?"

Holbrook and Hellerstein nodded. "Yes sir," they both said and left Semsch's office. As they exited, Holbrook said, "How about tomorrow morning, Norm, so we see a different perspective timewise? Maybe leave from here at 0930?"

"Sounds good, sir."

Across from Spandau Prison
Wilhelmstrasse, Borough of Spandau
British Sector
West Berlin
0940 hours, 29 September 1966

"Norm," said Holbrook as they climbed the still-under-construction staircase to the second floor of the new building, "this closed-in area around the stairwell would make a good place for us to hide while we wait for the sniper to show up and make his move."

"Yes, and we can stash on the third-floor landing the items you requested from Colonel Semsch." Holbrook's list, which he had worked on overnight and shown to Hellerstein, included a couple of bath towels, two handheld radios operating on the same frequency, a hypodermic needle with a knockout drug in it, a nightstick or billy club, two sets of handcuffs, the Speed Graphic camera which Holbrook would add to the inventory, a surgical scalpel, and some bandages, all to be fitted into a small gym bag.

"Good thought, Norm. We get here early, stash the bag up one flight of stairs, then hide up there until we hear the sniper arrive. But the more I think about it," Holbrook said, "the more I'm inclined to have you wait in my Chevy, out of sight. You could radio me when his rental car pulls into its space, take note of where he parks it, and then wait in my car while we see what develops."

"Won't you need some help upstairs?"

"I don't think so, Norm. I'll have the element of surprise. I'm going to come up behind him and stun him with the billy club. That'll put him out of commission for a few minutes. I'll radio you to come up and join me. We'll handcuff him, give him a shot from the hypodermic to knock him out, take his car keys and weapon, along with our gym bag, and carry him to his rental car.

"I'll drive his car, while you follow in mine. He'll be asleep in the back seat of his Opel, or whatever it is. We'll drive to Tegel, where I've learned there's a back entrance for the private airplanes that wealthy folks and business execs use. We'll deliver him to his buddies, hopefully still fast asleep, make sure that they fly out of here, and then turn in his car to the rental agency."

"What about his rifle?"

"Yes, of course. You'll stash that in the trunk of my car, where it'll stay overnight until we deliver it to Colonel Semsch tomorrow morning."

"You're assuming that it won't be necessary to kill him."

"That's right. You make a strong argument, Norm, that it would totally mess up relations with your contacts in East Berlin. Disposing of the body would pose a big problem, and when the Israelis learn that their shooter isn't coming home, they're likely to stir up a fuss. No, we want to avoid killing him—only as a last resort. But we're both going to be toting loaded .45s just in case."

"What's the scalpel for, sir?"

"We're gonna take us a souvenir, Norm. Let's scout around some, double-check the area, and then report back to Colonel Semsch that we're all set for Friday night."

Office of the Intelligence Officer
Headquarters, U.S. Commander Berlin
Clayallee and Saargemünder Strasse
Dahlem, Zehlendorf
West Berlin
1335 hours, 29 September 1966

On the drive back to USCOB headquarters, Holbrook had stopped at a *Konditorei* (pastry shop/café) and bought meat loaf sandwiches and Cokes for Hellerstein and himself. Thus fortified, they drove on to USCOB headquarters to update Semsch.

The intelligence officer listened to both reports. Neither Holbrook nor Hellerstein mentioned the scalpel that Holbrook planned to include in the gym bag, but Semsch didn't raise any questions about it.

"There is in fact an Israeli business jet due in to Tegel around 2030 hours tomorrow night," Semsch reported. "That's been confirmed by our guy in the air safety center. It belongs to an Israeli construction firm that's planning to buy some property in Steglitz and build apartment units. We know, of course," he noted, "that the company is a Mossad front and that the plane will be used to bring in and then extricate the sniper.

"Harry, your gym bag is all ready," Semsch said, pointing to a red and black bag near his desk, "and you can pick it up from here anytime tomorrow."

"What have we forgotten to do? What else should we be doing?" Semsch asked the two soldiers facing him.

Holbrook and Hellerstein looked at each other and shrugged. "If we've forgotten anything," said Holbrook, "I'm sure it will occur to us when it's too damn late to do anything about it."

"I think we're pretty well set, sir," said Hellerstein.

"All right," Semsch said. "Get there early, of course. The *Polizei* are anticipating a crowd of up to a thousand people who want to take in the prisoner release, take pictures, and tell their grandchildren that they saw the release of two of the last three Nazis in Spandau. Hess will never be released, according to the Russians, and will die there. So Speer and von Schirach are the last of their breed.

"Okay, you two," Semsch continued, "get on with your regular duties this afternoon, check with me first thing tomorrow and then again before your drive to the prison. Sound good?"

They agreed and exited Semsch's office.

Information Division (ID)
Headquarters, U.S. Commander Berlin
Clayallee and Saargemünder Strasse
Dahlem, Zehlendorf
West Berlin
1355 hours, 29 September 1966

Holbrook entered his office wearing his grubby blue jeans and a well-worn Penn State sweatshirt.

Frau Haupt, who had never seen her boss looking as tawdry as this, did a double take, as did Paul Scholl, who apparently had been waiting to see Harry.

"Been slumming, Major?" asked Scholl with a grin.

"Kinda, Paul, just doing a little recon out in the boondocks."

Neither Scholl nor Frau Haupt seemed satisfied with this lame explanation, Holbrook knew, but that was all they were going to get.

"Come on in, Paul," said Holbrook as he entered his office. What's up?"

"I drafted a press release about the Billy Graham Crusade coming up next month. *Stripes*"—Stars and Stripes, the military newspaper serving U.S. personnel in Europe—"asked me about it and I thought we ought to get a release out, with a photo of Graham."

"Good thought. Give me a minute to catch up with my in-box. I'll go over the release and get back to you. Thanks, Paul."

Frau Haupt came in with a stack of pink telephone message forms. "Anything important in there, Gertie? Anything that won't wait?"

"Mr. Erb was looking for a statement from the American Command about the release of the two prisoners tomorrow night. That is the only urgent matter."

"Good. Please get him on the line."

Two minutes later, Frau Haupt called out, "Mr. Erb is on Line 1, Major."

"What's up, Hugh?"

"About the release of Speer and von Schirach tomorrow night, Major ... I mean Harry. What's the position of the U.S. Command?"

Holbrook and Scholl had drafted a response to query on this and cleared it with Caraway and USBER. Holbrook fished the paper out of his wooden hold box and began to relay it to the AP bureau chief.

"Hugh, the Nuremberg tribunals, international in scope, weighed the activities of these two Nazi civilian leaders and found them guilty of multiple crimes against humanity. Each man was sentenced to 20 years' confinement in Spandau Prison, sentences which expire at midnight, September 30, 1966.

"They will be released promptly at that hour and will be free to resume the rest of their lives with family and friends. Both of them have been excellent prisoners and there is no reason to confine them beyond their original sentencing.

"The U.S. Commander Berlin feels that justice has been served, that the prison sentences imposed at the International Military Tribunal at Nuremberg in 1946 have been fulfilled, and that the freeing of both prisoners at this time is warranted."

Erb was either copying it down or recording it, maybe both, Holbrook suspected.

"What happens to Spandau Prison now, Harry? Surely it's not worth keeping it open for just one lone prisoner who's lost his marbles?"

"Hugh, the U.S. Mission here has already begun discussions with representatives of the Soviet Union about the future of Spandau Prison. The U.S. government hopes that an accommodation can be reached with regard to Spandau that scales down the size of the prison and reduces the burden of its costs upon the Berlin Senat."

Erb knew, of course, that Holbrook was quoting from a prepared statement that had been coordinated with the military and diplomatic chains of command in Berlin, maybe even in Washington. So he wasn't going to get any real news this way.

"The Russians have made it clear, Harry, that Hess will never be set free from Spandau—that he'll die in prison. He's 72 now and could live another ten or 15 years. I can't see the rotation of guard forces and prison commandants continuing much longer."

"That's pretty much up to the Soviets, Hugh. The three Western Allies have made it clear to them that all of us favor a revised approach that scales down the prison significantly."

"The Russians are going to hold out for something in return, Harry. Any idea what it's going to be?"

"Hugh, USBER is handling those discussions. I'm not in the loop and not likely to be."

Erb realized he wasn't going to coax much more out of the USCOB spokesman. "Say, Harry, Krista was very impressed with that young lady, Carolyn, whom you brought to dinner at our house. How did the two of you meet?"

The business part of the conversation over, Holbrook relaxed. "Carolyn is a sixth-grade math teacher at Thomas A. Roberts. I met her there at a PTA meeting."

"PTA meeting? What were you doing at a PTA gathering?"

"Long story Hugh. But the bottom line is that General Caraway wanted to increase the command's presence at the school which so many of our youngsters attend, so I was tapped to be a kind of good-will ambassador. Carolyn and I were at a PTA meeting a couple of months ago and began dating. She was my date at the USCOB dinner-dance a couple of weeks ago."

"Krista will want to know if it's serious. Are your intentions honorable, Major," Hugh joked, "and what does the future hold?"

"I wish I knew, Hugh. She's a lovely young woman, seven years younger than I am and innocent in a lot of very nice ways. I guess you could say that she's very special and we'll see what develops in the next few months before I leave for Vietnam."

"Is it true that O'Meara is going to push the Pentagon for a replacement for you as PIO so you can get to Vietnam and get on with your career?"

"Who told you that, Hugh?" Holbrook was astonished that anyone was aware of that conversation.

"Ve haf our vays," joked the AP bureau chief as he hung up his phone.

18

With no further news about the Israeli sniper and no new developments, Holbrook and Hellerstein began the drive to the Spandau Prison neighborhood. The small red and black gym bag, filled with the items Holbrook had requested from Semsch, sat on the back seat.

Both men, as agreed, were wearing blue jeans, windbreakers, and tennis shoes. Their haircuts were the only identifiers that stamped them as American military personnel, except for the pistol belt that each wore around his waist with a loaded .45 caliber pistol in its holster.

Holbrook parked his Chevy in an apartment complex parking lot a few blocks from the sniper's building. There it wouldn't arouse any suspicions and could be quickly moved by Hellerstein when the sniper had been neutralized by Holbrook.

The Spandau Prison courtyard was fully lighted, and crowds had begun to gather behind police barricades. The sniper would have a clear, unobstructed line of sight to take out both prisoners with two shots fired in quick succession from an automatic or semiautomatic rifle.

The second-floor landing appeared undisturbed since their visit yesterday. Holbrook carried the gym bag through the doors of the landing well and up the stairs to the third floor, where he hid the bag in a dark corner. It was doubtful, he felt, that the sniper would take time to investigate the third floor, but if he found the bag he'd likely attribute it to something forgotten by a workman at the site.

"Norm, let's do a commo check and then you can leave to wait in the car." Both radios worked fine, loud and clear, so Hellerstein slipped out and headed to the parking area.

Holbrook decided to wait on the stairs leading to the third floor. There would be two doors on the second-floor landing between the sniper and him, but he'd tested them several times. They were newly installed, freshly oiled, and opened and closed soundlessly.

He checked his watch: 2335 hours. Twenty-five minutes before the scheduled release time.

He stood, motionless, on the staircase connecting the second and third floors.

A few minutes later he heard a car drive up and park next to the building. Next, he heard faint footsteps on the bare concrete staircase. He could see through a small glass window in the stairwell door a well-built man wearing a dark baseball cap and carrying a case of some kind, together with a rolled-up mat.

As the man moved stealthily up the staircase to the second floor, Holbrook got a better look at his face, aided by the spotlights across the street in the Spandau Prison yard. Yes, definitely Samuel/Schmuel, definitely the "visitor from the east" that he'd met in Rabbi Halbfinger's office.

The assassin laid the mat down in the place he intended to fire from. The mat was about 6 feet long so it could accommodate his whole body in a comfortable firing position. Next, Samuel removed his weapon from its case and began to assemble its components.

Semsch had shared with Holbrook and Hellerstein photos and descriptions of likely weapons the sniper might use. The Soviet Dragunov SVD was a likely choice, along with two American sniper rifles used by the military: the Army's M-24 and the Navy's Mk13, both chambered for the 300 Winchester Magnum adopted a few years earlier.

As Samuel put the weapon together, it became clear to Holbrook that it was in fact the semiautomatic Dragunov. As Holbrook peeked through the glass door, he could see Samuel attaching the bipod legs and adjusting the telescopic sight. With a well-lighted courtyard at the prison, there would apparently be no need for a night-vision sight.

With the rifle in readiness, Samuel inserted a ten-round curved box magazine. His preparations complete, the sniper checked his watch—2353 hours, Holbrook noted—and relaxed, waiting for his targets to appear.

Across from Spandau Prison
British Sector, West Berlin
2355 hours, 29 September 1966

With five minutes to go before the prisoners' release, the crowd awaiting the event had swelled and was straining the barricades. But Berliners, like most Germans, followed the law implicitly and the police had no difficulty maintaining control.

Promptly at midnight, the huge prison gates opened and uniformed prison warders escorted the two prisoners being released to their waiting vehicles, both parked about 60 yards away.

His pulse quickening, Holbrook watched intently as the sniper moved into firing position, took aim, and prepared to squeeze the trigger. Just then, Holbrook bolted from the stairwell and smashed the sniper across the back of his head with a billy club, knocking him senseless.

The assassin collapsed across his weapon's stock. Holbrook pulled the inert body clear of the weapon, extricated the magazine and put the weapon on safe, after making sure that the man was out cold. Then, he sped up the stairs to retrieve his gym bag. First, he injected the hypodermic into the sniper's right arm, ensuring that he'd stay unconscious for another few hours.

Holbrook had taken note of the fact that Samuel was right-handed. He withdrew the surgical scalpel from the bag and sliced off the index finger of the shooter's right hand. He wrapped the finger in a bandage. It would be quite some time, Holbrook thought to himself, before this man fired a weapon again.

Holbrook used the handcuffs provided by Semsch to cuff his prisoner's limp hands behind his back. The man was still unconscious, bleeding somewhat from the blow to his head and from his severed finger. Holbrook took the Speed Graphic camera from the gym bag and snapped about a dozen photos of the Mossad agent and the weapon lying beside him, so that there was an indelible record of the assassination attempt.

Fingering his radio, he called Hellerstein. "Eagle 2, all clear here. Report for duty." While waiting for Hellerstein, Holbrook removed Samuel's car keys from a pants pocket and took his wallet and a small notebook with writing in Hebrew that he couldn't decipher.

As Hellerstein came up the stairs, Holbrook showed it to him. "What does it say, Norm?"

"Phone numbers in Berlin in case of trouble. Rabbi Halbfinger and his buddy Meier Grossman are at the top of the list, along with several other names I can't identify."

Holbrook had found in the man's wallet a West Berlin driving license in the name of Benjamin Ashkenazi. "I wonder if that's his real name or not, Norm," he said.

Hellerstein suddenly noted the condition of the sniper's right hand. "Sir," he told Holbrook, "his hand is bleeding quite a bit."

"So it is, Norm, so it is," said Holbrook, depositing the surgically removed digit into a small zip-lock bag that he put in his pocket. "He won't be shooting anyone for a long, long time, if ever again."

Down below, they could see the cars carrying the two newly freed men leaving the Spandau grounds, each escorted by a pair of West Berlin motorcycle *Polizei.*

"Norm, bring my car around and park it next to his. But first, help me carry him downstairs and put him in the back seat of his car."

Ashkenazi's vehicle was in fact a rented Opel Kadett bearing a Hertz decal on its rear bumper.

They laid the would-be assassin across the car's rear seat and used a second set of handcuffs to tie him to a chrome fitting over a rear door.

"Okay, Norm, I'm going back up to get the weapon, its case, the firing mat, and our gym bag. I don't think he brought anything else. Meet you down here in five."

Upstairs, Holbrook gathered everything up, including the baseball cap he had knocked off the sniper's head when he hit him with the billy club. Everything was put in the trunk of Holbrook's car for delivery to Colonel Semsch.

Private Plane Terminal and Facility
Flughafen Tegel
French Sector, West Berlin
0137 hours, 1 October 1966

Holbrook and Hellerstein drew their cars up alongside the sleek Dassault Falcon Mystere 20 jet that lay waiting to take off from Tegel Airport.

The three-man crew seemed surprised at the arrival of a second car, since they had been expecting only the Opel.

Holbrook dismounted and signaled to one of the crew members. "Do any of you speak English?" he asked. All three shook their heads. "Okay, my colleague here gets by pretty fluently in Hebrew. He'll translate for me." He turned to Hellerstein. "Norm, please do the translation," said Holbrook, noting that he'd just confirmed where the plotters had come from. "Tell them that we need a hand with Ashkenazi. He's been hurt and he's still unconscious. Here's a couple of clean towels to wrap around his right hand. He was in an accident and it looks like it's still bleeding."

"What happened to him?" asked the group's leader, who was wearing an airplane captain's four stripes on his white uniform shirt. They helped get the sniper into their airplane and made him as comfortable as possible.

"Can't tell. Looks like he may have gotten it caught in some sort of machinery. Maybe a weapon. But we were able to save the finger after he lost it and kept it in a plastic bag. Here it is," Holbrook said, and handed over the small zip-lock bag containing one sawed-off finger. "I figure you guys need to head back to Tel Aviv in a hurry," Holbrook said, waiting to see if anyone contradicted him. None did. "Would it be helpful if we turned the rental car in for you?"

"Yes, that would be most helpful. Why is our man in handcuffs?"

"That's the way we found him," Holbrook lied.

"What about the key?"

"We don't have it," he lied again. The key was in his hip pocket. "Can you carry a message to General Amit?"

"Of course. We have to report back to him."

"Please tell him that the operation was unsuccessful and that the West Berlin police are searching for Ashkenazi. That's his name, isn't it?"

"Yes, yes, of course we will inform General Amit. Is there anything else?"

"Please tell the general that I don't think Ashkenazi should return to Berlin anytime soon."

"Thank you, my friend."

"*Shalom*," said Holbrook.

"*Shalom*," said the three Israelis. The sniper was still unconscious.

Holbrook and Hellerstein waved goodbye as the sleek jet took off. "Good job, Norm," said Holbrook. "Let's drive both cars over to the Hertz counter."

Hertz was apparently staffed round the clock. A young man greeted Holbrook and asked how he could help.

"We're returning our Opel Kadett. Very fine car. It served us very well," Holbrook, said, handing over the car keys. The handcuff keys came out of his pocket with the car keys, and he tossed them into a nearby trashcan.

"We are pleased to learn that, Herr … " and he searched his rental files, "Ashkenazi."

"And please print out a complete set of our paperwork. Our bosses are very fussy about reimbursing us for money we spend."

"Of course, Herr Ashkenazi," the clerk said, handing Holbrook a thick packet of the rental paperwork.

"*Danke schön*," said Holbrook.

"My pleasure," said the clerk.

Holbrook and Hellerstein got into the Chevy and headed southward to their home turf. "Well, Norm, just another day at the office," Holbrook joked. "Say, your Hebrew is pretty good."

"I use it sometimes with Rabbi Halbfinger," Hellerstein explained.

"Sure came in handy tonight. It helped us confirm who was behind this operation."

They drove in silence for a while, each reflecting on what had happened in the past few hours.

"Major, was it really necessary to cut off the man's finger?"

"It was his trigger finger, Norm. I just wanted to put him out of commission for a while. Maybe their doctors can sew it back on, maybe not. In either case, I want the Israelis to know that we take our responsibilities about keeping the peace in Berlin very seriously and they'd better think twice before they try to pull off something like this ever again."

A few minutes later Holbrook asked, "When do we tell Colonel Semsch? It's almost 3 a.m. Do we wake him now?"

"No, let's wait till 7, sir. I'll phone him and tell him we stopped the attempt." Norm thought a moment longer. "What do I tell him about the finger, sir?"

"Tell him that Ashkenazi lost it in the line of duty. That I hacked it off so the son of a bitch can't shoot anyone ever again."

"Yes sir."

"And ask the good colonel what he wants me to do with the rifle, its ammunition, the .45s, the wallet, paperwork, etc. I can't very well go carrying a Dragunov sniper's rifle into the USCOB headquarters tomorrow morn ... I mean, later this morning. Charley Hines's MPs would mow me down like a terrorist."

"I agree, sir. I'll ask the colonel where he wants the weapon delivered."

"Thanks, Norm. Pleasure working with you."

"I'm not so sure, sir, but things are always interesting around you." Holbrook couldn't tell if his partner was serious or not.

Office of the Intelligence Officer
Headquarters, U.S. Commander Berlin
Clayallee and Saargemünder Strasse
1037 hours, 1 October 1966

"You've delivered the weapon to Halvorsen, Harry?"

"Right, Phil. I'm just back from the Outpost Theater. There's an overflow parking lot behind the theater that's deserted in the mornings, so Halvorsen wanted to meet there. One of his men took the weapon, the magazine for it, the wallet, the baseball cap, the little notebook, the car-rental paperwork—everything.

"I brought with me the two .45s, unloaded of course, one set of handcuffs, and the scalpel, since I didn't think they came from the CIA. They were in your gym bag."

"You're right. I scrounged them from other sources."

"I lost one of the two pairs of handcuffs though. I wanted the sniper to be as uncomfortable as possible during his long flight back home to Tel Aviv. The second set is here in your gym bag with the other items."

"You didn't think that losing a finger from his right hand would make him sufficiently uncomfortable?" asked Semsch. "That you had to keep him handcuffed during his trip home?"

"Maybe yes, maybe no, Phil. I wanted to send a message to King Saul Boulevard not to mess with us."

"I'm sure they got the message, Harry."

"Have you briefed Caraway yet?"

Semsch nodded in affirmation. "First thing this morning, right after Norm briefed me. Say, that was pretty clever of you two, using Norm's knowledge of Hebrew to imply that you both were part of the plot. I wonder, though, if they really swallowed your yarn that he caught the finger in a piece of machinery or in his weapon."

"Who really gives a shit, Phil? They can believe whatever they want. Once Ashkenazi regained consciousness, I'm sure he told the whole story to the Mossad brass and they know what actually took place."

"Did you consider killing him?" asked Semsch.

"Just for a moment, but never seriously. I remember what Norm said about maintaining his ties with people in East Berlin and I wanted to respect that. I felt that knocking the man out, aborting his mission, and crippling his future ability to fire a weapon were sufficient punishments. How did Caraway react when you told him?" Holbrook asked. He was curious.

"He went white. Turned ashy gray. Told me to stay in close touch with Halvorsen and his people and keep our headquarters out of it."

"Fair enough," said Harry. "What about USBER?"

"They sure as hell won't learn anything from me. If Halvorsen tips them, that's on him. Caraway wants us—you and me—to back away from the incident and pretend it never happened."

"Caraway also said that he hopes Speer and von Schirach live out the rest of their miserable, demented lives in peaceful anonymity before they end up in hell."

"Amen to that," said the USCOB information officer.

19

As before, Hellerstein's sedan was met at the synagogue's side door by the congregation's lay leader, Meier Grossman, a man in his fifties who had survived the war as a male nurse in a Berlin hospital that treated severely wounded soldiers of the *Wehrmacht*.

Grossman shook hands with Holbrook and Hellerstein and then led them into Rabbi Halbfinger's private office.

"Good evening, Major Holbrook and Norman," said the rabbi. "I suspect you have something to tell me, but before we get down to business, may we enjoy a glass of wine?"

Grossman produced four heavy, sparkling crystal water glasses and began pouring grape wine into them. "This is the last of our Manischewitz wine, Major Holbrook. It has become increasingly difficult to obtain here in the East. And very expensive too," he added.

Holbrook held his glass up to the light, scrutinizing the rich dark wine. "A nice, sweet wine, made from Concord grapes, Rabbi.

211

The Manischewitz winery is in western New York State, not far from Lake Erie, but the Concord grape was developed in Concord, Massachusetts in the 1850s, about the same time that Emerson and Thoreau were living there." Holbrook continued with his sudden display of wine erudition. "And, of course, Concord and Lexington were the very first battles of the American Revolution, so they're famous in our history, as I'm sure you were taught in your Milwaukee schools. Manischewitz, of course, is a kosher wine, very inexpensive in the States. It sells for maybe three-and a-half or four dollars a bottle. A lot of street winos are partial to Manischewitz because of its low cost and they aren't particular about whether it's kosher or not."

Rabbi Halbfinger was about to inquire how it was that the major was so familiar with kosher wines, when Holbrook said, "I'm not sure if our PX Class VI store stocks Manischewitz wine, Rabbi, but I'll see that they order some. In a few weeks I'll see that it's delivered here to you."

The rabbi wanted to continue the discussion with this unexpected oenophile sitting in his office but, sipping from his glass of wine, he knew that Holbrook and Hellerstein had come with a purpose and that a lecture of sorts was imminent.

Holbrook came to the point. "Rabbi, there must be no further reprisals against Speer or von Schirach. I gave Samuel or Schmuel or Benjamin Ashkenazi a pass last week because he was following orders from Tel Aviv and perhaps he'll be useful to his nation at some future date. But I need you to get word to King Saul Boulevard that the situation in West Berlin is that the status quo is to be protected at all costs and that no one rocks the boat. Had Ashkenazi been successful in his mission, all kinds of hell would have broken loose, and neo-Nazis would have rushed from their rat holes to threaten the city's stability and perhaps provoke some reaction from the Russians."

Holbrook took a sip of his wine before continuing. "Rabbi, I suspect that you have some sort of pipeline to General Amit at

Mossad headquarters and that's why the assassin met us here. You need to tell Amit that Speer and von Schirach were sentenced by an international tribunal in Nuremberg to each serve 20 years in Spandau. That sentence has been fulfilled. Hess was sentenced to life imprisonment and there's no doubt that he'll die in Spandau, but Speer and von Schirach are now free men and they're entitled to live out the rest of their miserable lives and die in peace."

Rabbi Halbfinger stroked his yellowish gray beard and thought carefully before responding to Harry Holbrook. "Major, on behalf of the Jewish people, we are grateful to you for sparing the life of the Mossad agent. But you have no idea of the crimes that these two Nazi fanatics committed against our people, indeed against all humankind. They do not deserve to live out the rest of their lives. After all, it is written in the holy bible that one should take an eye for an eye."

"That's not entirely accurate, Rabbi. When Moses wrote in Leviticus that 'Fracture for fracture, eye for eye, tooth for tooth, the same sort of injury he inflicted should be inflicted on him,' he was referring to appropriate punishment that suited the crime. Moses meant that the sentence for crimes committed should be commensurate with the severity of the crime. He was in no way sanctioning vigilante justice, such as Samuel was instructed to impose. The judges at Nuremberg—the wisest justices the Allies could summon up—imposed appropriate sentences on the Nazi war criminals and sent seven of them here to Spandau. With the exception of Hess, who's still in prison, the others have all done their time or died. What's done is done, Rabbi."

Rabbi Halbfinger was unused to having scripture quoted against him but Harry Holbrook—he of the legendary memory—was making a fair stab at it. Halbfinger began to respond, but the infantry major cut him off.

"Rabbi, you're well aware that Leviticus also says that 'You must not take vengeance nor hold a grudge against the sons of your people.'"

"Yes, Major, that's true but—"

Holbrook interrupted again as another biblical passage occurred to him. "And somewhere in Deuteronomy it says that instead of personal vengeance, the laws of Moses encourage people to trust God and the legal system to right any wrongs. When Jesus said in the Sermon on the Mount, 'You heard that it was said: 'Eye for eye and tooth for tooth,'' Jesus knew that some had misinterpreted what Moses had in mind. So, Jesus insisted instead that 'whoever slaps you on the right cheek, turn the other cheek.' That's in Matthew 5, a New Testament book written primarily for a Jewish audience."

The rabbi was speechless, unused to being on the receiving end of a homily. Holbrook drained his glass of the sweet wine and, turning to Hellerstein, said, "Norm, we've got a Wall patrol to finish up. We'd better be on our way."

Rabbi Halbfinger held up a hand to delay their departure. "Major, might one inquire how it is that you are so familiar with holy scripture from both our bible and yours?"

"That's easy, Rabbi. My dad was a Methodist minister in Youngstown."

"Youngstown?"

"Yes, Rabbi, it's a city in Ohio, in case you didn't know," said Holbrook, toying with the learned man. "I was supposed to follow my father into the ministry but then I got exposed to the military during ROTC at Penn State and I kind of eased into the Army as a career. My younger brother, Blake, graduated from the divinity school at Duke University and he's taken over my father's congregation in Youngstown."

The two Americans rose and shook hands with Rabbi Halbfinger and Meier Grossman.

"*Shalom*, Rabbi," Holbrook said, placing his famed service cap firmly on his head as they left the synagogue.

The rabbi sat in stunned silence, staring into space. Eventually, speaking in the Yiddish language he'd learned from his parents in Milwaukee, he turned to Grossman and said, "Meier, am I correct that I have just been given a lesson in the Holy Book by a young American Army officer?"

"Not necessarily, Rabbi. The major was just expressing—"

The rabbi interrupted his dear friend of many years. "Meier, if you find that there might be perhaps a little more wine at the bottom of that bottle, perhaps it would be well to finish it tonight. Somehow I feel confident that Major Holbrook will manage to resupply us with more Manischewitz. Undoubtedly he's familiar with what happened in John's gospel when they ran out of wine at the wedding in Cana."

20

Office of the U.S. Minister
Headquarters, U.S. Commander Berlin
Clayallee and Saargemünder Strasse
Dahlem, Zehlendorf
West Berlin
1400 hours, 13 October 1966

"Have a seat please, Holbrook," said Ernest Calhoun, the United States Minister in West Berlin, the senior State Department representative in the divided city, who reported directly to Ambassador George McGhee in Bonn and was very much on a co-equal line of command with General Caraway, the USCOB.

Holbrook was a little antsy. He had never before been in Calhoun's office, much less in the U.S. Mission (USBER) section of the headquarters building at 127 Clayallee.

But when Phil Semsch had phoned shortly before noon that he and Holbrook were expected in Calhoun's office at 1400, Holbrook told Frau Haupt to reschedule all his afternoon commitments for the next day.

Semsch had previously been in the USBER wing of the building, but it was all new to Holbrook. Marine sentries in dress uniforms were posted at the large glass doors leading into the section, and people in civilian clothes did double-takes, wondering what the two Army officers in their green uniforms were doing on the State Department's turf.

With neither preliminaries nor the offer of a cup of coffee or tea, Calhoun came quickly to the point. He was joined by his deputy, Pete Day—whom Holbrook knew—by the USBER legal advisor, Marten van Heuven, and by the CIA station chief, Roger Halvorson.

"Phil, Major Holbrook," Calhoun began, "with the release from Spandau of Speer and von Schirach, several new situations have arisen, some of them promising and some not so sanguine." Glancing around his conference table, he noted that Day and van Heuven were nodding appropriately in agreement.

"Pending the release on October 1, we communicated to the Soviets that perhaps it was time to rethink the ongoing status of the Spandau Prison. With only Rudolf Hess imprisoned in a facility built with one 134 cells, there is clearly a significant waste of manpower and resources.

"Our British and French partners here in Berlin," Calhoun intoned, clearly pleased with the sound of his delivery, "are very much with us in wanting to relocate Hess to a less costly environment involving far fewer warders and military personnel. In late September, with the release date of Speer and von Schirach approaching, we communicated to the Soviets our interest in a meeting to discuss some form of modification to the Spandau infrastructure."

Holbrook listened intently to the posturing and gobbledygook. He interpreted the minister's message thus far as "We want to meet with the Russians about finding a smaller cellblock for Hess."

"The Berliners, of course," Calhoun sailed along, "are very much with us. Governing Mayor Brandt puts the cost to the Senat of maintaining Spandau at 800,000 dollars annually, which presumably could be appreciably reduced by confining Hess in a smaller facility."

Holbrook was beginning to fully appreciate Paul Scholl's standing description of their State Department colleagues as "striped pants bastards." What Calhoun was saying—taking a long time to get it out—was that the Berlin government could save a bundle by moving Hess, since it was picking up most of the costs for running Spandau.

"Somewhat surprisingly," Calhoun continued, with a measured degree of skepticism in his voice, "the Soviets have hinted that they might be amenable to the possibility of discussing the feasibility of incarcerating Hess in a small building within the larger Spandau complex. He would still have access, of course, to his beloved gardens and gardening equipment, but all would be on a vastly reduced scale. Is everyone with me thus far?"

All nodded in agreement at these pearls of wisdom emanating from the minister's golden tongue, Holbrook among them.

"What's vitally important to the Soviets, of course, is that Spandau Prison continues to be maintained in some form, even if only for one man. It gives them a continued presence here in West Berlin, along with their role in the air safety center. Those are their only two ongoing presences here, other than the small ceremonial guard force at their War Memorial in the British sector.

"Before I continue, I should like to diverge a moment to ask Mr. Halvorsen to update us on the latest intel"—Calhoun used the term "intel" proudly to demonstrate his proficiency in spycraft—"we have on Speer and von Schirach. Roger, if you would, please."

Halvorsen had obviously been forewarned that Calhoun would call on him for this report, and he adjusted his reading glasses as he scrutinized a set of 5x7 notecards in front of him.

"Thank you, Minister Calhoun," the CIA station chief began. At this point Holbrook panicked a bit and wondered if Halvorsen might spill the beans about his role in thwarting the Mossad plot to assassinate the two Nazis. Semsch had promised Holbrook that he was duty bound to report the incident to Halvorsen, who would in turn relay it to CIA headquarters in Langley, Virginia. But that was to have been the extent of it, Semsch had reassured Holbrook. Nevertheless, Holbrook was edgy as Halvorsen began his report.

"Speer, like von Schirach, exited Spandau wearing the same set of civilian clothes he had on when he was confined there 20 years ago. He was met at the Spandau gate by several members of his family. He is only 59 years old and has a wife, four sons, and two daughters. They were picked up by several sedans and were driven to the Hotel Gerhus in the Grunewald district, where family members had arranged a press conference. About a dozen media were present and Speer spoke to them in German, French, and English.

"He commented that ever since Stalin's death in 1953 the prisoners at Spandau have been treated politely and with dignity. He described the prison food as good and sufficient. He was asked about his future plans, and he said that the family plans to live in Heidelberg, where he hopes to resume his prewar career as an architect.

"Von Schirach's situation is a little different. He was not met by anyone except a hired sedan, which drove quickly away. As we know, he is blind in one eye and has poor vision in the other. He is 61. His wife, Henriette, a writer who is known to have challenged Hitler in person about his persecution of the Jewish people, divorced him in 1950. Von Schirach, we understand, plans to live with his son in Munich. He has no financial worries because he still has money from his large interest in a Philadelphia engineering firm that belonged to his American mother."

Halvorsen looked up from his notes and removed his eyeglasses. "That's what we know about them and their plans at the moment, Minister," he said. "Are there any questions?"

Pete Day, the USBER spokesman, said, "Roger, UPI"—United Press International, the other American news bureau—"reported that there were a number of pro-Nazi banners and protest signs outside Spandau when the prisoners were released last week at midnight. Is there any truth to that report?"

As Halvorsen searched for an answer, Holbrook intervened. "Pete, I spoke with Hugh Erb about that. Joe Fleming of UPI didn't bother to get up and attend the release from Spandau. He relied upon the reports of his German stringer. It was the stringer who told Fleming about the Nazi demonstrations, but Erb was there and he swears they never happened. Matter of fact, according to Erb, Fleming got a rocket"—a negative telegram—"from UPI headquarters in New York City about reporting something that no other news media witnessed or reported on."

Holbrook adroitly avoided mentioning that he too had been present across the street from the prisoners' release and that no noticeable neo-Nazi activity had taken place. But admitting that he'd been there would have opened up a can of worms and he kept his mouth judiciously shut.

All present were silent, apparently impressed with Holbrook's awareness of doings within the media. Calhoun used this as an opportunity for moving on to his next item of business, which involved Holbrook.

"Major Holbrook," he said, "how well do you know Colonel Lazarev, the Soviet commandant of Spandau?"

Holbrook was taken aback by the direct question and change of subject. "I met him only once, at the monthly commandant's luncheon at Spandau, sir. You and Pete also attended. That's the only time I've ever spoken to him. His office did call mine before the Volksfest opening in August to ask for a seat in the reviewing stand, which we supplied."

"Lazarev seated you next to him at the luncheon table," Calhoun said. "What was behind that and what did the two of you discuss?"

"Sir, I was as surprised as anyone to be seated near him, right across from General Binoche. He asked me if I'd been to Vietnam yet, he bragged about his daughter's A-plus grades in aeronautical engineering, and encouraged me to try their vodka. At the very end of the luncheon he advised me to be sure I left with the correct uniform cap. On the drive back here, Colonel Semsch discovered the small note in my cap telling me to meet someone in the shoe department at KaDeWe, which you're all familiar with. That's the extent of my involvement with Colonel Lazarev, sir."

Calhoun digested this information. "Colonel Semsch, do you know offhand what level of security clearance Major Holbrook has?"

"Yes, Minister. He's cleared for information up to and including Top Secret/Crypto. That's one level higher than Top Secret. He earned that high-level clearance about five or six years ago when he was aide-de-camp to the chief of the Army Security Agency. Holbrook had access to every piece of communications intel, signals intel or human intel that came across his boss's desk."

Calhoun nodded and cleared his throat. He reached for a glass of water and took a sip. "The reason I ask, Holbrook, is because Colonel Lazarev has asked us, through diplomatic channels, to make you available for a meeting next week at the Soviet Embassy in East Berlin and we have absolutely no idea what's involved.

"To be perfectly candid, we of the U.S. Mission here totally oppose the involvement in discussions between the Russians, East Germans and ourselves of anyone not properly schooled in international relations." He looked around the table and got ardent nods of approval from Day and van Heuven.

"Nevertheless," Calhoun continued, "since the Soviets were insistent that you were the only person they were interested in negotiating with, we reluctantly assented. We, of course, consulted General Caraway to obtain his concurrence and he strongly advised against involving you."

Holbrook was about to comment but Semsch spoke first. "The USCOB is of the opinion, Minister, that Major Holbrook stretches the role of an information officer beyond his assigned areas of responsibilities."

Holbrook was of a mind to kick his friend in the shins under the table. *I didn't ask for any of this shit,* he thought to himself. *It just keeps landing on me!*

"Nevertheless, Holbrook, we will be dispatching you to meet next week with the Soviets at their embassy on Unter den Linden. You know, of course, where it is."

"Yes sir, just east of the Brandenburg Gate. I've been by there many times on Wall patrols."

"The Soviets sent an envelope via diplomatic pouch"—here Calhoun gestured with his fingers toward Day, who handed the minister an 8 by 11-inch manila envelope, which Calhoun opened—"which contains instructions and passes." Opening the envelope, Calhoun brought forth a map of the Soviet embassy grounds, with an X indicating parking areas. He also held up a placard to be displayed for access to the parking area and a badge with a chain to be worn around the neck. "That's a very good photo of you on the badge, Holbrook," said the minister, a little sarcastically.

Holbrook looked at it. A very recent head and shoulders photo of him in his Army Green uniform. Could have been taken anywhere, he assumed.

Finally, Calhoun came to the date and time. "You're expected at the Embassy at 1130 hours, Monday, October 17. There's no mention of lunch, but the time suggests that Colonel Lazarev plans a meeting over a luncheon. Do you need to write that down, Major?"

"No sir, I have—"

"Ah yes, of course, that memory. We'll expect a written report the afternoon of the 17th. I think that does it, gentlemen," said Calhoun with a self-satisfied grin and a flexing of his shoulders. "Is there anything else?" No one spoke. Clearly the United States Minister to West Berlin was ready to end this gathering and get away. All rose as Calhoun left his chair and exited.

Office of the Intelligence Officer
Headquarters, U.S. Commander Berlin
Clayallee and Saargemünder Strasse
Dahlem, Zehlendorf
West Berlin
1505 hours, 15 October 1966

"What's going on, Phil?" asked Holbrook when he and Colonel Semsch were seated in Semsch's secure office. "Why do I keep getting involved in all this crap?"

"Harry, I have no earthly idea. It's clear, however, that Colonel Lazarev took a liking to you at the Spandau luncheon and that he has a high regard for your ability to follow through. The defection of the Russian pilot, which you helped orchestrate, was a textbook case of exfiltration and it's obvious that Lazarev appreciated it."

"It strikes me that there's more to this than Calhoun was letting on," said Holbrook.

"I wouldn't be surprised. These State Department types are a devious breed, and they don't always know when they're telling the truth and when they're lying. It's best that you go into this thing with your eyes wide open. You and I have the weekend to think about it and figure out how to cover your ass when things go sour, as they inevitably will, so that USBER can scream, 'We told you so!' when they hang your carcass out to dry."

"Thanks, Phil. You sure know how to cheer a guy up." Holbrook rose and headed down the hall to the safety and sanctity of his own office.

Carolyn looked lovely, reflected Holbrook as they sat on the back porch of the Semsch family quarters on a beautiful sunlit mid-October afternoon.

Phil Semsch, who had called Harry on Friday and had invited the couple to their home after church services on Sunday for a barbecue dinner, was busy at the grill, wearing an apron proclaiming him as the top chef. Alicia Semsch was inside in the kitchen, preparing salads and ears of fresh corn that would accompany her husband's grilled T-bone steaks.

Alicia, women's intuition and all, had sensed that in Carolyn Mattersdorf their friend Harry may finally have found the woman he needed after the failure of his first marriage, and she, with a woman's protective, maternal instincts, wanted to ensure that Harry didn't get hurt yet again.

Alicia invited Carolyn into her kitchen, leaving the men outside to "talk shop."

"Would you help me slice the veggies for our salads, Carolyn?" she asked, handing her an apron. "How did you and Harry meet?" she asked innocently, beginning the interrogation.

"At a PTA meeting at Thomas A. Roberts School, of all places," Carolyn replied. She went on to explain Harry's role as liaison between the command and the school. "Miss Drew asked me to link up with him, since he'd told us that they would be donating some of the proceeds from the Volksfest to the school. It was the nicest assignment she's ever given me," Carolyn recalled.

Alicia, wife of a career military intelligence officer, continued her questioning. "So you've been dating a couple of months?" Carolyn nodded as she sliced raw carrots for the salads. "What do you think of him?"

Carolyn chose her next words with care. After all, she was baring her soul. "I haven't dated all that many men, Alicia. I've had a couple of dates with Army officers here in Berlin and one Air Force pilot. They were all very fine young men and they all treated me with courtesy and respect. But Harry ... Harry is a little bit different from everyone else."

"What makes him so different?"

"It's hard to explain. I mean he's a perfect gentleman and all that, but so were my other dates. Harry has a certain quality about him, I don't know how to define it, but it makes him stand out from anyone else. At least as far as I'm concerned."

As Carolyn paused, looking for the right words to describe her innermost feelings, Alicia tried to help her out a little. "I can't go into details, you understand, but Harry has some very special gifts. For one thing, he has a fantastic memory."

"And yet," Carolyn interrupted, "he forgot to call me after we first met at the PTA meeting. I had to jog his memory and invite him to see *The Sound of Music* with me."

"That may very well be because it was supposed to play out in that manner," Alicia said. "Maybe the fact that he forgot—and I can assure you that doesn't happen very often—was supposed to keep reminding him that you are someone special in his life."

"You may be right, Alicia. I know that I enjoy being with him. He's wonderful company and a perfect gentleman. He's an awful dancer though; at the USCOB dinner-dance he stepped all over my new gold shoes." She laughed.

"So is Phil, for that matter. Lousy dancer, but an excellent husband and father to our children."

"I enjoy my time with Harry very much," Carolyn seemed to sum up, without drawing any conclusions about where the relationship might be headed. "Can I help toss the salad for you?"

"Yes, that would be a great help. Thanks, Carolyn."

Out on the back patio, Semsch and Holbrook were indeed talking shop as the former kept flipping his T-bones to grill them to perfection.

"It's difficult to know exactly what the Russians have in mind, Harry," Semsch said. "The fact that Lazarev asked specifically for you indicates that he trusts you and has a high degree of confidence in you. Additionally, the fact that he'll be meeting you at his embassy, in wide-open view of everyone in the Russian and East German hierarchy, is another indication that whatever he's going to propose has been sanctioned at high levels, maybe even all the way up to the Kremlin. This is no clandestine meeting with a shoe clerk at KaDeWe. No, it's a structured, preplanned event that probably has high-level authorization from somewhere in the Soviet government."

"What do I need to be concerned about?' Holbrook asked.

"Whatever proposal is made, or whatever questions are asked of you, just take the standard diplomatic approach. That is, nod judiciously and say that you will take the matter up with your superiors. The Russians know you're just an Army major and that you don't speak for the USCOB in making decisions. So, they're expecting you to respond something along the lines of 'That's very interesting, Colonel Lazarev, and I'll be glad to pass it along to General Caraway.' That way, you become the messenger, not the decision maker, which is your appropriate role: to hear them out and convey their message accurately back to Caraway and Calhoun."

"That's good advice, Phil. I'll try to act accordingly. To change the subject, what did you think of Father Mulcahy's sermon today?"

"On why God lets bad things happen to good people? I thought it went over very well. You know, Mulcahy's not your typical Catholic priest. He's got kind of a checkered past."

"How's that?" Holbrook asked.

"Mulcahy grew up in a tough neighborhood on Chicago's south side. His father was an alcoholic who beat his wife regularly and was particularly nasty when he was drinking. More than once the young Mulcahy had to restrain his father from punching out his mother.

"To bring in some money to offset the father's alcohol expenditures, Mulcahy started dealing drugs, never telling his mother where the money came from. If she knew or suspected, she never let on. When he was about 17, he got caught by the Chicago cops and the judge told him it was either juvie or the Army."

"Juvie?"

"Juvenile detention, Harry. A softened form of jail for underage offenders. Mulcahy said he'd take the Army. He got sent to Korea, fought with the 17th Infantry Regiment in the hard fighting around the Iron Triangle and came home with sergeant's stripes, a Bronze Star for valor, and a Purple Heart. He got out of the Army, went to Northwestern on the GI Bill, and decided to go to seminary to become a priest and help out young men who were struggling, as had happened to him."

"How do you know all this, Phil? It's pretty personal information."

"Remember that I'm an intelligence officer, my lad, and I can get anyone—even a Catholic priest—to confess to me." Semsch chuckled a little at his attempt at humor. "Someday, Harry, I'll even get you to tell me what makes you tick."

"Good luck with that," said Holbrook, just as Semsch pronounced that the steaks and ears of corn were ready. Semsch put them on large serving platers that he and Holbrook carried inside, where the ladies had set a table with wine and water goblets and with empty salad bowls in place.

"What a pretty table!" Holbrook commented as he scrutinized the place settings and floral decorations that Alicia and Carolyn had set. Semsch said grace and the salad bowl was passed around as the host asked each person whether they wanted their steak rare or well-done. He'd prepared some of each.

Holbrook had brought with him two bottles of a Pinot Noir called *Spätburgunder*, which he'd bought at the Class VI store. Everyone agreed that the wine made an excellent complement to the steak dinner.

"So, what did you two girls talk about?" asked Semsch, the professional interrogator.

"Oh, just the usual girl talk," Alicia replied. "How about you guys?"

"Harry's been invited to the Soviet Embassy tomorrow," replied Semsch, "and we talked about how he'd better use the right fork if they invite him to lunch."

Carolyn's ears perked up. She paused with her steak knife in midair and looked at her date. "You didn't mention that this morning, Harry."

Holbrook reddened a bit and tamped his eyeglasses down on his nose. "It's no big deal. Phil and I were just talking about it and how I should handle it."

Carolyn's furrowed brow suggested she knew that this wasn't the entire story. No doubt she would ask Harry about it on their drive home.

The visit ended by midafternoon, with everyone sated and stuffed. All promised to stay in touch socially and to visit again. On the drive back to Carolyn's BOQ, as expected, she grilled Harry on additional details about his forthcoming adventure with the Russians.

"Okay, Harry, just the facts," she said, echoing a popular TV program, *Dragnet*, which had aired in the late 1950s.

And Harry told her.

Embassy of the Soviet Union to the German Democratic Republic
63–65 Unter den Linden
East Berlin
1115 hours, 17 October 1966

The Soviet Embassy on the southern side of Unter den Linden boulevard, just east of the historic Brandenburg Gate, looked like a 19th-century palace of some sort, Harry Holbrook thought as he drove up to the front gate and displayed his authorization.

But he knew that the huge, sprawling four-story complex had been built in fairly recent years—in the 1949–52 time period to be precise—employing the pretentious neoclassical architectural style favored by Soviet dictator Josef Stalin. The structure was, in fact, the first major postwar building project in East Berlin following the 1945 end of hostilities in World War II. Stalin had wanted to impress his East German vassals with the Soviet Union's steadfast support of the German Democratic Republic, so sculptures of working-class laborers looked out from the white building.

A large hammer-and-sickle flag of the Soviet Union flew atop the building, alongside the black, red, and gold banner of the GDR in an image of solidarity, although decorations with a hammer and sickle motif framed many of the embassy's windows.

Holbrook had been instructed by Minister Calhoun to wear his regular Army Green uniform, since it was an official visit and he was there as a representative of the United States government.

A sharp-looking Soviet Army captain greeted him as he parked his Chevy in a designated space.

"I am Captain Antonov," said the Russian officer in passable English, saluting the major, "adjutant to Colonel Lazarev. Welcome to our embassy, Major Holbrook. Please follow me."

As they entered the building's large rotunda, heading for the elevators, Holbrook and his uniform drew more than a few inquisitive glances. But the presence of the Soviet officer indicated that nothing was amiss and the onlookers had best be advised to stick to their own business. The two army officers rode the elevator in silence until they reached the fourth floor.

"Follow me, please, Major Holbrook," said Antonov. "We are going to Colonel Lazarev's office at the end of this corridor."

Lazarev rose as they entered his office and greeted Holbrook like a long-lost nephew. He gave him a warm bear hug.

"Major Holbrook, it is very, very good to see you again," he exclaimed. "I thank you for saving my life and that of many others at the Volksfest. I was sitting in the stands directly behind your ambassador and general. I would have been blown up with them."

Holbrook was stunned. No one except a close-hold few was supposed to know about the RPG-7 incident at the Volksfest. And yet it apparently was common knowledge among the Soviet contingent in Berlin.

"That was just lucky timing, Colonel," he tried to explain. "We were able to confront the terrorist just as he—"

"Nonsense, Holbrook, nonsense. I know all about your meetings at the Jewish church and with the Mossad operative. But nothing more about that incident needs to be said today. We have other matters to discuss. Come, wash your hands and refresh yourself here in my private bathroom and we shall go to lunch on the third floor."

Holbrook complied and he and Lazarev rode the elevator down one floor. There Captain Antonov awaited them and escorted them to a private dining room off the main dining area. Antonov led them to a small table set for three and saw them to their seats.

Hot tea was served in cut crystal glasses. Lazarev took a sugar cube from a bowl, placed it between his teeth, and drank the tea with a satisfied expression. "Ah," he said, "that is excellent tea and that is how it should be enjoyed. Try it," he said to Holbrook, extending a bowl of sugar cubes.

Holbrook took one and placed it between his teeth as the Russian had done. Carefully, so as not to spill any of the tea on his freshly pressed uniform, he sipped at the tea. "Very good tea, Colonel," he said. "Somewhat stronger than the Lipton tea bags I'm used to."

"Yes, we in the Soviet Union take our tea very seriously. We are famous for drinking vodka, of course, but black tea is very much our national beverage. Now, let me tell you why you are here."

But before Lazarev could begin, the door to the small dining room opened and Captain Antonov ushered in Soviet Ambassador Pyotr

Andreyevich Abrassimov, who took his seat at the unoccupied place setting. Lazarev and Holbrook rose as the ambassador approached their table and were seated when he gestured for them to do so.

"Good day, Excellency," said Lazarev, while Holbrook added, "Good morning, sir," uncertain whether it was morning or afternoon. "*Dobroe utro*," replied the ambassador in Russian, adding, "Good day, Major Holbrook."

As the 54-year-old Abrassimov unfolded his starched linen napkin and carefully placed it on his lap, a waiter in a white mess jacket brought him a glass of tea as Lazarev passed him the bowl of sugar cubes. The waiter then replaced the tea glasses of Lazarev and Holbrook with steaming fresh ones.

Abrassimov waited until the waiter was gone before speaking. "How much have you told the good major, Dmitri?"

"I was just beginning, Ambassador. In fact, I haven't even started. Perhaps you would be kind enough to explain to Major Holbrook why he is here."

The ambassador wiped his lips with his napkin as he planned his explanation. Holbrook knew that Abrassimov was a former textile factory worker, a behind-the-German-lines hero of the Great Patriotic War, that he was plugged into the highest levels of the Kremlin, including former premier Nikita Khrushchev and now Leonid Brezhnev, and that he represented a new breed of Soviet statesman. Abrassimov was a full member of the Soviet Communist Party's Central Committee, although Holbrook had no knowledge of this fact. Unlike many of his predecessors, Abrassimov was available to the news media, made television appearances during visits to schools, factories and trade fairs, and could be counted on for some headline-inducing quotes more often than not.

Holbrook knew that he was in the presence of considerable power, diplomatic and otherwise.

"To begin with, Holbrook"—his English was excellent—"we are grateful to you for saving the life of my colleague here, Colonel

Lazarev, as well as many other members of the governing powers in Berlin. Had the terrorist succeeded, it would have caused serious disruptions to the Allied presence in Berlin, and neither your president, nor our leader, wants anything to happen which disrupts the status quo here.

"Your president is waging a war in Southeast Asia that he doesn't really want. He would much prefer to be spending his resources and manpower for building his 'Great Society,' as he terms it, and improving the lot of underprivileged Americans of all colors. Similarly, our Soviet economy is experiencing diminishing productivity, we are behind in technological advances such as computer usage, and some of our satellite brethren are on the verge of making noises about wanting to leave the fold. Neither your nation nor ours wants to 'rock the boat,' as President Johnson has phrased it.

"That is a very candid assessment of the situation, Major, from your country's point of view and ours," the ambassador summed up. "Do you comprehend what I am saying?"

"Yes sir."

"Dmitri, let's eat lunch and then we can continue." Lazarev pressed a hidden button under the table that summoned Captain Antonov. "We are ready for lunch now, Yuri."

Antonov withdrew to the kitchen and moments later cold borscht was being served. The entrée consisted of an excellent trout known as *sevani ishkhan*, a freshwater fish found only in Armenia's Lake Sevan.

"Excellent meal, Dmitri," complimented the ambassador, even though Lazarev's only involvement had been to choose the menu. Plates were cleared, raspberry sherbet was served along with more hot tea, and the wait staff was told by Captain Antonov to stay out of the dining room.

"So, where were we?" asked the ambassador. "Oh yes. Dmitri, would you be kind enough to bring Major Holbrook up to speed while I enjoy this nice cigar that Comrade Fidel sent me last week?" He proceeded to light up his Cuban cigar.

Lazarev shifted his body posture and chair so that he was facing Holbrook directly. "First let us talk about Spandau Prison. Ambassador Abrassimov does not disagree with the three Allies in the western zones that it may well be counterproductive to retain the prison in its current large form. Obviously, we do not require almost 150 cells to house one lone prisoner."

Lazarev was eyeing Abrassimov as he spoke, ascertaining that he was on the same sheet of music as the ambassador. But the Soviet emissary was puffing contentedly on his hand-rolled Hoyo de Monterrey imported cigar, apparently satisfied with Lazarev's intro to the discussion.

"So, in principle, Major Holbrook," Lazarev continued, "the Soviet Union is basically in agreement that some concessions can be made with respect to reducing the scope of the Spandau Prison. But that would entail for us a considerable loss of our presence in the western zone. As a personal matter, I would experience the loss of my responsibilities as commandant three times a year since there would presumably be no need for a rotating four-power guard force. The Berlin police units and the professional warders at Spandau are clearly capable of administering to and controlling one deranged old man.

"In other words, Major, let us assume as a starting point that the Soviet Union is amenable to an agreed-upon restructuring of the facilities at Spandau and a consequent reduction in the guard force requirement. Perhaps the use of one single building with adequate bathroom facilities for Hess. Are you with me so far?"

Holbrook nodded. "Please continue, Colonel."

Lazarev glanced over at the ambassador. "You are aware, Excellency, are you not, that Major Holbrook has an exceptionally acute memory?"

"Yes, I am. I can see him even now taking mental notes of everything that has been said. And isn't that one of the reasons why we have invited him here to our embassy today?"

"That is correct, Ambassador. Major Holbrook, do I need to repeat anything that we have said to date?"

"No sir, I've got it all."

"In return for our agreement to modify arrangements at Spandau Prison, the Soviet Union feels that certain quid pro quos from the Western Allies are necessary. That should be a given, am I correct, Major?"

"I understand, Colonel Lazarev."

"Then, to continue—" Here Lazarev was interrupted by the ambassador.

"I will take it from here, Dmitri." Turning to Holbrook, the ambassador said, "You have certain plans, Major Holbrook, that we desire."

Holbrook was confused. Thoroughly confused. What the hell kind of Secret or Top Secret documents did he have access to? He was a lowly PIO, as CINC Andrew P. O'Meara had described it, and had no knowledge of the inner classified workings of the Berlin Command.

"What kind of plans, Mr. Ambassador? I don't have any access to classified documents. I just deal with the press."

"Not so, Major," Abrassimov corrected. "Who is in charge of your Volksfest?"

"I am, sir."

"We want your plans for the Volksfest. We require them before any movement vis-à-vis Spandau can take place.

"My plans, Ambassador? I have memos that I've written, blueprints for the layout of the Volksfest Village and construction specifications, minutes from meetings of my Volksfest committee, coordinating instructions, that's all. There are no 'secret' documents."

"Who said anything about 'secret' documents? What we want, Major, are copies of every single document, including blueprints and financial statements, that involve or relate to your Volksfest. We took photographs in August of everything that went on at the Volksfest. But now we want to know how it was done, how it was coordinated, how it was financed."

"And," added Lazarev, "that includes how arrangements were made to show the John Wayne movies in the German language. Who was responsible for that stroke of good fortune?"

"I guess that was my idea, Colonel Lazarev." Turning to Abrassimov, Holbrook said, "Mr. Ambassador, can I ask what is so important about my Volksfest files? What does that have to do with Soviet-American relations?"

Abrassimov took a long drag from his stogie and watched the smoke from it curl upward as he exhaled in a state of near euphoria. "It's quite simple, Holbrook. We will conduct a Volksfest in East Berlin next summer and it will put yours to shame."

The ambassador rose from the table as Holbrook and Lazarev stood with him. "I have to be at some stupid meeting in a few minutes. Those are our conditions. Tell General Caraway and Calhoun and his minions that if they want to scale down Spandau, we want to know everything—and I mean *everything*—about the Volksfest!"

He shook Holbrook's hand, waved goodbye to Lazarev, and left in a hurry.

Holbrook was in shock. What the hell had just happened? "Colonel Lazarev, what's so important about the Volksfest? How does the future of Spandau Prison hinge on a common, ordinary Volksfest?"

Lazarev motioned for Holbrook to resume his seat, as he took his. He pressed the unseen buzzer and a waiter arrived with two fresh glasses of hot tea.

"Allow me to explain, Major Holbrook. Are you familiar with the term 'bread and circuses' as it was employed in ancient Rome?'

"A little, perhaps. It meant keeping the people satisfied by throwing them some crumbs, some amusements, to take their minds off how bad conditions really were. To help keep the populace in line, the emperors handed out free wheat to their citizens, along with other forms of entertainment—gladiators, circuses—so the people would be satisfied with their condition, wouldn't bother to vote and change regimes, and would neglect their civic duties as Roman citizens. Kind of pulling the wool over their eyes."

"Exactly. Very well said. The Soviet Union has much the same problem with our comrades here in East Berlin and, to a certain extent, throughout the GDR. Here in Berlin, for example, we are well aware that laborers on your side of the Wall have much better living conditions than here in the East. Workers in West Berlin enjoy much higher pay scales and standards of living than here in East Berlin, and that difference is being recognized more and more each day by our comrades, who are growing increasingly restless.

"You know, of course," Lazarev continued, "that a primary rationale for building the Wall in 1961 was to prevent skilled workers from escaping to West Berlin and West Germany. We need those workers very urgently. As the ambassador told you, we are lacking in technological progress such as electronics and computers, so every skilled worker who leaves us is a considerable loss.

"The ambassador, after consulting with his colleagues in the Kremlin, has determined that perhaps a little bread and circuses would be useful in winning back the hearts and minds—that's your term being used in Vietnam, I believe—of the local population. He intends to stage in East Berlin next summer a massive Volksfest using many of the techniques that you and your predecessors have initiated over the past five years. Your Volksfest files may seem trivial and unimportant to you, but believe me, they could be critically important to the success of our 'bread and circus' interests. I hope we have convinced you and I hope you will be able to persuade your superiors accordingly.

"This is a complication over Spandau that will need to be resolved if we are to move ahead with scaling down the prison," Lazarev summed up. "Will you communicate our views accurately to your headquarters?" he asked as he rose from his chair.

"Of course I will, Colonel Lazarev. It has been a most interesting meeting. Thank you for a wonderful lunch and please tell Ambassador Abrassimov how impressed I was to meet him."

"You're very welcome, Harry," said Lazarev, using Holbrook's first name for the first time. "I hope we shall meet again. Captain Antonov will take you to your car."

"Thank you, sir," said Holbrook and left.

Information Division (ID)
Headquaters, U.S. Commander Berlin
Clayallee and Saargemünder Strasse
Dahlem, Zehlendorf
West Berlin
1445 hours, 17 October 1966

"How did the Russians treat you, Major Holbrook?" asked Frau Haupt as Harry entered his office. Like many other middle-aged female Berliners, she had been abused and mistreated by Russian soldiers when they overwhelmed the city in 1945.

"Gertie, they were surprisingly nice. I even got to meet their ambassador, Abrassimov. Please see if Colonel Semsch is available while I wash my hands."

Holbrook's bladder was bursting with Russian tea and he hurried to relieve himself. As he returned to his office, Frau Haupt said, "Colonel Semsch can see you now."

Holbrook hurried down the corridor connecting his office with that of the intelligence officer, where he was waved in and was offered a seat in front of Semsch's desk.

"Phil, you won't believe what the hell that was all about."

"Just tell me, Harry, and calm down. You look a little flustered."

"Maybe I am. The bottom line is that the Russians are agreeable to scaling Spandau Prison down. But they want something in return."

"Of course, they do. What is it? A sample tactical nuke?"

"Not exactly." Here Holbrook paused to draw a breath. "They want my plans and files for the Volksfest."

"The *what*?"

"Exactly. They want to know every little bit of information about the Volksfest so they can replicate it in East Berlin next summer. Blueprints, construction documents, costs of building supplies, how we hired the laborers and dancehall girls, security. In short, everything."

Semsch sat back, amazed. "So Lazarev is willing to more or less close down Spandau Prison in return for your Volksfest files?"

"Not just Lazarev, Phil. The ambassador was there the whole time, eating lunch with us and smoking a big fat Cuban cigar."

"Abrassimov sat in with Lazarev and you?" Semsch couldn't believe it.

"Just about the entire time. He had to leave for some meeting."

"Why? Why is the Volksfest so important to them?"

Holbrook recited almost verbatim Colonel Lazarev's explanation of the bread and circuses analogy that had been used to describe the Soviet problem in keeping East Berlin and much of the entire GDR under its thumb.

"Harry, we need to brief the general on this right away. He'll be astonished."

"I'll bet he will. But would you mind filling him in without me? Calhoun wants a contemporaneous memo for the record about the meeting this afternoon and I need to get started. I've got all the conversation in my head but I need to get it down on paper. I do my own typing, of course, so I'll need about an hour.

"I'll bring the original to Calhoun's office and make copies for Caraway, Pete Day, you, and Halvorsen. Anyone else need a copy, Phil?"

"No, that'll do it. And label your memo 'Confidential' with a blue 'Confidential' cover on top of it. There's nothing in it that's really classified except the fact that we're talking to the Russians about shrinking the size of Spandau Prison.

"And, Harry, one word of caution: nothing about this yet to your buddies in the news media, understood?"

"Got it, Phil."

Office of the U.S. Commander Berlin
Clayallee and Saargemünder Strasse
Dahlem, Zehlendorf
West Berlin
0930 hours, 18 October 1966

General Caraway convened the meeting of this latest iteration of his Volksfest task force. In attendance were Minister Calhoun and Pete Day of USBER; Halvorsen of the CIA; General Hay of the Berlin Brigade; Colonel Hazeltine, Caraway's chief of staff; Phil Semsch; and Major Holbrook.

"Has everyone had an opportunity to read and digest Holbrook's memo of yesterday afternoon?" Caraway asked.

All nodded. "Good report, Harry," said Hazeltine, although some of the others—Caraway and the two USBER representatives—seemed to be reserving final judgment.

"Holbrook," said Caraway, "is there anything you might have left out? Anything you forgot to include?" Caraway apparently was the only person in Berlin who was still unaware of Holbrook's vaunted memory gifts, but no one at the round table opted to point this out.

"Sir, that's everything. I've reconstructed the meeting as fully and accurately as possible." Holbrook had even included details of the sugar-cube-between-the-teeth routine and the origins of Ambassador Abrassimov's cigar.

"So, what are your thoughts, gentlemen?" asked Caraway. "Ernest, what do you and your people think?"

Calhoun paused for maximum effect, giving his weightiest thoughts to this thorniest of Cold War problems. "We are still assessing and reassessing the situation, of course, General, so my reaction—and that of our colleagues here in Berlin, as well as in Bonn and Washington—is very much a preliminary one."

"I understand, of course. It's only preliminary," said the USCOB, apparently in deep sympathy with Calhoun's dilemma.

Calhoun continued, enjoying the situation as he wrestled with this moment in history. "The personal involvement in this matter of Abrassimov himself is what gives us pause." He looked over at Pete Day, who nodded in agreement. Halvorsen was looking down, apparently studying something in Holbrook's memo.

"Frankly, General, we are surprised that the Soviets appear to be acquiescent"—he rolled the word around lovingly, almost squeezing an extra syllable out of it—"in a reduction at Spandau, which is very much in line with what we had proposed to them. Quite frankly, we had expected a counteroffer involving keeping the four-power rotating guard force and monthly rotation of prison commandants. By the way, General, one wonders why our commandant, Colonel Bird, isn't here with us?"

Caraway glanced down, uncertain about his response, so Hazeltine intervened. "Minister, Bird is currently under investigation. There are indications that he's gotten too cozy with Hess and that the two of them may be collaborating on a book about Hess's time in

Spandau. Bird has been suspended from his duties, pending the outcome of the investigation."

Hazeltine glanced around the table. "Gentlemen, that information is very close hold and is not to leave this room. We don't want to read about it in the newspapers," he said, whereupon all heads turned momentarily to Holbrook, before turning away.

Holbrook nodded his understanding, wondering why the hell the members of this group were so hostile toward him. Probably just following Caraway's lead, he concluded.

Calhoun finally seemed to be coming to the point. "Holbrook's comment about 'bread and circuses' may well help explain the Soviets' motivation in all this. Roger, what does Langley think about it?"

So far, Holbrook thought to himself, Calhoun hadn't said a damn thing except comment on the State Department's surprise that the Russians might be agreeable to the Spandau-reduction proposal. Maybe Halvorsen could say something meaningful.

The thoughtful, circumspect Halvorsen looked up from his perusal of Holbrook's memo for the record. "General, Minister," he began, "we've known for some time that there are rumblings of discontent in East Berlin and throughout some of the Soviet republics When Khrushchev was ousted two years ago, there were hopes among the Soviet peoples that the economy could be turned around and prosperity might be achieved under Brezhnev.

"Those hopes and expectations," Halvorsen continued, "haven't been fulfilled, nor are they likely to happen. Soviet military expenditures arising from the Cold War are taking a huge bite out of their gross domestic product and the people are feeling it. Last year, as an example, Moscow decided to acquire an IBM/360 to jump into the computer age, and that proved to be yet another setback, because it locked Soviet scientists and engineers into a system that shortly became outdated. The Soviets were unable to manufacture reliable computer chips in adequate quantities and then found that they couldn't create dependable computer programs or adequate computer-support systems.

"These factors, and many others, all took their toll on the Soviet economy and on the standards of living for the average Soviet citizen and for the people living in most of the 15 or so Soviet Socialist Republics, or SSRs.

"The Wall here in Berlin provides a good example. As we all know, when skilled workers from the East began fleeing westward through West Berlin for better-paying jobs here in West Berlin or in the Federal Republic, Khrushchev had to put a stop to it by walling his people in. Five years later, those people are getting increasingly unhappy as they learn from television and the news media that conditions in West Germany are far more sanguine than in the East.

"So the 'bread and circuses' analogy that Colonel Lazarev discussed with Harry comes into play. If you can't take care of your populace adequately enough to keep them satisfied, give them entertainment to take their minds off their misery. And that's why a Volksfest might just be the thing," Halvorsen concluded.

All nodded in agreement. "Excellent report, Roger," said Caraway. "So, what are our actions, gentlemen? Holbrook, what do you suggest?"

Holbrook had prepared for this since he knew that ultimately the responsibility for providing Volksfest plans to the Soviets would fall upon his shoulders. Yesterday afternoon he'd alerted Frau Jochem—his keeper of all Volksfest files and records—about what was going on and had directed her to create a one-page inventory of all documentation related to the Volksfest, including a listing of all blueprints and specifications. He passed copies of the inventory around the table so that each member had one.

"This is what we have, and this is what we can copy and give to the Russians," said Holbrook.

"Did they give you any timetable for when they want this done, Holbrook?" asked Calhoun.

"No sir, that wasn't discussed. Ambassador Abrassimov seemed very aware that we would be consulting our respective higher headquarters before arriving at a decision."

"How long do you estimate you'll need to copy all these documents for the Russians, Harry?" asked Hazeltine.

"Sir, my office Xerox machine is an old-model 914. I'll need one, maybe two, of the newer 813s to get this job done. With two of them, I could complete the job in a week, probably about the time it takes to get concurrence from Heidelberg, Bonn or D.C."

Hazeltine turned to the general. "Sir, we have a contingency fund for emergencies such as this. If you approve, I can order a pair of Xeroxes from the States this afternoon and authorize air-express shipment."

Caraway looked around the table. Everyone nodded in agreement. Holbrook was elated. He'd hold onto at least one of the new copiers when all was said and done and would fight to keep both. His office staff would adore him for it.

"All right, that's it for this meeting," said the USCOB. "We've all got to get busy establishing coordination on this with our higher headquarters. Let's shoot for nailing this down by this time next week, as Major Holbrook has suggested." Harry thought that Caraway grimaced a little at this, but perhaps that was just his imagination.

"Thank you all for coming," said Caraway, and the meeting was dismissed.

21

Information Division (ID)
Headquarters, U.S. Commander Berlin
Clayallee and Saargemünder Strasse
Dahlem, Zehlendorf
West Berlin
1050 hours, 20 October 1966

Frau Haupt came into Holbrook's office carrying a small calling card. "There is a Mr. Mooneyham waiting in my office to see you, Major Holbrook. He apologized for coming without an appointment but wonders if you could spare five minutes for him," she said, handing the card to Harry.

He read: "Reverend Dr. W. Stanley Mooneyham, Vice President, Billy Graham Evangelistic Association." Of course, Holbrook recalled, Billy Graham was coming to West Berlin next week for some kind of World Congress on Evangelism, which would include a big rally at the Olympic Stadium. Hugh Erb had written a lengthy article about it a few days ago.

"Sure thing, Gertie. Please show him in."

Holbrook rose from his chair to greet his visitor. "Welcome to Berlin, Dr. Mooneyham," he said, then realized he'd seen

Mooneyham before. "I know you!" he said. "You and your family live in that big modern house at one end of Goldfinkweg. I live at the other end."

The two shook hands. "Right you are, Major. Billy sent me here a couple of months ago to do advance work for the World Congress and the stadium rally. I'm his special assistant and in charge of coordinating the conference and the rally. I thought I'd do well to drop by and introduce myself to the Berlin Command's spokesman."

"I'm glad you did," Holbrook responded. "The city's been buzzing with interest about the events."

Mooneyham was a tall, dark-haired, bespectacled man who spoke with a distinctive southern accent, Holbrook noted. Mississippi maybe? Alabama? His navy blue suit was beautifully tailored, probably costing a month or two's worth of Holbrook's salary as an Army O-4, or major.

They chatted for a few more minutes about life on Goldfinkweg and about the series of events that Mooneyham was coordinating as advance man for the Billy Graham Crusade. Holbrook learned that an estimated twelve hundred delegates from than one hundred nations would be in attendance at the World Congress, all encouraged by Graham to wear their native dress in a demonstration of global solidarity. The gathering would take place over a ten-day span at the *Kongresshalle* (Congress Hall), a gift in 1957 from the United States to West Berlin, where President Kennedy had spoken during his June 1963 visit to the city.

As Mooneyham rose to leave, he held out a stack of what looked like tickets. "Here are some reserved-seat passes to the rally at the stadium on the 29th, Major. Perhaps you can distribute them to members of your staff?"

"Indeed I will, Dr. Mooneyham. Thank you very much. Is there anything we can do to help?"

"I think we've got everything under control, Major Holbrook, but thanks. I'll look forward to seeing you around the neighborhood."

They shook hands and Mooneyham left.

Wertheim Department Store Restaurant
Schlossstrasse and Treischkestrasse
Steglitz-Zehlendorf District
West Berlin
1330 hours, 22 October 1966

Carolyn and Harry were finishing up a very nice lunch of *Knockwurst*, sauerkraut, and *Bratkartoffeln* (pan-fried potatoes) at the massive Wertheim department store. Carolyn had wanted to go shopping for a winter coat and they decided to stay for lunch at the store's restaurant. Much like the KaDeWe store, Wertheim proudly boasted a very fine dining room and kitchen.

Carolyn had found a full-length maroon coat that fitted her very well and had been marked down to an affordable price. She was in high spirits and Holbrook decided to give her some more good news.

"Please don't make any plans with your girlfriends for next Saturday afternoon, Carolyn," he said.

That got her attention. "I won't if you say so, dear Harry. What did you have in mind?"

"Just this," and he pulled from his jacket pocket two passes to the Billy Graham Crusade at the Olympic Stadium.

"Oh, my goodness!" she exclaimed. "We're going to see and hear Billy Graham!"

"And Johnny Cash too," Holbrook added. "He's come along for the ride with the preacher."

"My parents will be so thrilled that I got to see Billy Graham in person!"

"You and about a hundred thousand Berliners, Carolyn, so we'll be seated some distance from him, you can be sure."

"How did you get these tickets?"

"Graham's event coordinator stopped by the office a couple of day ago to say hello. He and his family are leasing that beautiful modern house at the end of Goldfinkweg and he offered me a dozen or so reserved seat passes for the news media. I gave a pair to Phil and Alicia and told Paul Scholl to distribute the rest among members of our office who were interested. It should be very informative.

"But be sure to dress warmly," Holbrook cautioned. "Berlin in late October can be downright cool and windy, even in the afternoons."

"I know just what to wear, Harry!" she said, as she patted the shopping bag containing the box with her new maroon winter coat.

News Media Section
Billy Graham Crusade
Olympiastadion
British Sector, West Berlin
1400 hours, 29 October 1966

Showing their news media passes, Holbrook and Carolyn took their seats in the press section overlooking the platform from which the Reverend Billy Graham would address and hopefully inspire almost 100,000 ardent West Berliners.

Holbrook and Carolyn both waved to Hugh and Krista Erb. Erb, of course, was there to cover the epic event for the Associated Press. Harry waved to Colonel and Mrs. Semsch, Dieter Goos and his wife, Gary Stindt of NBC, Mark White of the AFN Berlin Radio Network, Pete Day of USBER and his wife, and Joe Fleming of UPI. Paul Scholl, Gertraud Haupt, and Ingeborg Jochem of his own office were there, using passes provided by Stan Mooneyham, who was seated on the dais not far from Graham.

Flags flying over the stadium honored the 104 nations attending Graham's World Conference on Evangelism, being held at the Congress Hall on the south bank of the River Spree in Berlin's central Tiergarten District. The building was named for John Foster Dulles, President Dwight Eisenhower's secretary of state, who had played a key role in the building's donation.

Johnny Cash entertained the crowd before Graham came on. The crowd was familiar with his "Ring of Fire" and "Folsom Prison Blues," and roared its approval as he sang these and a medley of his other hits, including several with religious themes.

On that cool, windswept, cloudy day, Graham held his audience spellbound. He spoke of ongoing discussions at the eight-day Congress, of the worldwide danger of international communism, and of the threat to the Western world posed by Soviet expansionism. He maintained that a return to the lessons of the bible—both in the Old and New Testaments—was fundamental to preserving a civilized, decent, respectful, and humane way of life.

Graham held a bible in his right hand as he spoke, raising it aloft from time to time to demonstrate its power and relevance in the days of the Cold War, which had divided the good peoples of Berlin, making it almost impossible for West Berliners to visit their relatives on the other side of the infamous Berlin Wall, a universal symbol of the failures of "godless communism," as he put it.

He spoke for an hour and 15 minutes, according to Holbrook's wristwatch. As he checked the time, Harry noticed a scratch on its face that he hadn't seen before. *Probably from my scuffle with the sniper a month ago*, he concluded, and wondered if Ashkenazi would ever squeeze a trigger again.

Billy Graham finished his speech with a rousing peroration intended to inspire his followers to go forth and evangelize. They loved it, rising from their seats as one and applauding Graham until he ran out of smiles and hand waves and left the stage.

As the crowd was exiting, Hugh and Krista Erb stopped by to say hello. "What a beautiful coat, Caroline!" said Krista, as she eyed both the coat and Caroline's right hand, which was linked closely with Holbrook's.

"Thank you Krista. Harry took me to Wertheim a few days ago and we found it there. It is certainly nice and warm on a chilly day like this."

Erb wasn't interested in learning about women's fashions. "What did you think of the speech, Harry?"

"Billy Graham sure knows how to motivate an audience, doesn't he?" said Holbrook.

"You know he's going to visit the troops in Vietnam at Christmas, Harry. He's a firm supporter of the war and Nixon's policies at present, but if things don't improve over there, I wonder how much longer he'll stay in Nixon's corner."

Krista told Carolyn that they needed to get together again very soon. Then, caught up in the tide of the exiting crowd, they waved their goodbyes and headed toward their vehicles and probably a late Saturday lunch or early dinner.

22

Office of the U.S. Commander Berlin
Clayallee and Saargemünder Strasse
Dahlem, Zehlendorf
West Berlin, West Germany
15 November 1966

With the arrival at USCOB headquarters of Lieutenant Colonel Richard C. Hansen, a well-qualified public information officer with a master's degree in journalism from the University of Missouri, Harry Holbrook felt at liberty to remind General Caraway of his commitment to release him for reassignment to Vietnam when a replacement had been found.

As an aside, Holbrook felt that the USCOB would be secretly delighted to get this troublesome major out of Berlin. After all, Camp Long Binh Junction was as far away as possible from Clayallee 127.

Soon afterwards, Holbrook received a TWX (teletypewriter exchange service, a military telegram) ordering him to report to U.S. Army Vietnam for further assignment to the 1st Cavalry Division (Airmobile). He thanked his lucky stars that General O'Meara and Colonel Boggs had gone to work in his behalf.

Colonel Hazeltine, the USCOB chief of staff, called Holbrook into his office for a farewell visit and handed him a third award of the Army Commendation Medal. "I had Lil Baker in Heidelberg help me write you up for a Legion of Merit, Harry, after all you've done here, but the General felt that that was a little much and downgraded it to an ARCOM."

"No sweat, sir," said Holbrook. "An ARCOM is fine." Hazeltine handed Harry the medal and its blue case and shook his hand. "Take care, Harry," he said.

The staff of his information office held a farewell party in his honor at the Harnack House. Paul Scholl delivered some fairly funny anecdotes about Harry's adventures in Berlin, and Carolyn Mattersdorf, Harry's invited guest, took it all in and wondered just how much more there was to learn about her beau.

23

Flughafen Tempelhof
Lufthansa Departure Gate
American Sector, West Berlin
1845 hours, 19 December 1966

Driven by Sergeant Norman Hellerstein, the official U.S. Army sedan carrying Lieutenant Colonel and Mrs. Philip Semsch, Major Harrison Holbrook and Miss Carolyn Mattersdorf arrived at the departure gate of Tempelhof Airport an hour before Holbrook's Lufthansa flight to Rhein-Main Airport in Frankfurt and then on to connecting flights to Newark International Airport, Seattle-Tacoma International Airport, Honolulu International Airport, Tokyo International Airport (commonly known as Haneda Airport), and terminating at Tan Son Nhut Air Base outside Saigon in the Republic of Vietnam.

Waiting near the departure gate were Hubert J. Erb of the Associated Press and Dieter Goos of *Die Berliner Morgenpost*. Both were there in an unofficial role, not as working journalists. There was, after all, nothing newsworthy in 1966 about yet another U.S. Army officer being reassigned from a tour of duty in Europe and being transferred to the ever-expanding U.S. war effort in South Vietnam.

Holbrook, carrying his military overcoat and wearing his Army Green uniform with his standard service cap, held hands with Carolyn Mattersdorf as the arriving group walked to their gate and sat down. Sergeant Hellerstein, after making arrangements for Holbrook's gray Val-Pak suitcase to be placed aboard the Lufthansa Boeing 707, joined the group a few minutes later.

After ten minutes or so, members of the party began to leave. Erb, who had served in the Korean War as an artillery forward observer, counseled Holbrook to keep his ass down when the going got rough. Goos shook hands and patted Holbrook's back: "It has been my honor to be working with you these past two years, Major Holbrook. May you come home safely."

"Thanks, Hugh and Dieter. I'll try not to make any waves over there. It's been a real pleasure to have worked with a couple of pros like you two."

The Semsches were next to take their leave. Alicia gave the young major a motherly peck on the cheek, saying, "Be careful, Harry, and do stay in touch."

Colonel Semsch, somewhat choked up, shook Holbrook's hand and said, "Bon voyage, Harry. Give 'em hell. Carolyn, we'll wait for you in the car."

Hellerstein, who needed to lead the Semsches to his illegally parked sedan, handed a sealed envelope to Holbrook, saying only, "From our friends at the synagogue, Major. Take care over there." Holbrook opened the envelope and found a Christmas card inside, on which had been written "*Shalom*" and signed "Rabbi Bernd Halbfinger."

"I'll do my best to come home in one piece. Norm. Good luck with your studies at NYU. I expect to see you as a top judge in New York in a couple of years."

"I'll try, Major. Keep in touch."

Carolyn and Holbrook sat side-by-side in the departure lounge, holding hands, both uncertain about what needed to be said, what should be said, what promises exchanged.

Not knowing what to say that would be meaningful, they made small talk.

"I bought a book for you to read on the plane, Harry. It just arrived in the PX and it's been a bestseller back home."

"That's very thoughtful, Carolyn," said Holbrook as she handed him a paperback copy of *The Spy Who Came in from the Cold*, by John le Carré.

"I've heard of this," Holbrook said. "It's a spy story that takes place here in Berlin. It's gotten wonderful reviews and they've just made a movie from it, starring Richard Burton. This is a great gift! Thanks very much, Carolyn."

He tucked the book into an overcoat pocket. Time for some important talk.

"So, you'll be going back home to Rockford and staying with your folks, Carolyn?"

"Yes, Harry. I've told the school that I'll finish up this school year in June and then I plan to return to the States. I'll live with my mom and dad for a couple of months while I'm getting resettled and then we'll see what happens."

Holbrook—nobody's fool—saw his opening. "Carolyn, we have a wonderful future together. By the time I get home from Vietnam in 12 months, I think we should get married, then finish up my 20 years in the Army. We'll retire to your hometown in Rockford so your parents can see their grandchildren as often as they'd like and maybe we'd both teach school there. Does that make any sense?"

"Oh, yes, Harry. That's exactly what I'd like to see happen!" she beamed. "I know that your mail deliveries in Vietnam will be erratic and that you won't be able to write me as often as I'd like, but I'll be writing three or four letters a week to you. Will that be okay?"

"I'd love it, Carolyn."

"Let me write down my parents' mailing address for you."

"That's not necessary; just tell it to me," Holbrook said, as an announcement in German and then English came over the

PA system that his flight to Rhein-Main was about to board. "I have a pretty good memory."

They kissed and held hands for a moment, each of them a little misty-eyed.

Holbrook placed his well-worn service cap on his head and headed for the departure gate. As he left, he turned to wave goodbye to Carolyn Mattersdorf and threw her a farewell kiss.

He passed through the gate and left for the war.

Epilogue

The following events took place subsequent to this narrative:

Major General Paul Caraway, U.S. Commander Berlin, completed his normal tour of duty in Berlin and was reassigned to St. Louis, Missouri, as commanding general of XI U.S. Army Corps, which had jurisdiction over Army Reserve and ROTC activities in the Midwestern states. He retired from that post, returned to his native Kentucky, and died at age 71 from cirrhosis of the liver.

Sergeant Norman Hellerstein completed his three years of active duty and returned to his studies at New York University's School of Law. He graduated first in his class, simultaneously earning a Ph.D. degree. He is currently chief judge of the Southern District of New York, covering Manhattan and its 3 million residents, plus the Bronx and several counties. He is in demand as a speaker on legal issues and reportedly is under consideration by the current administration in Washington for a high-level position at the Department of Justice.

Rudolph Hess, the last remaining prisoner at Spandau Prison, hanged himself in his cell in 1987. He was 93. Following his death,

Spandau Prison was razed to the ground to prevent its becoming a neo-Nazi shrine. The site currently houses a shopping center.

Colonel Philip Semsch, upon completion of his tour of duty in Berlin, was reassigned to the Pentagon as deputy assistant chief of staff for intelligence (ACSI). He retired as a brigadier general, lives in Arlington, Virginia, and lectures in intelligence acquisition as the National War College in Washington, D.C. His wife Alicia passed away from ovarian cancer several years ago.

Major Lillian Baker spent a successful year in the Personnel Division of Headquarters, U.S. Army Europe in Heidelberg. Upon completion of that assignment, she was reassigned to Vietnam and became G-1 (Personnel) of the U.S. Army Headquarters Area Command in Saigon. She retired as a lieutenant colonel and never married.

Hubert (Hugh) J. Erb was reassigned by the Associated Press to its New York City bureau, with wide-ranging responsibilities. While covering heavy fighting in Vietnam during the 1968 Tet Offensive, he was wounded in the right arm by fragments from a North Vietnamese 122mm rocket. He lost the use of the arm and decided to retire from news gathering. Erb and his wife Christa live in a suburb of New York City. Their son Klaus is a high school teacher of the German language.

J. Paul Scholl, deputy information officer in the USCOB headquarters, retired from the civil service in 1973 but continues to live in Berlin. Shortly after his retirement, he divorced his wife Anna and married a 26-year-old secretary from one of the USCOB offices. They were divorced two years later, apparently because of his infidelity.

Willy Brandt, West Berlin's governing mayor, became chancellor of the Federal Republic of Germany (West Germany) in 1969. He was awarded the Nobel Peace Prize in 1971 for his work in improving relations with former Iron Curtain nations, including the USSR. He resigned as chancellor in 1974 after one of his personal assistants was found to be a spy for East German intelligence organizations. Brandt died of colon cancer in 1992 at age 78, received a state funeral, and was buried in a cemetery in the Zehlendorf district of the reunited city of Berlin.

Captain Charles A. ("Charley") Hines retired from the Army in 1994 as a major general. In his final assignment, he commanded the Army's Chemical and Military Police Center at Fort McClellan, Alabama, the first African American to command a major Army installation in the South. He earned a doctorate in sociology from Johns Hopkins University. Hines served as president of Prairie View A&M University near Houston, Texas, from 1994 to 2002 but left after continuing disputes with the trustees. He died in Houston on July 4, 2013 from a heart attack. He was 77.

General Andrew P. O'Meara, commander-in-chief of U.S. Army Europe, retired from active duty in 1967, following completion of his assignment in Heidelberg. He lived in the Washington, D.C., area and died of a stroke in 2005. He was 98.

Rabbi Bernd Halbfinger, chief rabbi of the New Synagogue in East Berlin, died in June 1989 as a result of complications from pneumonia. He therefore missed by five months the fall of the Berlin Wall and the reunification of Berlin's Jewish population. He was 86 years old at the time of his death. His older son, Nathaniel, is currently chief rabbi at a synagogue in the Spandau district of Berlin, while his younger son, Daniel, is a professor of religious studies at the University of Wisconsin-Milwaukee.

Frau Gertraud Haupt, secretary to a succession of USCOB information officers for almost 17 years, retired from that position in 1972 and was honored with the highest civilian service award that USCOB granted. Her husband, an economics professor at the Freie Universität in Berlin, passed away in 1969. Frau Haupt resides in the Dahlem area of Berlin with her married daughter.

Captain Dmitri Vasilevsky, formerly of the Soviet Air Forces, lives in Monterey, California, where he teaches Slavic languages, including Russian, at the Defense Language Institute. His wife, Natalya, is a violinist with the San Francisco Philharmonic Orchestra. Their son, Yuri, enlisted in the U.S. Army and is currently attending infantry officer candidate school at Fort Benning, Georgia.

Lyndon Baines Johnson, 36th American President, in a nationally televised address to the nation on March 31, 1968, declined to be nominated by the Democratic Party for a second full term in office. Despite his success in coordinating and leading the passage of more significant civil-rights legislation than any president before or since, Johnson was heartbroken over the tragic failure of his policies regarding the Vietnam War. He retired to his ranch in Stonewall, Texas, in the state's Hill Country, where he died of a massive heart attack on January 22, 1973. He was 64 years old. Two days before his death, Richard Milhous Nixon, who became President when Johnson declined to run again, was sworn in for his second term as president. Nixon resigned in disgrace in August 1974 after covering up the Watergate burglary, the only American President ever to resign.

Samuel/Schmuel (true name unknown, although it may have been Benjamin Ashkenazi) returned to Mossad headquarters in Tel Aviv after his life was spared by Major Harry Holbrook. He was appointed aide-de-camp to Mossad director Major General Meir

Amit despite his failure to assassinate the two Nazi war criminals upon their release from Spandau Prison. Following the massacres of 11 Israeli athletes and coaches at the Summer Olympics in Munich in September 1972, Samuel/Schmuel led the reprisals that resulted in the tracking down of many of the Black September gunmen and their executions by Mossad hitmen.

Dieter Goos, military affairs reporter for the *Berliner Morgenpost* newspaper, rose through the ranks to become the paper's editor-in-chief. His hardline stance against unchecked immigration irked many German industrialists who profited from the source of cheap labor. He and his wife narrowly escaped serious injury in May 1993 when a fragmentation hand grenade thrown through an open window of their living room failed to detonate. The perpetrators have never been found, although the case is still marked "open" by the Berlin *Polizei*.

Frau Angelika Bausch, owner of Bausch Porzellan, sold her porcelain retail establishment in 1974 to a husband-wife team that had worked with her at the store for many years. Although Frau Bausch steadfastly maintained that her husband had been killed in World War II during fighting on the Eastern Front, later research by a reporter working discreetly for *Morgenpost* editor-in-chief Dieter Goos determined that her husband, a Jew, had been arrested by Nazi storm troopers one night after closing the store and was never seen again. It was speculated by the reporter that he died of malnutrition in early 1943 as a slave laborer in the Birkenau concentration camp, a subcamp of the Auschwitz complex in German-occupied Poland. Frau Bausch never remarried and died in Berlin in 1981 at the age of 67.

Colonel Dmitri Lazarev, Soviet commandant of Spandau Prison, retired from that post and active duty in 1967. His involvement in the defection of Captain Vasilevsky and compromise of the MiG-21 aircraft never became known to Soviet officials, although an investigation took place. During CIA debriefings at the IG Farben building in 1966, Vasilevsky's wife Natalya disclosed that she was Lazarev's niece and that her husband felt constrained by the Soviet political and military establishments and wanted new opportunities in the West.

Baldur von Schirach, released from Spandau Prison on October 1, 1966 after completing his 20-year sentence for "crimes against humanity," moved in with his son Klaus in a fashionable suburb of Munich, where he lived in seclusion. He died in August 1974 while on vacation in the wine-growing village of Kroev. He was 67. Von Schirach was the first leader of the Hitler Youth movement and played a key role in the deportation and execution of approximately 50,000 Austrian Jews.

Albert Speer, released from Spandau Prison at the same time as Baldur von Schirach, was Hitler's minister of armaments and war production, in charge of resupplying the German armed forces during World War II. After his release from Spandau, he published two bestselling autobiographical books, *Inside the Third Reich* and *Spandau: The Secret Diaries*. Speer, an architect by profession, helped design Berlin's Olympiastadion, site of the 1936 Olympics Games and last defensive position of the Berlin Brigade in the event of a Russian attack. Speer's personal involvement in the Holocaust has never been definitively established. Unlike the reticent von Schirach, Speer spoke openly to interviewers and historians about the Hitler regime. While in London in September 1981 for an interview with the BBC, Speer suffered a stroke and died. He was 76.

Major General Meir Amit (birth name Meir Slutsky) was chief director of the Mossad and head of the Israeli intelligence organization's global operations from 1963 to 1968, at which point he went into politics, serving in the Knesset (the Israeli parliament) and as a cabinet minister. He earned an MBA degree from Columbia University.

Unrelated to *The Spandau Complication*, Amit was successful in 1966 in bringing an Iraqi MiG-21 and its pilot to Israel, sharing the coup with the United States and affording the West an early look at the advanced Soviet aircraft. Amit, ever mindful that Harry Holbrook had not only spared the life of his operative named Samuel or Schmuel, but had also saved the Mossad from a major international embarrassment by concealing its role in the ill-fated assassination plot, kept in touch with Holbrook and sent him Christmas cards each year. Amit died in July 2009 in Tel Aviv at age 88 and was honored by Israeli President Shimon Peres as a national hero.

The Berlin Wall stood from August 13, 1961 to November 9, 1989 as the ultimate symbol of the four-decades-long Cold War era. With the collapse of the East German government following massive pro-democracy demonstrations in East Berlin, the Wall was breached and Germans from both sides began tearing it down. With the Berlin Wall dismantled, the pathway was open for the reunification of West and East Germany, which officially took place October 3, 1990. In effect, the Cold War was over and the West had won.

Harrison ("Harry") Holbrook retired from the U.S. Army as a lieutenant colonel of infantry. He and his wife reside in her hometown of Rockford, Illinois, where he teaches English and language arts at Rockford East High School. He is called upon each year—largely because of his prior ROTC experience at Penn State—to evaluate the Junior ROTC program at the high school, an assignment he looks forward to. His wife, Carolyn Holbrook (née Mattersdorf), teaches sixth-grade mathematics at Eisenhower Middle School in Rockford. The Holbrooks have two daughters: Meredith, age 14, and Jennifer, 12. Holbrook has been working on and off for several years on a book about his Cold War experiences in Berlin, the working title of which is *The Spandau Complication*. At last report, he was still searching for a publisher.

Dedication

The Spandau Complication is humbly dedicated to the memory of John le Carré (October 19, 1931–December 12, 2020), who passed away from pneumonia while this novel was being fashioned.

Born David John Moore Cornwell in Poole, Dorset, England, he joined MI6—the British Secret Intelligence Service—in 1960 and worked undercover at the British Embassy in Bonn. With his cover blown to the KGB by the revelations about British intelligence secrets by double agent Kim Philby, Cornwell became a full-time novelist.

Using the pen name John le Carré (French for "the square") because British foreign-service agents weren't allowed to write under their own names, he authored in 1963 the international bestseller, *The Spy Who Came in from the Cold.* Two years later, a film made from the book starring Sir Richard Burton as over-the-hill spy Alec Leamas—the MI6 station chief in West Berlin—won an Academy Award best-actor nomination for Burton.

At le Carré's death, *The New York Times* said that his "exquisitely nuanced, intricately plotted Cold War thrillers elevated the spy novel to high art," adding that "many critics considered his books literature of the first order."

As an example of what *The Times* was referring to, consider this passage from Chapter 13 of *The Spy Who Came in from the Cold*:

> Aware of the overwhelming temptations which assail a man permanently isolated in his deceit, Leamas resorted to the course which suited him best; even when he was alone, he compelled himself to live with the personality he had assumed. It is said that Balzac on his deathbed inquired anxiously after the health and prosperity of characters he had created. Similarly Leamas, without relinquishing the power of invention, identified himself with what he had invented.

To pay fitting tribute to John le Carré, upon news of his death at 89—while finishing up *The Spandau Complication*—I felt compelled to add something to the book's final scene. *Spoiler Alert*: as protagonist Major Harrison Holbrook Jr. prepares to depart from Tempelhof Airport for his coming assignment in Vietnam, a friend gives him a paperback copy of *The Spy Who Came in from the Cold* to read during the lengthy airplane voyages awaiting him as he travels from Berlin to Saigon, like Christopher Columbus heading westward to the East. (The paperback edition—published January 1, 1964—had only recently become available in the Berlin PX when the friend bought it for Holbrook in December 1966 as a farewell present.

Holbrook digests the entire le Carré novel as he waits interminably in terminals and endures endless airplane voyages in cramped seats, all the while wishing that he could write half as well as John le Carré, to whom this novel is reverently dedicated.